T0149319

Stalk the Darkness

Books by Alexandra Ivy

Guardians of Eternity
WHEN DARKNESS COMES
EMBRACE THE DARNKESS
DARKNESS EVERLASTING
DARKNESS REVEALED
DARKNESS UNLEASHED
BEYOND THE DARKNESS
DEVOURED BY DARKNESS
BOUND BY DARKNESS
FEAR THE DARKNESS
DARKNESS AVENGED
HUNT THE DARKNESS
WHEN DARKNESS ENDS
DARKNESS RETURNS
BEWARE THE DARKNESS
CONQUER THE DARKNESS
SHADES OF DARKNESS
DARKNESS BETRAYED
BEWITCH THE DARKNESS
STALK THE DARKNESS

The Immortal Rogues
MY LORD VAMPIRE
MY LORD ETERNITY
MY LORD IMMORTALITY

The Sentinels
BORN IN BLOOD
BLOOD ASSASSIN
BLOOD LUST

Ares Security
KILL WITHOUT MERCY
KILL WITHOUT SHAME

Historical Romance

SOME LIKE IT WICKED
SOME LIKE IT SINFUL
SOME LIKE IT BRAZEN

Romantic Suspense
PRETEND YOU'RE SAFE
WHAT ARE YOU AFRAID OF?
YOU WILL SUFFER
THE INTENDED VICTIM
DON'T LOOK
FACELESS
UNSTABLE

And don't miss these Guardians of Eternity novellas
TAKEN BY DARKNESS in YOURS FOR ETERNITY
DARKNESS ETERNAL in SUPERNATURAL
WHERE DARKNESS LIVES in THE REAL WEREWIVES OF
VAMPIRE COUNTY
LEVET (ebook only)
A VERY LEVET CHRISTMAS (ebook only)

And don't miss these Sentinel novellas
OUT OF CONTROL
ON THE HUNT

Published by Kensington Publishing Corp.

Stalk the Darkness

Alexandra Ivy

LYRICAL PRESS
Kensington Publishing Corp.
www.kensingtonbooks.com

LYRICAL PRESS BOOKS are published by

Kensington Publishing Corp.
119 West 40th Street
New York, NY 10018

All Kensington titles, imprints, and distributed lines are available at special quantity discounts for bulk purchases for sales promotion, premiums, fund-raising, educational, or institutional use.

Special book excerpts or customized printings can also be created to fit specific needs. For details, write or phone the office of the Kensington Sales Manager: Kensington Publishing Corp., 119 West 40th Street, New York, NY 10018. Attn. Sales Department. Phone: 1-800-221-2647.

First Electronic Edition: August 2022
ISBN: 978-1-5161-1134-3 (ebook)

First Print Edition: August 2022
ISBN: 978-1-5161-1135-0

Printed in the United States of America

To my boys Chance and Alex. Always my inspiration.

Chapter 1

Every demon in Chicago could recognize Satin. It wasn't just the fact that she was a stunningly beautiful vampire with thick black hair that tumbled down her back and a pale face dominated by eyes the precise shade of aged cognac. Or that she managed the Viper Pit, the most exclusive demon club in the city. It was the thunderous power that vibrated around her reed-slender body. The sort of power that was usually reserved for a clan chief.

Her notoriety meant that she was rarely challenged. By anyone. Something she appreciated when she was working, but it did ensure there wasn't much variety in her life.

Until now.

Standing at the edge of the clearing, Satin absorbed the pulse of her surroundings. If her heart could beat, it would be thumping with excitement. Instead, it was her fully extended fangs that throbbed in anticipation.

The night air was laced with the scent of her prey. A rich male musk that was unique to pure-blooded Were. It whispered of power and sex and the most delicious pain. Relishing the raw, primitive sensations that vibrated through her, Satin stepped out of the thick fringe of trees and allowed the moonlight to bathe her in silver.

When she'd first sought out this secret club that sprawled over a thousand empty acres an hour south of Chicago, it had been to scope out the competition. Viper, the local clan chief and owner of the Viper Pit, wasn't a male who shared his territory. If the Were was attempting to steal their customers, then she would shut him down. Permanently.

It had only taken one visit to realize that the Hunting Grounds was nothing like Viper's club. There was no elegant building, no plush booths, nor any beautiful waiters delivering the finest champagne while soft music played in the background. This place was woodlands and overgrown fields and meadows that were shrouded in layers of magic. The demons didn't come here to mingle or seek their eternal mates. They came to hunt and fight and enjoy meaningless sex with complete abandon.

Even better, the owner of the club, Marco, had strict rules that kept the bloodshed to a minimum. Every guest was there of their own free will, and any of them could call a halt to the game whenever they wanted.

It was a place for the most powerful demons to test their strength against each other without fear of lasting consequences. And if the night ended with a bout of sizzling sex...so much the better.

Which was exactly why Satin had returned over and over again. There were few creatures who could match her in a one-on-one battle. Perhaps Viper or Styx, who was the current King of Vampires. And there were even fewer demons who could stir her icy passions to a fever pitch.

As if on cue, a large male joined her in the clearing.

She hissed, as always stunned by the sight of Marco. Even for a pure-blooded Were, he was tall with broad shoulders and muscles that rippled beneath his white silk shirt and black slacks. His dark hair was cut short, emphasizing the chiseled symmetry of his features and his eyes, which were as dark as the pits of hell and circled with a rim of shimmering gold. It was the brutal heat and savage strength in the air when he was near that enticed Satin. He was not only the local pack master, but he was a cousin to Salvatore, King of Weres.

A perfect opponent.

In more ways than one.

Marco flashed a smug smile, folding his arms over his impressive chest. "I knew you would be here tonight."

Satin felt a stab of irritation. Was the jerk implying she was predictable? Or that she simply couldn't stay away? Either one pissed her off.

"You can read the future? Impressive."

His smile widened. "I can't read the future, but I can read you."

The air dropped by several degrees. "Doubtful."

His nose flared, a hint of his wolf flashing gold in the depths of his dark eyes. "I can smell your hunger."

"Actually, I ate before I left my lair," she drawled.

"You're not hungry for food."

"No?"

"You're hungry for me."

He was right, of course. It'd been nearly a week since she'd last visited the Hunting Grounds, and she'd grown increasingly restless. As if she had an itch she couldn't scratch. But she'd have her fangs extracted before she let him know he'd struck a nerve.

"Of course, you would assume every female desires you." She lifted her hand to her lips, as if stifling a yawn. "Males are so predictable."

He tilted back his head, sniffing the soft breeze. "I can smell it in the air." His voice thickened with his own desire. "But it's not just sex. You want to prove you can match me in combat. And what better night to prove your superiority than on the night of the full moon?"

Satin stilled. She wasn't a werewolf. She didn't pay attention to the cycles of the moon. But she couldn't deny the possibility that he was right. There might be an inner instinct to seek out this male when he was at the apex of his powers.

So what?

It didn't change anything, did it?

No. Of course not.

Satin spread her arms in a mocking gesture. "I know one thing I didn't come here for."

He arched a dark brow. "What's that?"

"Talking."

He blinked, as if caught off-guard by her response. Heat prickled through the clearing, then with a flash of his snowy-white fangs, he lifted his hand and wiggled his fingers.

"Fine. Let's do this."

Satin smiled in anticipation, reaching up to make sure her hair was still tightly braided. She didn't want any distractions. Before coming to the Hunting Grounds, she'd changed out of her designer gown and three-inch heels. The black spandex pants and sports bra clung to her rail-thin body like a second skin, and the soft leather boots were designed to allow her to move in complete silence. Perfect attire to kick some sexy Were ass.

Striding forward with the bold assurance of a predator who was at the top of the evolutionary ladder, Satin kept close watch on Marco. He pretended to be an arrogant brute like most of the customers at the club, with more ego than skill, but Satin wasn't fooled. He was a lethal competitor who could shift into his wolf form at any moment.

Marco pulled back his lips, revealing his razor-sharp fangs that could rip through flesh and bone. The sight of them ignited a blast of desire that seared through her. She'd discovered a shocking addiction to fangs and claws and hot male skin pressed against her naked body.

They met in the center of the opening, the air sizzling with an electric energy that sent the local wildlife scurrying for cover. It was a battle between titans, and no one wanted to get caught in the crossfire.

For a long moment, they stared at one another, allowing the anticipation to build to a crescendo. Then, with a blur of motion, Satin was leaping forward, crashing into the male with enough force to knock him backward. With a grunt, he grabbed her arm, flinging her over his head as he regained his balance. Satin twirled to land on her feet and swiftly reversed his grip on her arm to yank him toward her. Marco growled, his eyes burning with the golden fire of his wolf as he snapped his teeth a breath from her face. Satin flashed her own fully extended fangs, a sharp chill clashing against Marco's ferocious heat.

A heady musk teased Satin's senses, promising pleasure beyond her wildest dreams. She leaned against Marco's hard body, pretending to melt in submission. Marco released another growl, wrapping his arms around her slender waist as he lowered his head.

Using his distraction to her advantage, Satin whirled in a circle, kicking out to sweep his legs from beneath him.

Blindsided by her move, Marco did a complete backflip before he was flowing to his feet and pouncing toward her. Grabbing her by her shoulders, Marco leaned down to speak directly against her ear.

"Run."

Any other time or place, Satin would have punished a male who dared to give her orders. She had a low tolerance for bossy creatures. No, not low. Zero. Zero tolerance. Even Viper took care when he was requesting her to deal with a task for him.

But this was part of the game. The rare occasion she could release the rigid grip she kept on her emotions and give in to her primitive desires.

With a speed impossible to track, Satin was flowing toward the nearby trees and disappearing into the shadows. Behind her, the howl of a wolf pierced the night. Satin laughed as she raced through the darkness, feeling the press of Marco's power just behind her. It was exhilarating.

The scent of wolf was laced on the breeze, but the footsteps that were gaining on her were human. Marco had never shifted during their encounters. She didn't know if it was because she was a vampire and he feared reminding her that they were natural enemies. Or if he simply didn't have ample control when he was in his animal form.

Leaping over a fallen log, Satin was about to double back when hands grabbed her from behind.

Satin felt herself lifted off her feet and then tossed on the mossy ground. She didn't struggle as she landed flat on her back. Instead, she studied Marco in silence as he crouched over her, his dark beauty emphasized by the feral glow in his eyes.

His wolf was just below the surface, watching her with a ruthless desire that was tangible. He was gloriously, decadently sexy.

And for tonight, he was all hers.

She stretched up her arms, wrapping them around his neck before she was using her leverage to flip their positions. In one smooth movement, Marco was lodged beneath her and Satin was perched on top, her legs straddling his hips.

A slow, wicked smile curved his lips.

"Do you always have to be on top, *cara*?"

She grasped his silk shirt, holding his smoldering gaze as she ripped the silk material to expose the smooth expanse of his chest.

Her fangs throbbed with an unexpected hunger. What the hell? She had a sudden, violent urge to drink his blood. As if she was starved for the taste of him.

No. She squashed the dangerous thought. What she wanted from this male was nothing more complicated than a primitive release. Anything else was a product of the adrenaline pumping through her.

Focusing on the raw passion that pulsated between them, Satin scored her nails down his chest. Not hard enough to cut through his skin, but enough to wrench a groan of pleasure from his lips.

"You're rough on a man's wardrobe, *cara*," he murmured, his Italian accent thicker than usual.

"Are you complaining?"

He reached up to grasp her stretchy sports bra. With one yank he had it over her head and tossed on the nearby brush. Then he cupped her breasts in the searing heat of his hands.

"No complaints," he assured her. "No complaints at all."

Satin shivered, drowning in his rich musk.

"Your wolf is close tonight."

"Full moon." The words came out as a guttural rasp, his hands skimming down her rib cage to slide beneath the waistband of her pants. "And you."

Satin wriggled, helping Marco strip off the thin spandex. He muttered a curse as he fumbled with the lacing on her boots, but Satin didn't mind. Their sex was always hard and fast. She enjoyed having a minute to admire his fierce male features and the bulge of muscles beneath his smooth, golden skin.

Once she was naked, Satin ran her palms down his rock-hard stomach, investigating each ripple of his washboard abs. Even for a pureblood Were, this male was a beast. White-hot passion flared through her as the heat of his body seeped through her bare skin, igniting the fire that had smoldered since she'd arrived at the Hunting Grounds and caught his scent.

Savage impatience replaced her desire to savor the moment, and with zero guilt, she grabbed his expensive slacks and ripped them off his body. He could send her the bill to have them replaced. She relished the sensation that she was unwrapping him like a long-desired gift.

She grinned at the sound of his soul-deep groan. Her wolf liked it rough.

She froze. No. Not *her* wolf.

Just a temporary boy toy to sate her hunger. She'd forget all about him the second she found a new diversion.

Refusing to consider that this was anything more than sex, Satin leaned down to press her lips against his chest, using her lips and fangs to stir his desire to a fever pitch.

She liked him hot and bothered.

A lot.

"Satin," he ground out, his fingers digging into her lower back as he spanned her waist.

In answer, she wrapped her lips around the tip of his rigid erection. The taste of him exploded through her. A spicy musk that was tastier than ambrosia.

"Now," he abruptly barked, and Satin realized she'd pushed him to the edge of his control. Positioning herself over him, she slowly slid onto his massive length, feeling stretched to the limit as she at last had him fully inside her.

"Now," she agreed, bracing herself as he lifted his hips off the ground and began to pound their bodies together with glorious abandon.

Satin tilted back her head, her gaze blindly locked on the star-splattered sky as ecstasy cascaded through her. It was stunningly perfect. As if Marco had been created just to sate her deepest needs. Releasing the tension and aggravations of the past week, Satin gave herself completely to the barbaric coupling.

But as her orgasm loomed, she lowered her head, locking her gaze with the golden fire in Marco's eyes. In the midst of the chaotic hunger threatening to consume her, he was her touchstone. The only truth in a world that was spinning out of her control.

That's when she felt the sharp press of his claws raking down her back, and a primal cry was wrenched from her throat as the pleasure-pain vaulted her over the edge into utter bliss.

* * * *

Three weeks later

The mansion on the outskirts of Chicago was an impressive sight. It was a massive, sweeping structure that consumed a vast amount of the manicured grounds. Inside, there was plenty of the mandatory marble and gilt with fluted columns that might have come straight from Greece. It was the sort of place that should have belonged to a hedge-fund manager who skimmed money from his clients and smuggled drugs with his yacht on the weekends.

Instead, it was home to a far more exotic power couple. The King of Vampires, Styx, and his vegetarian werewolf mate, Darcy.

Currently Styx was watching the tiny gargoyle pace across his office. Levet was barely three feet tall, with large fairy wings and an impressive ability to scrape his nerves raw. Styx, on the other hand, stood well over six foot with the chiseled beauty of his Aztec ancestors. His long black hair was held from his face with thin gold bands, and he was covered from neck to toe in leather. He wasn't trying to look like a badass. He *was* a badass.

Settling on the corner of the massive desk, Styx folded his arms over the broad width of his chest, wishing he'd never gotten out of bed.

Being the Anasso—the official title of the leader of the vampires—meant that he spent the first few hours of each night dealing with the endless squabbles between various clans or complaints from demons about a vampire damaging their property or committing violence against them. It was an expected annoyance.

But after sending away the last petitioner and preparing to spend some quality time with his lovely mate, Styx had been cornered in his office by the tiny gargoyle. He'd tried to order the annoying creature to go away, but Levet had immediately started babbling about his aunt Bertha and Hong Kong and blah, blah, blah. Or at least that's what it had sounded like to Styx.

"Stop," he finally snapped, rubbing his temple. "You're giving me a headache."

Levet came to a halt, regarding him with a curious expression. "Do vampires get headaches?"

It shouldn't be possible. Vampires were impervious to human sickness. But there was no denying the throb behind his right eye.

"Only when they're being besieged by a chatterbox who keeps yammering about people I don't know and have zero interest in hearing about."

Levet blinked. "How can you not have interest in my aunt Bertha? She is *tres* fascinating."

Styx scowled. He'd heard the gargoyle babbling about his aunt, but he'd assumed he was making up the wild stories.

"She's real?"

"Of course she's real."

"And she's in Hong Kong?"

"*Non*. She *was* in Hong Kong, but I caught sight of her last night near Navy Pier when I was test-driving Viper's new Jag."

Styx blinked. "Viper asked you to test-drive his new Jag?"

Levet's tail twitched at the question. "Perhaps he did not specifically ask, but I assumed he would desire a friend to ensure it was in good working order. And he is lucky that I did. I discovered several scratches on the bumper when I eventually returned it to his garage. He should contact the dealer and complain."

Styx rolled his eyes. "When Viper finds out you destroyed his car, he's going to have your head chopped off and mounted as a hood ornament."

"*Destroyed* is such an ugly word." Levet clicked his tongue. "Besides, what Viper does not know does not hurt *moi*, right?"

With a shake of his head, Styx dismissed the hope that Viper might rid the world of the gargoyle once and for all. Levet always managed to survive. Like a cockroach. Only more irritating.

"And I should care about your aunt Bertha because...?" He turned the conversation back to the original reason Levet was in his office making him nuts.

"Because she wasn't in her gargoyle form."

"Is that unusual?"

"Would it be unusual if you woke up in the shape of a dew fairy?"

The overhead chandelier flickered as Styx released a small thread of power. He could destroy the entire electrical grid of Chicago if he wanted.

"Careful, gargoyle."

Levet held up his hands, as if sensing he was treading on Styx's last nerve. "I am worried about her."

Styx swallowed a curse. The sooner he could get the stupid creature to spit out what he wanted, the sooner Styx could get rid of him.

"What shape was she in?"

"She looked like a human."

"And you have no idea how it happened?"

"*Non*. When I first saw her in Hong Kong, she said she woke from one of her epic naps to discover she'd been transformed."

"Is she in danger?"

Levet wrinkled his snout. "I am not sure."

Styx stared down at the miniature demon. Levet aggravated the hell out of him, but he couldn't deny a small amount of sympathy for being born different from other gargoyles. He wasn't only a fraction of the normal size, but his large wings were as thin as gossamer instead of leather and his magic was sketchy as hell.

"Why do you care?" he demanded. "I thought your family banished you from the Gargoyle Guild?"

"They did." Levet heaved a gusty sigh. "Which was much worse than my mother attempting to kill me."

"So, why help any of them?"

Levet shrugged. "Aunt Bertha is the only one who ever showed me any kindness." The gargoyle paused before clearing his throat. "Besides, she might have a teeny-tiny habit of causing disasters."

Uh-oh. A bad feeling formed in the pit of Styx's gut. Levet was notorious for creating chaos. If he was worried about his aunt, then things were bad. Really bad.

"Disasters?"

"You know..." Levet gave an airy wave of his hands. "The Ice Age. The Great Fire of London. The breakup of the Beatles."

Styx shuddered. "Obviously she's related to you. Which means she'll be fine, even if she does destroy Chicago."

"Not in her human form. She is too vulnerable to be wandering around alone."

"If that's true, you have the skills necessary to track her." Styx pointed out the obvious. "Knock yourself out."

Levet stomped his foot, his hands on his hips as he glared the long distance up at Styx. "You owe me."

"I *owe* you?" Styx lifted a hand to touch the spot where he'd been recently injured. "You hit me on the head with a rock."

"*Oui*." The gargoyle revealed zero regret for nearly splitting open Styx's skull. "To save you from the evil vampire. In fact, I have saved you from several evil creatures. You owe me double. Or triple."

Unfortunately, he wasn't exaggerating. Over the past decade, the irritating demon had revealed an astonishing talent for possessing the magic necessary to battle back a variety of enemies. Styx, however, was more concerned with the reason Levet wanted help in chasing down his relative.

"There's something you're not telling me."

Levet widened his eyes. "*Moi?*"

"Spit it out," Styx snapped. "Now."

The sparkling wings drooped as Levet heaved a small sigh. "I cannot locate Bertha."

"Why not?"

There was a long pause, as if the gargoyle was reluctant to confess the truth. "I presume she has placed a protective spell around herself to avoid my detection."

"That's possible?" Styx demanded in genuine surprise. It hadn't occurred to him that there might be a way to avoid the pest. Probably because vampires detested magic with the force of a thousand suns. "More importantly, will she provide me with the same spell? I'm willing to pay whatever she asks."

"Be serious."

"I've never been more serious."

Levet gave another stomp of his foot. "Are you going to help me, or must I speak to Darcy?"

Styx grimaced, conceding to the inevitable. His beautiful mate would nag at him until he did what Levet wanted. She had a ridiculous soft spot for the creature.

"I'll help," he grudgingly conceded, leaning down to pluck a hair from between the gargoyle's stunted horns.

"Hey." Levet rubbed the spot, glaring up at Styx. "Why did you do that?"

"I need something connected to the gargoyle. You should have the same DNA." Styx tucked the hair in the front pocket of his pants before pointing his finger directly in Levet's face. "Once your aunt has been located, all debts between us are cancelled. Got it?"

"*Oui.* I got it."

"Good." Styx headed toward the door.

"Where are you going?" Levet called out.

"To find the one vampire capable of tracking a gargoyle who doesn't want to be found."

Chapter 2

The lodge at the Hunting Grounds wasn't the biggest or most elegant demon club around. The main floor of the split-log building had a long room with a massive fireplace where the customers gathered before a hunt, a large bar area, and kitchens. The second floor was reserved for Marco's private rooms, as well as his office.

The appeal of this place wasn't the lodge; it was the rolling fields and thick woodlands that were populated with wild animals, fish, and fowl. Plus, there were always plenty of curs who were hanging around, prepared for a good fight with any demon who needed to blow off steam. All he needed to offer was plenty of privacy and strict guidelines that kept the bloodshed to an acceptable level.

Currently Marco was pacing from one end of his office to the other. It was a large room with floor-to-ceiling windows that overlooked the nearby meadow. Unlike many demons, a pure-blooded Were enjoyed sunshine and fresh air. More importantly, the windows allowed him to keep a constant watch on his considerable investment. The furniture was carved out of wood and reinforced to bear the weight of demons. Overhead, the ceiling was open-beamed with muted lighting, and at the far end was a stone fireplace big enough to roast an entire pig.

It reminded him of the lair he'd left behind in Italy. It'd been hard to leave their traditional hunting grounds, but with his cousin Salvatore in Kansas City, he'd made the decision a year ago to try his luck at the American dream. And he'd succeeded beyond his wildest imagination. The Hunting Grounds had expanded from a hundred-acre farm with a decaying barn and brackish pond to a thousand-acre playground with the lodge, private cabins, and a huge lake with an island in the center that could be reserved for fights between his more aggressive demons. It prevented the lesser creatures from being accidentally caught up in the battle.

The initial success of the Hunting Grounds was a result of Marco's hard work and innate knowledge of the innermost desires of his fellow demons. But the expansion of his business was increasingly in the hands of the manager he'd brought in a few months ago.

Troy was…well, Marco hadn't exactly decided. To say he was an imp, was like saying Liberace was a piano player. Or that the sun was warm. Troy was as large and muscular as Marco with long hair that shimmered like fire as it flowed down his back. He had bright green eyes that smoldered with a sensuality that he shared indiscriminately with the various guests. Most unnerving was his wardrobe. Leather, lace, feathers, or nothing more than a thong. It was always designed to shock. The first day they'd met, he was wearing a tiger-striped spandex onesie that stretched tight over his body. *Too* tight.

He wasn't the sort of creature whom Marco would have expected to enjoy the often-tedious tasks of operating a business. He was too flamboyant, too flighty, too…extra. But Salvatore's mate, Harley, had mentioned that her mother had opened a strip club in Chicago with the help of Troy and it had become a raging sensation. In fact, they now had a chain of them across the States and in Europe.

Marco was ambitious enough to want the same global expansion. Or at least he had been. Until the past three weeks.

Now he didn't know what the hell he wanted. Well, besides a few hours of sleep that wasn't plagued with strange nightmares. And the ability to concentrate on work without being interrupted with thoughts of a certain female vampire. Oh, and if someone was handing out wishes, he'd take a nice bottle of double-oaked bourbon from the highlands of Scotland. It wouldn't solve anything, but it would smooth the annoyance of the nightmares and the relentless obsessing over a female who'd ghosted him.

He was on yet another circuit around the office when the door was shoved open and Troy stepped inside. Marco came to an abrupt halt at the sight of his manager. This evening he was wearing black-and-white-striped spandex pants and a sleeveless vest made from thick white fur. His hair was braided and decorated with metal feathers studded with rare gems.

"I have the list of supplies that need to be ordered," Troy said, waving the clipboard he held in his hand.

Marco scowled. "Not now."

"That's what you said yesterday. And the day before. And the—"

"Are you deliberately trying to piss me off?" Marco interrupted.

"I'm attempting to manage your club and make both of us a great deal of money," the imp chided, his emerald eyes hardening. Troy acted like a flighty, exotic butterfly until it came to money. Then he was a lethal opponent. "Something I'm very good at. Or have you forgotten why you hired me?"

The imp was right, of course. He'd asked Troy to become the manager because he could help Marco build his empire. Unfortunately, he wasn't currently in the mood for empire building.

"Do your managing elsewhere," he commanded. "I'm busy."

"Busy?"

"Yes."

Troy pointedly glanced around the empty office. "Polishing the bottom of your shoes on the carpet? Practicing your manly growls and very explicit Italian curses?"

Marco drew back his lips to expose his extended fangs in a blatant warning. Troy, however, remained unimpressed, the pungent scent of plums suddenly thick in the air. Marco felt a violent urge to punch something. Or someone. But even as his hands curled into tight fists, he heaved a harsh sigh. He was part wolf, not jackass. He was obviously being unreasonable.

Striding forward, he grabbed the clipboard and scanned the long list of supplies.

"Double the amount of ambrosia. We've had more fey creatures than I originally anticipated. And…wait." Marco glanced up as he reached the bottom of the list. "Why are there two vats of grog? They cost a fortune."

"I convinced the local orc tribe to use the Hunting Grounds to celebrate their annual tribute to the goddess." Troy smiled with smug satisfaction. "You're welcome."

"What does this tribute include?"

"Best not to ask."

Marco scowled. He didn't like the sound of that. "They're not going to destroy my club, are they?"

"Are you a betting man?"

The air prickled with a sudden heat as his wolf stirred inside him. For Marco, this place was a stepping-stone to greatness. For his animal, it was the place he called home. And no one screwed with that.

"No."

"Easy." Troy lifted a slender hand. "I required a deposit large enough to rebuild this place if necessary. Orcs are crude and smelly and have rocks as brains, but they are willing to pay to honor their goddess."

Marco resisted the urge to cancel the ritual. As Troy said, they usually had large amounts of treasure, and they were willing to spend it. If this became an annual occasion, he could make a small fortune.

"Is that all?"

Troy shook his head. "The staffing schedules still need to be completed, plus we need to interview for a new bartender."

Marco swallowed a curse. "Can you deal with that?"

"I can." There was a deliberate pause. "But only if you agree to my request."

"If it's money—"

"It's not," Troy interrupted, his brows arching as if struck by a sudden thought. "Although I never say no to money." He shrugged. "Or sex. Or designer shoes."

Marco snapped his teeth. "Troy, what is your request?"

"I want you to find Satin and get her out of your system."

It was the last thing Marco had been expecting. A low growl rumbled in his throat. "I don't know what you're talking about."

Troy rolled his eyes. "Then let me clarify. You've been in a foul mood for the past three weeks. You snarl at anyone unfortunate enough to cross your path. You've put your fist through walls. You busted windows and ripped through the priceless tapestry in the main lobby. And now you lock yourself away for endless hours, pacing and muttering. Either you have rabies or you're missing the beautiful vampire who no longer comes to play with you. Go." Troy waved his hands in a get-the-hell-out-of-here motion. "Find her."

Marco folded his arms over his chest, his wolf pressing against his skin. It was bad enough to be obsessed to the point of insanity with a female without the realization everyone was aware of his enthrallment. It was… embarrassing.

"I hired you to manage the club, not to offer advice on my private life," he snapped.

"The club is what I'm concerned about," Troy insisted. "You have scared off our bartender, the tribe of wood sprites who tended the grounds, and at least a dozen customers. You won't have a business for me to oversee if you don't get her out of your system."

Marco spun away. Dammit. He'd been so focused on his tangled emotions that he hadn't allowed himself to consider the price his club was paying for his foul mood. Not just the physical damage, but the destruction of the atmosphere he'd carefully cultivated. This was supposed to be a place of electric excitement, where everyone went for a good time.

Like Vegas for demons.

"And how do you suggest I do that?"

"Do you want written instructions or a demonstration?"

With a low hiss, Marco headed for the door. Enough was enough. He was going to find Satin and...

Actually, he didn't know what was going to happen once he found her. He'd worry about that when he was standing face-to-face with the aggravating leech.

"Take care of the club. I might be gone a few days," he called out as he jogged out of the office and toward the nearby stairs.

Once he was outside, he halted in the shadows of the lodge and tilted back his head. With his gaze locked on the star-spattered sky, he called on his inner magic.

Hot, searing pleasure jolted through him. A combination of pain and ecstasy as his bones popped and his muscles stretched. There was nothing that could compare to shifting into his wolf. It was a primal force that expanded from the core of his soul and exploded through him.

Seconds later, his human form had been transformed into a large wolf with dark fur and golden eyes. With a howl of sheer relief at being out of his office and on the hunt, Marco put his nose to the ground and headed toward Chicago. Satin would no doubt be at the Viper Pit. But he'd taken less than a dozen steps when he slowed at the realization that he could actually 'sense' Satin. Not by the usual means. He couldn't smell her or feel the cool wash of her power. No. It was as if there was a mental connection between them that was tugging him in the opposite direction.

Marco briefly hesitated. What was happening? A trick of his fevered obsession? Or something more nefarious?

Impossible to know until he finally managed to track her down. Turning to the west, Marco released another growl and began to lope in pursuit of his delectable prey.

* * * *

The small town in central Oklahoma appeared oddly trapped in time. The redbrick buildings lined the cobblestone sidewalks with old-time saloons and mercantile shops. The focal point, however, appeared to be a large white temple. Bertha had no idea what it was used for, and she had zero interest in finding out. Instead, she headed toward the edge of town.

Walking along the narrow creek that was bathed in moonlight, she at last stopped next to a dead tree trunk that had been weathered to a pale gray. Lifting her hand, she pressed against the layer of magic and slowly stepped through the illusion.

Instantly she was standing in the hidden demon bar. Like the nearby town, the taproom was trapped in the past. The large wooden building had an open-beamed ceiling and worn floors with roughly carved tables and chairs scattered through the narrow space. It smelled of stale ale, wet fur, and what she suspected were troll farts.

Wrinkling her nose, Bertha halted in the center of the floor. She'd been in worse places. Then again, she'd been in better ones. Much better. But it wasn't the stench or the sense of decay hanging heavy in the air that caused her to turn in a hesitant circle, her brow furrowed with confusion.

She was still turning when a male voice intruded into her bewilderment. "Are you lost?"

"Hmm." Bertha considered the question as she aimlessly wandered toward the back of the room. The imp looked vaguely familiar, although most of the fey looked alike. This one had flame-red hair that he wore in a short, spiky style and a pale, narrow face with large emerald eyes. He was dressed in black leather with a wide gold band around his neck. Like a dog collar, only studded with emeralds. "I haven't decided," she told her companion as she crawled onto one of the high stools.

The male blinked. "You haven't decided if you're lost?"

Bertha placed her elbow on the smooth wood and planted her chin in her open palm.

"I suppose it depends on your definition of 'lost'," she pointed out.

"Is there more than one definition?"

"I don't know where I am," Bertha admitted. "But then again, I'm not sure where I'm going." She'd been quite happy spending time in Chicago. At least as happy as she could be in her current form. She'd been indulging in various entertainments around the city, including a strip club called Sophia's Menagerie, which had the most delicious pure-blooded Were dancers. Then a strange voice had started to whisper in her mind. It insisted she had to leave Chicago and travel west. At first, she'd ignored the stupid thing. She didn't want to go west. If she ever decided to leave Chicago, she would go to Paris and visit her family. But as the voice had become more and more insistent, she'd been unable to sleep. And then her appetite had disappeared. That was unacceptable. Life was not worth living without cheesecake and roasted pork and deep-dish pizza. Mmm. Pizza. At last, she'd given into the inevitable and began her long, tedious trek. Anything to shut up the voice. So now she was standing in this remote bar with no idea why. "If I don't have a destination, can I actually be lost?" she concluded.

"I…" The male seemed to struggle for words, as if he wasn't quite sure what to say. That happened a lot. Bertha assumed that other creatures were dazzled by her deep thoughts and unique philosophy. Finally, he cleared his throat, his gaze skimming over her. "This isn't a place for a female like you. Not once the nearby fighting pits are closed and the crowd comes here to celebrate their victory. Or more likely, to drown their sorrow. There's another bar in Tulsa you should check out. They serve lots of fruity punch in coconut shells with umbrellas."

Bertha frowned at his suggestion before heaving a sigh. She forgot she wasn't currently a seven-foot-tall gargoyle covered with gray skin coated in moss and leather wings that had a span as wide as this bar. Instead, she was smaller than the majority of demons, with a delicate structure that made her appear as fragile as a dew fairy. Her pale gold hair was twisted into wild spirals to her shoulders, and her eyes were a misty gray. Only the faintest outline of ephemeral wings revealed that she was something other than human. At the moment she was wearing a sheer gown with rhinestones that floated down to her ankles because she liked the sparkles. She hadn't bothered with shoes.

"I don't like fruity drinks." She pointed toward the iron vat that was brewing over an open fire in the far corner. "Get me a grog."

"Grog?" The imp appeared shocked by the request. "Are you sure?"

"Please stop asking me questions." Bertha pressed a finger against her temple. There was a pain directly behind her right eye. "I really need that drink."

The scent of gingersnaps laced with granite swirled through the air, and the imp hurriedly backed away. Clearly, he could sense her thunderous power despite the fact she was doing her best to keep it leashed. It occasionally leaked out. Like the gooey marshmallow in a s'more when you bit into it. Mmm. S'mores.

"One grog coming up," he muttered, grabbing a tankard and dipping it into the steaming vat.

"Make it a double," Bertha called out. If one was good, then two was better, right?

The imp did a second dip of the tankard before returning to the bar to set it in front of her. "Double grog."

"Thanks." Bertha grabbed the tankard and downed the contents in one gulp.

The fiery liquid seared down her throat and hit her stomach with an explosive impact. Bertha parted her lips to release a belch that sent flames flying, accidentally melting the empty tankard. She dropped the lump of bronze on the floor as the male hissed in shock.

"What are you?" he demanded.

She belched again. This time it was thankfully fire-free. "A gargoyle."

"Gargoyle?"

"Yep."

The imp blinked. Did he have something in his eye? That was always a drag.

"You don't look like a gargoyle."

"Right?" Bertha glanced down, giving a sad shake of her head at the sight of her pathetically weak body. "I don't know what happened. I fell asleep on a mountain in Nepal. I think there was an earthquake. Or maybe I was magically attacked. Whatever the case, I woke up a century later buried beneath a ton of rubble and in this human shape."

"Gargoyle..." The male studied her in disbelief.

Bertha shifted uncomfortably on the stool. "Are you going to stare at me all night?"

"Nope." Holding up his hands in an apologetic gesture, the imp backed away. Most fey creatures were terrified of gargoyles. With good reason. "I'm just going to stand over here until you need me."

"Probably a good idea."

Bertha drummed her fingers on the bar, impatiently waiting for the urge to move along to hit her. That was how it'd been happening. She felt an odd tug that led her from location to location. Sometimes she would stop for an hour or so to eat or drink. And, of course, during the day she would rest in a spot with plenty of shade. She might not look like a gargoyle, but she would turn to stone in the sun. But as soon as she woke, she would be moving again.

"Well?" she at last snapped.

"I didn't say anything." The words came from the imp, who was now plastered against the back wall.

Bertha glared in his direction. "I wasn't talking to you."

"Oh. Right. Okay." The male forced a stiff smile to his lips. "Carry on."

With a click of her tongue, Bertha swiveled on the stool until she was facing the door. She didn't want to be distracted again.

"Hello. I'm waiting," she said out loud.

"For what?" This time it was the voice in her head.

"To go."

"Not yet. You need to get ready."

Bertha scowled. She didn't like this place, with its smell of troll farts. Especially now that she could feel a sharp chill in the air. It was causing goose bumps to crawl over her too-delicate skin.

"Get ready for what?"

"That."

The word whispered through her mind at the precise moment the door was shoved open and a tall, slender vampire with black hair pulled into a braid and pale features set in lines of grim determination entered the bar. Bertha whistled in appreciation as she allowed her gaze to skim over the female's red leather vest that laced up the front and the stretchy yoga pants. If she was going to be stuck in this body for more than a few years, then she was going to need to develop a kick-ass style. Maybe this female could give her some tips.

The vampire narrowed her cognac eyes as she caught sight of Bertha. "There you are."

"Am I?" Bertha glanced down. "I suppose so," she conceded, glancing back at the female. "Although it's all a matter of perspective, isn't it? The reality of existence."

The female made a sound of impatience. "You're Bertha, right?"

"Yes." Bertha tilted her head to the side. "Do I know you?"

"I'm Satin." She cast a quick glance around the room, as if searching for potential enemies. Only when she was satisfied that there was no one lurking beyond the imp in the corner did she move forward. Bertha silently applauded her caution. A woman could never be too careful. "Styx sent me," she informed Bertha.

"Styx?" Bertha searched her brain. At last she hit on the most reasonable guess. "The band?"

It was the leech's turn to be confused. "What band?"

"You said that Styx sent you," Bertha reminded her. "I'm sure the river to the underworld didn't send you, so it has to be the band. I'm not stupid."

The female rolled her eyes. "Styx is the Anasso."

"Oh." *Anasso* was the official title to the King of Vampires. The last Bertha had heard about the Anasso was that he'd gone bat-shit crazy and was hiding in some cave near Chicago. Of course, now that she actually thought about it, one of the king's most trusted guards was named Styx. He'd obviously decided to give himself a promotion. "I must have slept through the overthrow of the previous king. No matter." She waved her hand in an airy motion. "What does he want?"

Satin shrugged. "Something to do with your nephew."

"I have several dozen nephews. Perhaps hundreds. Who keeps track?"

"Levet."

Bertha heaved a sigh. When she'd left Chicago, she'd placed a protective spell around herself. Until she knew exactly who or what was leading her around like a puppet, she wasn't going to put Levet in danger.

"I should have known," she muttered. "He is quite special to me, but he can be annoyingly persistent."

"So I hear." Satin jerked her head toward the door. "Let's go."

"Go?" Bertha arched her brows. "Go where?"

"I just told you."

"No, you didn't. You said that Styx—who isn't the band or the river to the underworld—sent you and that it was because of Levet. But you never mentioned going anywhere."

"I'm taking you to Chicago."

Bertha slid off the stool. An argument was brewing. And since vampires were nearly as stubborn as gargoyles, there was a better-than-average chance things could get ugly.

"Yeah, I don't think so."

The temperature in the bar dropped by several degrees. "This isn't a debate. Styx wants you in Chicago, and that's where you're going."

Bertha folded her arms over her chest. "No."

"I'm not leaving here without you."

"Then you're staying, I guess. I'll warn you, there's more than a whiff of troll farts in the air."

Ice crawled over the wooden floor. "Why are you being so stubborn?"

"Because I'm on a mission."

"What mission?"

"I'm not sure yet." Bertha wrinkled her nose. "But I think it might be important."

Satin glared down at her, the line of her jaw hardening as she revealed a hint of fang. "This is bullshit. I don't have the energy to argue." She reached down as if intending to grab Bertha by the arm. "Let's go."

Bertha hurriedly darted to the side, holding out her hand in warning. "Stay back. I don't want to hurt you."

"As if you could."

"Not a 'female in your condition'."

"Just come with me and…" The annoyed words trailed away as Satin absorbed Bertha's words. "What do you mean? A female in my condition?"

"You know." Bertha leaned forward, whispering in case the leech didn't want anyone to know her secret. "The baby."

Satin blinked, and Bertha sighed. Yet another demon blinking when she was talking to them.

"Baby?" The word fell awkwardly from the female's lips.

"*Oui. Le bébé. Pequeño. Il bambino,*" Bertha clarified.

"I understand the word *baby*," Satin snapped. "What I don't understand is what it has to do with me."

It was Bertha's turn to blink. Was this a joke? Was the vampire truly oblivious to the fact she was pregnant? Or was she attempting to pretend ignorance to fool Bertha? A waste of time, of course. Bertha had detected the presence of the child the moment the female had walked through the door. She could not only hear the heartbeat, but it was a soft ball of warmth in the center of the icy leech.

"I'm referring to the one you're currently carrying, of course. There's no use in pretending it's not there. Not with me."

"Did you hit your head?" Satin demanded, even as she lifted a hand to press it against her gently rounded stomach.

Bertha gave the question serious consideration. "Numerous times. Would you like me to list them all?"

"No." Satin released a hiss of annoyance. "I'm a vampire."

"True. What does that have to do with hitting my head?"

"Vampires sire offspring with their bite." Each word was slow and concise, as if Satin assumed Bertha was too stupid to comprehend what she was telling her. "They don't have actual children."

Bertha boldly strolled forward to touch the hand that Satin cradled over her stomach. "Then why is there a baby in here?" Bertha's eyes widened in surprise, suddenly realizing why the baby was putting out such a fierce heat. "Oh. A 'Were'."

The female's lips parted in shock. "Did you say Were?"

"Pureblood." Bertha pursed her lips to whistle in admiration. The kid was already more powerful than many full-grown demons. "And very strong."

Satin knocked Bertha's hand away, her fangs fully exposed. "Impossible."

"You can keep saying that, but it doesn't change the fact that you are expecting a baby."

"It has to be a spell," Satin muttered, speaking more to herself than Bertha. "Some sort of illusion."

"*Non,* not an illusion. The baby is very real." Bertha paused, abruptly noticing the energy that pulsed around the vampire. She hadn't sensed it until she forced herself to directly concentrate on the female. As if it was deliberately deflecting attention. Hmm. Odd. "But there is magic," she murmured.

Satin appeared predictably unnerved. Vamps hated magic. "What kind?"

Bertha lifted her hands in a gesture of confusion. "I can't tell, but I suspect that it's connected to the evil presence that's shrouded around you."

"The…" Satin struggled to get the word past her stiff lips. "Baby?"

"Not directly." Bertha couldn't sense evil in the child. It was attached directly to the vampire. "It's seeped into your very essence," she said.

Satin jerked. "What the hell does that mean?"

"Perhaps a curse," Bertha suggested. "Or a demonic possession. Or a…" Bertha lost her train of thought as the familiar voice spoke directly into her mind.

"Time to go."

She stomped her foot. "Stop yammering in my head. You made me forget what I was going to say."

"Bertha, feel the air," the voice warned with a harsh insistence. "Get out of there."

Bertha paused, closing her eyes to allow her senses to spread outward. Instantly she encountered the sizzling heat of an approaching Were. No. Not just a Were. A super-duper pissed-off pure-blooded Were who was on the hunt for the female he considered his own. Only an idiot would get involved in the looming confrontation.

"Perhaps you're right," she muttered, grabbing the skirt of her gown and lifting her hand over her head. "*Au revoir.*"

With a snap of her fingers, Bertha created a portal, and in the blink of an eye, she had disappeared.

Chapter 3

Satin watched in numb disbelief as Bertha stepped through a portal and vanished from the bar. Or at least Satin assumed it was a portal. As a vampire she had no ability to detect magic. Which meant she couldn't follow the strange gargoyle.

Probably for the best. Satin was too busy processing the shocking claim that she was carrying a baby to wander into unfamiliar territory. The last thing she needed was to blindly stumble into a trap.

Standing in the center of the room, she ignored the imp who was regarding her with a wary gaze. Her thoughts were focused on the strange heat that burned in the center of her body.

It wasn't the first time she'd felt it. It'd started three weeks ago. The night after her pagan coupling with Marco beneath the full moon. At first, she'd thought it was caused by her growing addiction to the male Were. That's why she'd stopped going to the Hunting Grounds. The mere thought that she might not be in control of her emotions was horrifying. She was ruthlessly independent. No male would ever change that. But avoiding Marco hadn't eased the weird sensations. In fact, the heat had started to spread, as if there was a fire burning in the pit of her stomach. And worse, the massive powers that she'd come to depend on were slowly being leached away, leaving her feeling...vulnerable. A sensation that hadn't tormented her since the days she'd been a fledgling vampire cowering in her dark cave.

Her hand absently pressed against her stomach, feeling the soft bump that had made her choose the stretchy yoga pants instead of her jeans.

Was it possible?

It shouldn't be. No vampire had ever given birth to a baby. But there was no denying something strange was happening to her. It wasn't just the heat inside her and the relentless drain on her powers—but Marco's scent remained embedded in her skin. Add in her expanding waistline and it all combined to suggest that the Were had done something to her. Something that was screwing with her body.

As if on cue, a potent musk swirled through the air. A surge of anger laced with treacherous anticipation raced through Satin as she whirled toward the door. A second later it was slammed open, and a gorgeous male stormed into the bar.

"At last," Marco snarled, prowling directly toward her. He was wearing black slacks and a white silk shirt that should have made him look civilized. He'd even combed his short black hair until it lay smooth against his head. But not even a human would think this Were was civilized. His eyes glowed with the power of his wolf, and the air snapped with his animal energy. "You can run, but you can't hide."

"You."

Satin was moving before she had the opportunity to consider what she was doing. Grabbing him by the throat, she hauled him across the floor and pinned him against the wall.

Marco scowled, but oddly he made no effort to fight against her hold. "Easy, leech," he warned.

Satin glared at his elegantly sculpted features. Why did they have to be so perfect?

"Tell me what you did to me."

"Did to you?" He arched a brow, his eyes darkening as if he was recalling their time together. "In detail? Or just the highlights?"

"You used some sort of animal magic on me."

A slow, wicked smile curved his lips. "You're welcome."

"This isn't funny," Satin hissed.

"Look, I don't know what the hell you're..." Marco's words trailed away, his nose flaring as if he'd caught an unexpected scent. He leaned his head forward, sniffing her.

"Stop that."

He ignored her command. "You smell like Were."

His words intensified her anger. "Because of you."

"Me?" Marco narrowed his eyes. "I haven't been near you in weeks."

"Your magic did something to me." Satin muttered a curse as Marco knocked aside her hand that was holding him captive to lean down and press his nose against her belly. "I told you to stop that."

"A baby?" He froze, his heat suddenly thundering through the air as he straightened to regard her with a shocked expression. "My baby." He made a harsh sound, like he'd just taken a blow to the gut. "Impossible."

"That's what I said."

"Seriously." He shook his head. "I don't understand."

"Really?" She glared at him. "You're responsible."

"Me?"

"Yes." Satin's icy anger cut through the thick heat in the room. "You put your baby inside me…somehow."

His brows snapped together at her accusation. "That's absurd."

It had sounded absurd when she said the words out loud. Like she was telling a cheesy fairy tale. Unfortunately, this was all too real.

"Careful, dog," she warned.

"If it was possible to put my child into random females, I would have a hundred pups running around," he said, his voice harsh with barely suppressed emotions. "The Weres have struggled for centuries to procreate. Even after Salvatore destroyed the wolf spirit that was draining our powers, we have precious few babies. Each child is a miracle."

Satin paused. From the second Bertha had spoken the word "baby," she'd been too overwhelmed to think clearly. And she was *still* overwhelmed. But his fierce words forced her to actually consider her accusation. It was true that the Weres had struggled for centuries to have pups. Salvatore had eventually turned to science to help create babies, and even then, their powers were muted. They had hopes that the future would be brighter, but she had to admit that if they had the ability to magically create offspring, they wouldn't waste the opportunity by putting one into a vampire.

With an effort, she tried to control the panic lurking just below the surface. "If you aren't responsible for the insanity happening to me, then why are you here?"

Marco cleared his throat, appearing oddly uncomfortable at her question. "I think we have more important matters to discuss."

She eyed him in suspicion. "Why did you follow me?"

His jaw tightened. He was an alpha male who was used to other creatures eagerly trying to please him. She'd witnessed a few actually fall to their knees when he strolled past. They certainly never talked back. But he no doubt sensed she was on the edge. In truth, she was way over the edge.

"I wanted to know why you stopped coming to the Hunting Grounds," he grudgingly answered.

She waited. When he didn't continue, she frowned in confusion. "That's it?"

"*Si.*"

"How did you find me?"

"I'm a pureblood Were." He shrugged. "I could follow your scent to the pits of the netherworld."

"You tracked me eight hundred miles to discover why I haven't been at your club?" She didn't try to disguise her disbelief.

"I take my customer service very seriously."

Satin took a step back, her hand covering her stomach in an instinctively protective gesture.

"This is a trick," she muttered. "It has to be."

"What's a trick?"

"You appearing at the exact moment that I'm told about the baby."

"Told?" Marco didn't bother to insist on his innocence. Instead, he studied her with a puzzled expression. "By whom?"

"The gargoyle."

"A gargoyle told you about the baby?"

Satin was vaguely aware that she sounded like she'd lost her grip on reality, but at the moment she didn't care. She was suddenly remembering Bertha had told her more than just the fact that there was a child inside her.

"Yes," she murmured in distracted tones.

Marco stepped toward her, his expression worried. "Are you feeling okay?"

Satin stiffened. Not at the implication there was something wrong with her, but by the fact that this male was showing her concern. She wanted to be invincible. The badass of all badasses. Not a damsel in distress.

"No, I'm not feeling okay. And it's all your fault." She flashed her fangs, grabbing the small stone she'd hidden in the pocket of the leather vest.

It might not be fair to blame this male for her troubles, but she wasn't in the mood to be reasonable. Her life was spiraling out of control. Someone had to be punished.

And then, she needed answers.

The gargoyle had said she could sense the baby—along with another presence. She had to know what it was, and how the hell she could get rid of it.

"My fault? That's—" Marco bit off his frustrated words as he caught sight of the crystal she clutched in her fingers. It glowed to life as she tossed it directly toward him. There was a brilliant flash before the spell hidden in the crystal exploded and Marco was trapped in strands of magic. Satin had intended the snare for Bertha in case she proved to be a problem. Right now, it was more important to leash the Were so she could return to her hunt without having him hot on her trail. Marco growled in frustration, struggling against the invisible web. "What the hell are you doing?"

"I'll deal with you after I find the gargoyle." Satin whirled around and headed for the door.

"You can't leave me here!"

"Watch me."

Satin jogged through the darkness, wanting to put space between her and the Were before she had to find a place to wait out the daylight. After that, she would use her powers to find the gargoyle and demand the answers she needed.

Marco had called the baby a miracle. The gargoyle had suggested it was a curse. Her hand moved to touch her stomach, and she grimaced at the heat that burned through her skin. Miracle or curse? Right now, it felt like both.

* * * *

Styx was seated alone on the private balcony overlooking the dance floor at Viper's club. It was nearing dawn, and Viper was busy convincing the thinning crowd to spend the last of their money on drinks or the gambling tables before seeking out their lairs. Styx needed to head to his mansion on the outskirts of town. Dawn was less than an hour away. But his mate, Darcy, was visiting her twin sister, who'd come into the city for a visit, and he had no doubt she would lose track of time. Returning to an empty bed held no appeal. Odd, considering he'd spent centuries sleeping alone.

So, he lingered, sipping the last of the expensive scotch that Viper had reluctantly offered him. Reluctantly, because Styx never paid his tab. There had to be some perks for being king, right?

Attempting to decide if he should order another drink, Styx scowled in annoyance as the dusty stench of granite assaulted his nose. A second later, Levet flapped his way over the railing of the balcony and landed on the table.

Styx jumped to his feet. "What the hell are you doing?"

The aggravating gargoyle pointed toward the nearby staircase. "I am here with a red-light special."

"Red-light special? What's that mean?"

"You know." He twirled his hands over his head. "Warning, warning, warning."

"Warning about what?"

"Salvatore just burst through the front door. And he does not appear to be happy."

Styx arched his brows in surprise. The King of Weres was supposed to be at the Hunting Grounds with his mate and pack of pups. At least that's where Darcy had said they would be when she took off to visit with them. Styx hadn't tried to convince her to stay home and have them come to her instead. The Were children were worse than full-grown adults. The last time they'd visited, it had been like having tiny tornadoes whipping from room to room, destroying everything in their path.

"What is he doing here?" he muttered his thoughts out loud. "I thought he was staying with Marco."

"Perhaps it is mutt night." Levet waggled his heavy brows. "Do you comprehend? Not Ladies' Night, but mutt because—"

"Yeah, I get it," Styx interrupted, glaring at the ridiculous creature.

Levet snorted. "I have encountered trolls who have a better sense of humor."

"Not now, gargoyle." Styx spread his feet, his hands clenched at his side as he caught the unmistakable stench of Were. A shame he'd left his big sword at the house, but then again, that wasn't his most formidable weapon.

"*Oui*," the gargoyle surprisingly agreed, hopping off the table. "It is probably time for me to depart."

There was a blast of heat in the air as Salvatore's power filled the club, sending dozens of lesser demons running for the exits. It sizzled and popped when it encountered Styx's icy energy.

"Don't move, gargoyle," Styx warned, a savage thrust of violence beating through him as Salvatore, the King of Weres, stepped onto the balcony.

The pure-blooded Were was smaller than Styx and attired in a Gucci suit. He had elegant features and black hair that brushed his shoulders. At a glance, he didn't appear to be a match for the Anasso. In fact, he looked like he should be on the cover of a fashion magazine. But one peek into his golden-brown eyes revealed the smoldering hunger of the wolf. Not to mention the searing power that thundered around him like a force field.

The two kings had made a tenuous peace treaty. Not only because Styx's mate was a Were and twin sister to Salvatore's mate, but they both understood that the eons of war between the two species had caused irreparable harm. In the modern world, it was important for demons to work together for the good of all.

Still, it hadn't been easy. And they both knew that the smallest incident could destroy the temporary cease-fire.

"Salvatore," Styx muttered as the Were halted directly in front of him, his wolf barely leashed.

"Did you approve the attack on my cousin, leech?" the male growled.

The overhead chandeliers flickered as Styx struggled to contain his temper. No one talked to him like that. No. One.

"Let's start this again, dog." He snapped his fangs together. "Good evening, Salvatore. How are you? Is Harley having a nice visit with Darcy?"

Salvatore ignored the sharp edge of warning in Styx's tone. "One of your minions assaulted Marco. I want to know why."

Styx scowled at the ridiculous accusation. "He runs a fight club, doesn't he? His business is literally getting attacked. If he doesn't like it, then tell him to open a bakery."

"He wasn't at the club," Salvatore bit out. "He was lured away by a bloodsucker who led him straight into her trap." Salvatore stepped close enough to surround Styx in his heat. "If he's been harmed, I'm going to hold you personally responsible."

Styx hissed, releasing enough of his power to shatter the overhead chandelier and cause the balcony to quake beneath their feet. Just a small reminder that he could flatten the entire city if he wanted. Distantly he was aware of demons screaming in fear, but his gaze never wavered from the feral glow of the wolf in Salvatore's eyes. The Were was a breath away from shifting and all hell breaking lose.

"A vampire doesn't need a trap to kick the ass of a mangy—"

Without warning, the rich smell of plums cut through the heavy musk in the air, and a tall imp stepped from behind Salvatore.

"Perhaps I should explain," Troy, the Prince of Imps, announced, smoothing his hands down the one-piece leather jumpsuit that was studded with silver stars.

Styx battled back the urge to toss the flamboyant creature over the edge of the railing. He was familiar with Troy. Along with the fact that he was often as annoying as the gargoyle who was currently hiding beneath the table.

"Explain what?" he demanded.

"I'm currently managing the Hunting Grounds for Marco."

"Am I supposed to be impressed?"

"In oh, so many ways," Troy drawled. "But my point is that my employment at the club is the reason I was in contact with Marco shortly before he went off the grid."

"Went off the grid?" Styx sent a suspicious frown toward Salvatore. "I thought you claimed he was attacked?"

Salvatore pointed toward the imp. "Continue," he commanded.

Styx narrowed his eyes. "From the beginning."

"As I said, I've been managing the Hunting Grounds over the past couple of months," Troy said. "Very successfully, I might add. Soon I will have it expanded to locations around the world, just as I did with your mother-in-law's strip clubs and my own coffee shops..." His arrogant boast faded away as both Styx and Salvatore released low growls of impatience. "Ah. Not interested. Got it. Back to my story." He cleared his throat. "My position as manager offered me the perfect opportunity to watch the relationship between Marco and Satin."

"Satin?" Styx muttered the name in surprise.

Troy nodded. "She would come at least twice a week. Sometimes more."

Styx hesitated. He wasn't close to the female. Like many vampires, she was aloof and fiercely independent. But he did know she was a ruthless manager who was utterly loyal to Viper. There was no way she could be cheating on her employer with another club.

"She's a professional," he finally said. "She was no doubt checking out the competition."

Troy tossed his long, fiery hair, a taunting smile curving his lips. "Oh, she checked it out. Repeatedly and in intimate detail."

Styx wasn't amused. "What's that supposed to mean?"

"You know..." Troy pursed his lips, as if blowing a kiss in his direction. "Her and Marco."

Styx ground his fangs together. Darcy was helping him with his anger-management issues, but no demon could be confronted with a moody hound and a pest of an imp without wanting to rip out a few throats.

"I presume you're implying they were lovers?"

"It was more than that," Troy insisted.

"More?"

Troy hesitated, as if considering how to explain what he'd witnessed. "It was like they were obsessed with each other. So obsessed that when Satin suddenly stopped coming to the club, Marco was a mess."

"You said *they*, but obviously it was just the dog who was obsessed if she decided to avoid him," Styx pointed out, unable to believe that Satin could ever be anything but icily detached.

Troy shook his head. "It wasn't just Marco. I've seen a million lovers over my long life. Those two..."

Styx felt a surge of impatience. "What?"

"They were destined for one another." A visible shiver raced through Troy's surprisingly muscular body. "Whether they liked it or not."

Instinctively, Styx and Salvatore shared an uncomfortable glance. They would never be besties, thank the goddess, but they were both leaders who cared about their people. And when they started hearing words like "obsessed" and "destined," it set off all sorts of alarms. Lust was one thing. Compulsion was another.

"What does any of this have to do with me?" Styx asked.

"When Satin stopped coming to the club, I suggested to Marco that he discover why she had disappeared." Troy grimaced. "It was that or have him sedated. His temper was somewhere between volatile and catastrophic."

"Typical dog," Styx retorted. "Always foaming at the mouth."

Salvatore flashed a smile that didn't reach his smoldering eyes. "I'll be sure to share your opinion with Darcy."

"Anyhoo," Troy quickly interrupted the brewing battle. "Marco left the Hunting Grounds, and last evening he called to say he was on Satin's trail."

"He was stalking her?" Styx hissed.

"That's one way of putting it, I suppose," Troy reluctantly agreed.

"My cousin has no need to stalk women," Salvatore snarled. "They swarm around him like bees to honey."

"That's another way of putting it." Troy heaved a loud sigh. "May I continue?"

Styx flashed his fangs at the imp. "Make it fast."

"I spoke with him a few hours ago. He'd reached a town called Guthrie in Oklahoma, which I think is…" Troy waved a slender hand. "In that direction. He told me he'd managed to track down Satin to a small demon bar."

Styx turned his attention back to the angry Were. "I can imagine she wasn't happy to discover she was being hounded by an ex."

"Unhappy or not, she had no right to imprison him," Salvatore growled.

"Imprison him? What the hell are you babbling about?"

It was Troy who answered the sharp question. "Shortly after I spoke to Marco, I lost contact with him."

"What contact?" Styx asked.

"Before Marco left the club, I placed a simple tracing spell on him." Troy took a hasty step to the side as Salvatore bared his lengthened fangs. "Only because I sensed he wasn't thinking clearly. I am a believer of better safe than sorry."

"You?" Without warning, Levet popped his head over the edge of the table. "Since when have you worried about anyone but yourself?"

Styx swallowed a curse. He'd forgotten all about the ugly lump of granite. Which proved just how focused he was on the potential violence that pulsed in the air.

"Fine." Troy rolled his eyes. "I was keeping track of him because he owed me money. A *lot* of money."

"Finish your story," Styx commanded.

Troy deliberately turned his back on the gargoyle. "I contacted the owner of the local demon bar in Guthrie," he told Styx. "He happens to be an old business partner of mine."

"Of course he is," Styx muttered. Troy possessed an amazing ability to amass enormous amounts of wealth. It gave him the sort of power that was rare for an imp. "And?"

"And he told me that his evening had started fine and then it went to hell when a strange female with pale gold curls and eyes the color of a London fog suddenly appeared." Troy halted, scratching the tip of his nose. "He also said she had wings that were there but not there. Whatever that means."

"Aunt Bertha!" Levet cried out.

Troy scowled down at the gargoyle. "I should have known she would be related to you. My friend told me she had bats in her belfry."

Levet snapped his fairy wings. "That is…" He paused, wrinkling his snout. "Potentially accurate."

"Satin seemingly arrived at the same bar not long after…Bertha arrived," Troy continued. "She was obviously searching for the female."

"She was," Styx said. "I sent her."

"Is she bringing Aunt Bertha back to Chicago?" Levet demanded.

"I'm not sure. There was a rather shocking turn of events."

The floor shook as Styx imagined Satin being captured, perhaps even harmed by the Were chasing her.

"Marco?"

"No." Troy sent an odd glance toward Levet. "Your aunt Bertha told Satin that she was pregnant with a Were pup, and then she vanished into thin air."

There was a shocked silence that stretched and stretched and stretched. As if Troy had dropped a grenade and they were all waiting for it to explode. It was at last Styx who managed to find his voice.

"What did you say?"

"And then the gargoyle vanished," Troy murmured.

Styx stepped forward, his hands curled into massive fists that were ready and willing to smash things. Starting with Troy's too-handsome face.

"Imp."

"Easy, big boy." Troy allowed his gaze to slide down Styx's massive body in blatant appreciation. "Big, big boy."

Another chandelier shattered, this one over the dance floor.

"Um...Troy." Levet reached out to tug on the imp's arm. "I would not."
Troy glanced at Styx's fangs, his face paling. "Perhaps you're right."

"Tell me exactly what Bertha said," Styx rasped.

"She told the vampire she was pregnant and that the child was a pure-blooded Were. Then she vanished. A second later, a Were appeared, whom I assume was Marco, and the vampire went feral." Troy shot a glance toward Salvatore. "She attacked Marco, claiming that he'd used some sort of animal magic on her. They argued, each convinced the other was lying, then the vampire tossed a pebble at the Were to freeze him in place before she ran out of the bar."

Styx tried to process what the imp was telling him. On a logical level, he understood the concept of a pregnancy. But not in the context of a vampire. For the moment, he futilely struggled with the outrageous implications, then he grimly shoved the thought to the back of his mind and concentrated on what he could understand.

"She must have used a snare spell." He folded his arms over the broad width of his chest. "What happened to Satin after she trapped the Were?"

Troy shrugged. "I have no idea."

"What about the Were?"

"While I was on the phone with my friend, he managed to bust out of the spell and left the bar. I assume he's back on Satin's trail."

Styx stepped toward Salvatore, a layer of ice forming on the nearby table. "If he hurts her..."

Salvatore held his ground, his power snarling and snapping as it smacked against the frigid air.

"She was the aggressor, leech. Plus, she is obviously unstable if she thinks she's pregnant."

Styx didn't bother to remind the Were that it was Levet's batty relative who'd claimed Satin was pregnant.

"So, call him home," he snapped, his eyes narrowing as Salvatore's jaw tightened. "You've tried, and he ignored you," Styx deduced. "That's why you're here. Your hound is on the run, isn't he?"

Salvatore refused to answer the question. "Call home your vampire, and we will clear up this mess," he stubbornly insisted.

"*Non.*" Levet flapped his wings, rising until he could perch on the railing of the balcony. "She is on a very important mission."

"Mission?" Salvatore's heavy brows snapped together. "What mission?"

"It is all very hush-hush," the gargoyle insisted.

"There you have it. Hush-hush," Styx taunted, happy that for once Levet was tormenting someone besides himself. "Go find your hound and leash him before I do."

Salvatore moved until he was standing an inch from Styx, the ripple of his wolf visibly pressing against his skin.

"Listen, you frigid lump—"

"I have a suggestion," Troy smoothly interrupted.

The two kings turned their heads in unison.

"What?" Styx barked.

Troy casually smoothed an imaginary wrinkle from the sleeve of his jumpsuit, as if he didn't have a care in the world. Styx, however, didn't miss the sharp scent of fruit. The male was well aware that a bloodbath could erupt at the least provocation.

"Why don't *I* go and speak with Marco?" Troy suggested. "He might listen to me."

"Why would he listen to an imp?" Salvatore demanded.

"I can remind him of what is truly important."

The Were snorted. "And what's that?"

"The Hunting Grounds." Troy glanced from Salvatore to Styx. "Plus, I won't go charging after him with my alpha ass in a twist, causing more problems than I solve."

Salvatore looked as if he had swallowed a lemon as he studied the imp. Then he glanced back at Styx.

"He has a point." The words sounded as if they were being forced through the male's stiff lips.

He did, but Styx wasn't satisfied. "I will check on Satin."

"No." Salvatore shook his head. "I don't want you anywhere near Marco."

"There's obviously something wrong with her."

"All the more reason I don't want you near my cousin," Salvatore warned. "He's already in enough danger."

"I'm going," Styx snapped.

"Then so am I," Salvatore retorted.

The building shuddered beneath the weight of Styx's power, but he managed to keep it from collapsing. More importantly, he forced himself to accept he was going to have to compromise with the mangy mutt. Something more painful than walking into the morning sun.

"Fine." He pointed toward the gargoyle. "Then Levet will go with Troy."

Levet widened his eyes in horror. "*Moi*? Impossible. I must return to Inga," he protested, referring to the Queen of the Merfolk, whom he'd been fluttering around for months. "I have been away from her for too long."

"That wasn't a request," Styx informed him.

"But—"

"No," Troy interrupted the gargoyle, looking equally horrified. "No way am I traveling with that disaster magnet."

"I am not the magnesium for disaster." Levet stomped his foot, pointing toward the imp. "It is you."

Salvatore glared toward Troy. "Just bring Marco home."

Chapter 4

Marco stretched out his legs, leaning his back against a large rock. Below him a narrow creek cut through the rolling hills that were sparsely covered with a prickly brush. Earlier there had been a handful of human hikers rambling along the remote paths, but as the sun sank over the horizon, the land was reclaimed by the natural inhabitants. Coyote, fox, and bats searched the barren landscape for their first meal of the night.

Marco was busy with his own hunt. His, however, was far more elusive than a scampering mouse.

Tilting back his head, he studied the entrance to the cave at the top of the peak. He could sense Satin was inside, despite her efforts to mute her presence. He didn't need her scent to track her. She called to him with a siren's song.

Marco heaved a deep sigh. He was a skilled predator. And even if he wasn't, it didn't take any brains to figure out that the time to attack his prey was when they were at their most vulnerable.

Right now Satin was cornered. She couldn't escape until the sun was completely gone. The perfect opportunity to demand the answers to the questions gnawing at him. But rather than take advantage of the situation, Marco had found a spot where he could keep guard on the entrance to the cave and wait for night.

He told himself it was a smart strategy. Last time he'd charged after Satin, he'd ended up caught in a snare. He wasn't going to risk stumbling into another trap. Not to mention the fact that he was exhausted. He couldn't remember when he'd last had a decent night's sleep. Add in a wild chase to track down Satin and then the struggle to escape the spell she'd tossed at him…it was no wonder his energy was sapped. It felt good to simply relax for a few hours.

But that wasn't the real reason he was waiting.

There'd been something in Satin's eyes when she'd talked about the baby that he'd never expected to see. Fear. He could understand confusion and suspicion and even anger. But the fear was disturbing. He didn't like the thought that his beautiful warrior was afraid. Especially when she was carrying his child.

His child.

Marco's stomach clenched with a sharp excitement. He had no idea what strange magic was at work. Or if it was potentially dangerous. He was simply overwhelmed with a euphoric joy that bubbled through him like the finest champagne.

Not sure whether to savor the sensation or to have his head examined, Marco was distracted by the soft sound of footsteps. With a fluid motion, he was on his feet, his inner wolf rumbling in pleasure at the sight of the female who stepped out of the cave. The moonlight spilled over her slender body and added a layer of silver beauty to her delicate features. Enchanting.

Desire seared through Marco. A desire that was unfazed when Satin planted her hands on her hips and glared in his direction.

"I can smell you, dog."

Marco stepped forward, a mocking smile on his lips. "I'm not trying to hide…leech."

Her eyes narrowed. "I knew Weres weren't overly bright, but even you should be able to take a hint."

"Actually, you're the one who missed the hint."

"What hint?"

With easy strides, he loped up the steep pathway, ignoring the blast of icy warning that thickened the air. He halted just inches from her rigid body.

"Don't start something you're not prepared to finish," he answered.

She arched a brow. "Oh, it's finished."

"On the contrary." He deliberately glanced down at her stomach, able to detect the warmth of the child inside her. "It's just begun."

She flinched, as if she'd taken a blow. "Marco."

Instant regret flowed through him. She'd always seemed indomitable. As if nothing could touch her. Not even when she was screaming in pleasure beneath him. Now he was beginning to suspect she wasn't nearly as self-assured as she pretended. Even before the child.

"Talk to me, Satin." He reached out to grasp her hands, his movements slow and cautious. Only an idiot grabbed at a vampire who was on edge. Usually a dead idiot. "Please."

Astonishingly, she didn't pull away. Instead, she turned her head, as if trying to hide the vulnerability in her eyes.

"I don't know what to say."

Marco paused, considering how to approach the conversation. If he pressed too hard about the baby, she was guaranteed to shut him down. Probably best to circle around to the subject.

"Let's start with what you're doing out in the middle of nowhere," he said. "Why aren't you busy managing the Viper Pit?"

She shrugged. "Styx asked me to track down a missing gargoyle."

He regarded her with genuine curiosity. "Why you?"

"That's my skill. Once I have the..." She considered the best way to explain her powers. "The essence of a demon, I can follow them anywhere."

Marco nodded. Each vampire had a unique talent. He'd heard that Viper could split open the earth, and of course, everyone knew that when Styx lost his temper, he could take out the entire power grid of Chicago.

"What's so important about the gargoyle?"

"I'm not sure. She's related to Levet, so I assume that's why Styx is involved."

"Levet." Marco shuddered in horror. The miniature gargoyle had arrived at the Hunting Grounds the first week he'd opened. It had taken less than an hour for the creature to burn a hole in his new lodge with a massive fireball and cause a riot among the fairies when he claimed the nectar was being watered down. Marco had banned the gargoyle from returning, but he didn't doubt the tiny bundle of trouble would return whenever he wanted.

"Darcy is fond of him."

Marco's lips twisted. The King of Vampires had one weakness. And that was his mate. He doted on the pure-blooded Were despite their differences.

"That explains the Anasso's willingness to help," he said. "Anything to keep Darcy happy."

"True."

Marco studied the elegant lines of Satin's profile. "You tracked the gargoyle to the bar?"

"Yes." Her jaw tightened, as if she was remembering the previous evening. "It was supposed to be a routine grab and bag."

"What happened?"

"I cornered her at the bar, but before I could convince her to return to Chicago with me, she started babbling about a baby."

That strange sense of joy shimmered through Marco. "*Our* baby."

"I don't know what it is," Satin muttered, pulling her hands from his light grasp.

Marco didn't bother to argue. She was still struggling to accept the chaos that had exploded in her life. And in her body.

"What else did the gargoyle tell you?"

There was a long silence before Satin grudgingly answered his question. "She said she sensed an evil spirit."

A blast of fear squeezed Marco's heart. There'd been a voice in the back of his mind whispering that there was a mysterious magic that had created the baby. Probably dark magic. But he hadn't wanted to believe this could be anything but a miracle. Now he braced himself to have his hope destroyed.

"The child?"

"No." She glanced back at his harsh sigh of relief. "It's somehow attached to me."

Marco hissed. He'd been worried about the baby, but he suddenly realized that the thought of Satin in danger was even more troubling. He didn't have any specialized knowledge of spirits or how they attached themselves to demons, but he had no doubt they could cause irreparable harm. Maybe even the destruction of an immortal.

Something had to be done. Immediately.

"We need to return to Chicago," he said, the words clipped as his barely leashed emotions warmed the night air. There was no way he was going to let Satin continue her errand when she was being haunted by an evil power. The mere thought made his wolf snarl in fury.

She appeared genuinely confused. "Why would I return to Chicago?"

"Your king surely has contacts in the demon world who can locate the spirit and exorcise it. If he can't, I'm sure Salvatore can."

She was shaking her head before he finished speaking. "No, I have to find the gargoyle."

Marco frowned. "I admire your loyalty, Satin, but—"

"It's not about loyalty," she interrupted, her eyes suddenly smoldering with a cognac fire. "I think the gargoyle I'm chasing has the answers."

"The answers to what?"

"Everything." She cupped a slender hand over her belly. "Including this."

Marco battled back the urge to insist on returning to Chicago. Not an easy task. He was an alpha. He barked out orders and expected them to be obeyed. In a hurry and without question.

This female, however, would rip out his throat before she'd meekly submit to being told what to do. Which meant he would have to use cunning, not brute strength, to get what he wanted.

"Okay." He squared his broad shoulders, preparing for a fight. "Then I go with you."

"Absolutely not," she snapped.

If nothing else, she was predictable. And so was he.

"I can go with you, or I can follow," he said, his tone warning he was digging in his size thirteen boots. End of story. "Either way, you're not getting rid of me."

Her brows snapped together. She was just as used to giving orders and having them obeyed as he was.

"Don't you have a club to take care of?"

"I left Troy in charge."

"And you trust him?"

Marco considered the question. He hadn't known the Prince of Imps for long, but he'd formed very specific opinions since Troy had become the manager of the Hunting Grounds.

"With my business? I trust him absolutely," he assured her. "With anything else? Not as far as I can throw him. Which isn't very damn far."

She sent him a frustrated glare. "I don't want you to come with me."

"Why not?"

"Because I work alone," she snapped. "I always have and always will."

"No. You might not want to accept it, but you'll never be alone again," he reminded her, his voice soft, but ruthless. "Let me help you."

* * * *

Levet wasn't a demon who complained. Well, not unless he was tired or hungry or trudging through a landscape that was more boring than the netherworld. Or missing the latest episode of *The Masked Singer*.

Currently he was all of the above. And not happy about it.

To make matters worse—if that was even possible—he was traveling with Troy, the Prince of Imps.

This wasn't their first adventure together. They'd worked together to track down a crazed vampire trying to resurrect the previous Anasso. And while they'd been successful, Troy had unfairly held Levet responsible for his debt to a power-hungry nymph who'd nearly killed him.

As if Levet could have known Cleo was a whackadoodle when he asked her for a favor.

"Try to keep up," the imp growled, taking unreasonably long strides as they climbed the steep slope.

The imp had opened a portal near his friend's demon club in Guthrie. From there they'd followed the trail west through Oklahoma.

Levet sniffed. "I cannot help that you have legs that are too long."

"My legs are perfect," Troy drawled, refusing to slow his fast pace. Levet glared up at him as he scrambled to keep up. The large creature should have looked ridiculous in his tight shirt with fringes on the arms and suede chaps. His hair was tucked beneath a cowboy hat, and his boots had spurs on the heels. Instead, he looked like true royalty as he glided through the barren darkness. It was annoying. "Yours are too short."

"They are not short," Levet protested. "They are pleasingly petite."

"Pleasing to whom?"

"To Inga."

"Doubtful," Troy muttered, but he'd lost a small portion of his arrogance.

The imp made no secret of his admiration for the Queen of the Merfolk, or his disbelief that the female could be genuinely fond of Levet. It was the one certain way to get beneath the male's skin.

"I would prove it if we could go and ask her," Levet said with utter confidence.

"Go." Troy waved a slender hand. "And don't come back."

That's what Levet wanted to do. He genuinely missed Inga. But Bertha was the only relative who had ever shown him any kindness.

"I have to find my aunt," he protested. "Besides, Styx was clearly in a pussy mood—"

"Pissy mood," Troy rudely interrupted.

Levet clicked his tongue. "That is what I said. And it is all your fault."

Troy halted, bending down to sniff at a rock that protruded from the arid ground.

"How is it my fault?"

"It was you who sent your employee to interfere with the return of my aunt Bertha," he reminded the imp. "And you who insisted on going to find the stupid Were."

"Yes, I volunteered. I certainly didn't want a yammering lump of stone with me."

"Fah." Levet frowned as Troy continued to sniff. "Why are you stopping?"

"Marco was here." The imp straightened and headed toward the peak of the hill. "He went this way."

Levet scrambled behind Troy, his claws dislodging small pebbles that bounced down the path behind him. They once again halted, and Levet caught the icy scent of a vampire.

"Satin," he said, easily recognizing the manager of the Viper Pit. She'd always remained aloof, but he'd caught her scent when he was visiting Viper's cellars to inspect his very fine collection of tequila. "She must have stayed in the cave."

"Yes." Troy's expression was distracted as he crouched down and touched the dirt with the tips of his fingers. "And something else."

Levet grimaced. He'd been doing his best to ignore the echoes of malignant energy pulsing through the air. He was a big believer in pretending a problem didn't exist in the hope it would...*poof.* Disappear.

"*Oui*," he reluctantly conceded. "I sense it. An evil."

Troy lifted his head, glancing around the empty landscape as if searching for an enemy. "It appears to be following them. But what the hell is it?"

Levet didn't know. Which was odd. There were few creatures in this world or any other that he didn't recognize. A tingle of anticipation raced through him. It was a mystery.

He adored mysteries.

"I can find out," he promised, holding out his hand as he concentrated on the vile residue that seemed to hang in the air.

"How?"

"My magic, of course."

"Forget it. Your magic is a disaster."

Levet clicked his tongue. What was the matter with the imp? Didn't he want to discover what sort of evil they were chasing? Besides, his magic was awesome.

"Do not be a *bébé*," he groused, releasing a burst of power.

He expected the magic to solidify the essence of the evil, allowing him to determine exactly what sort of creature had left it behind. Instead, it hit the residue and sizzled like ice being tossed into a fire. Bracing himself for an explosion—always a possibility—Levet was shocked when he instead felt himself being tugged forward. It was like a black hole had opened up and was pulling everything inside it. Including him and Troy.

"Levet! Stop!" Troy cried out.

"I cannot." Levet tried to grab at the nearby rock, only to be sucked off his feet and into a swirling pit that opened in the ground directly in front of him. "*Sacrebleu!*"

Chapter 5

Satin had no explanation why she had so easily conceded to the Were's insistence that he join her. Wasn't there some human thing called Baby Brain? Maybe the child inside her was sucking away her intelligence.

Or perhaps it was just the opposite, a voice whispered in the back of her mind. Her rest in the cave had done nothing to restore her energy. And while she was still a lethal predator who could destroy any demon stupid enough to cross her path, she was dangerously distracted when she was using her tracking powers. Didn't it make sense to have someone she trusted watching her back?

And she did trust Marco, she grudgingly acknowledged. Despite her initial suspicion that he was somehow responsible for her...predicament, she had spent the past few hours trying to make sense of the madness.

It was mostly a wasted effort. There was no logical explanation for the baby. Or the mysterious spirit that Bertha claimed was attached to her. But she accepted that Marco wasn't involved. His shock had been too genuine. She could actually smell it in the air. And if he'd wanted a litter of pups, the last creature he would have chosen to impregnate was a vampire. Not when there were dozens of female Weres desperate to capture his attention every night at his club.

Bitches.

Heading in a westerly direction, they walked in silence for several hours. Satin was busy concentrating on the distant essence of the gargoyle she was chasing, while Marco prowled beside her, his gaze relentlessly searching for any hint of danger.

"How do your powers work?" he abruptly asked. "Can you smell your prey?"

Satin took a second to consider the unexpected question. She didn't have the exact words to explain her particular skill. It was just...there.

"No. It's more of a feeling," she finally responded. "I can sense Bertha's presence in that direction." She pointed toward the horizon ahead of them. "Unfortunately, I won't be able to pinpoint the exact location until I'm closer to her. Which means I can't use a fey creature to create portals to follow her. And even human transportation can interfere."

His brow furrowed as he considered her explanation. "Odd."

The temperature dipped. "I'm odd?"

"No, I managed to track you down with a 'feeling'," he said, his gaze sliding down her body. "Or maybe it was the baby I could sense."

Satin leaped over a patch of shrubs that grew along the top of the ridge, refusing to consider the various implications of the baby. Right now, she had to concentrate on finding the gargoyle.

"I still don't believe you followed me just because I stopped coming to the club."

"There might have been more than one reason," he readily agreed.

"What?"

"I'll make a deal with you."

Satin glanced to the side, giving in to the urge to savor her companion's exquisite beauty. The crisp, noble lines of his profile. The solid width of his muscular body. The smoldering heat of his wolf that prowled just below the surface. It all combined to remind her why she'd been so obsessed with returning to the Hunting Grounds night after night.

If she had a heartbeat, it would be racing with a surge of fierce awareness.

"Always the businessman," she said, barely leashing the urge to grab the male and throw him onto the hard ground. "Negotiating for a deal."

Thankfully, Marco pretended not to notice the scent of her lust that perfumed the air. Instead, he sent her a teasing grin.

"Just like you."

A flare of pride raced through her at his words. "Tell me what's involved in your deal."

"You tell me why you stopped coming to the club, and I'll tell you why I followed you."

"Okay." She shrugged. "Styx asked me to track down Levet's mysterious Aunt Bertha and return her to Chicago."

Marco snorted. "Nice try. You started avoiding the Hunting Grounds before then. Why?"

Her jaw tightened, but she silently acknowledged she'd agreed to his bargain. A deal was a deal.

"I could feel my power fading," she admitted. "Not a lot, but enough to concern me that I was overextending my energies."

Heat prickled against her skin as Marco released a low, sexy chuckle. "I like how you overextend your energies."

Pleasure curled through the pit of Satin's stomach as she recalled the varied methods she'd employed. Including hunting for Marco through the thick trees before cornering him in a hidden cave. Nothing like a game of hide-and-seek to heighten her passions.

"I decided to take a break and restore my powers," she smoothly hedged.

Of course, the stubborn Were couldn't let it be. "And that's all?"

She sent him an annoyed frown. "No. I wanted to prove to myself I could stay away."

Satisfaction smoldered in his dark eyes. "Ah."

Satin snapped her fangs together, returning her gaze to the flat, barren landscape stretched out before her. The last thing she wanted was to inflate Marco's ego. It was swollen enough.

"Your turn," she sharply reminded him.

"It started with the nightmares," he replied without hesitation.

Her stab of annoyance was forgotten at his words. Weres possessed many strange powers. One of those was the rare ability to glimpse into the future.

"Wolf dreams?"

"I thought at first it was just regular dreams, but they kept returning." He heaved a harsh sigh. "Now I'm not so sure."

Satin felt a tingle of unease. Premonitions weren't actually magic, but they were just as disturbing to vampires. It was something they couldn't explain. And worse, something they couldn't control.

"What are the dreams about?"

"I'm standing in the middle of the desert, and there's a hole in the ground."

Satin arched a brow. "That doesn't sound like a nightmare."

"There's something bubbling out of the hole. An evil that's threatening to destroy me." His musk suddenly swirled through the air. A certain sign he was struggling to contain his emotions. "And you."

Satin sent him a startled glance. She hadn't been expecting that. "I'm in your dreams?"

He nodded, his jaw clenched tight. "You're screaming as if you're in unbearable pain."

Satin stumbled over a loose stone. It was one thing to worry that she might be heading into danger. It was another to have her impending torment featured in a wolf dream. With a fierce effort, she regained control over the fear that threatened to cloud her mind.

She had enough to worry about without adding future problems. Besides, she didn't want Marco to realize how disturbed she was by his dreams.

"Great." She kept her tone deliberately light, easily regaining her balance. "You couldn't have a premonition that I won the lottery and retired to Monaco?"

He grimaced. "Trust me, I tried everything to get rid of it. Including drinking several gallons of my finest bourbon. But the compulsion to find you and make sure you were okay became overwhelming."

Compulsion? Satin didn't know whether to be flattered or offended that Marco had tracked her down because some mysterious urge had forced him to do so. What did it matter why he was there?

It didn't, of course. So why did a tiny prick of disappointment stab through her unbeating heart?

Annoyed by her ridiculous thoughts, Satin shook her head, as if hoping to dislodge them.

"Do all wolf dreams come true?" she demanded, focusing on more important matters.

He hesitated, clearly choosing his words with care. "The visions are one possibility of our future."

"Nicely vague."

Marco shrugged. "Let's just say we should be careful."

"I'm always careful."

He abruptly chuckled, his heat brushing over her skin like a caress. "Not always," he countered. "I remember a few reckless moments during our time together."

Satin remembered a lot of reckless moments. More than one night she'd returned to Chicago covered in scrapes and bruises and bite marks that had taken hours to heal. It had been glorious.

"Everyone needs a chance to blow off steam."

"And that's what I was?" he asked. "A way to blow off steam?"

She sent him a confused glance. "Isn't that the whole point of the Hunting Grounds?"

"*Si*. But with us…" He allowed his words to trail away.

"What?"

His jaw clenched, his musk deepening as if he was regretting the direction of the conversation.

"It felt different," he forced himself to confess. "Special."

Satin nearly stumbled again. This time from the unexpected joy that blasted through her. Like she'd been desperately waiting for him to confirm that what they shared was extraordinary, despite her efforts to pretend it was nothing more than lust.

Satin clenched her hands. If she hadn't been a vampire, she would have blushed.

"I'm sure you say that to all the females," she muttered.

"There have been no other females. Not since the first night you strolled into my lodge." His lips twisted as she made a sound of disbelief. "It's true," he insisted. "Once you've tasted paradise, nothing else will do."

A strange apprehension whispered through her. A warning that whatever was happening between her and the Were was just as dangerous as the child she carried inside her.

"I don't need flattery."

"It's not flattery."

"Right."

"The truth is, I've never joined in the entertainment before," he insisted. "I'm there to make sure my guests are having a good time without things getting out of hand." He reached out to brush his fingers down the curve of her neck. "And then I saw you."

* * * *

Bertha was nearing a gaping split in the ground that the humans called the Grand Canyon when a heavy mist formed around her. It could have been natural. Dawn wasn't far off, and the air was beginning to warm, skimming over the ground that had cooled during the night.

But Bertha had been around a long time and her spidey-senses were tingling. It wasn't just the distant pulse of magic. Or the unmistakable smell of sulfur. It was the change in air pressure as she moved from one dimension to another.

Someone had opened a portal, and she'd just stepped through it.

More curious than alarmed, Bertha waited for the mist to dissipate. If there was something here waiting to devour her, she wasn't going to make it easier for the monster. Plus, the last time she'd walked through the fog, she'd stubbed her toe on a rock. The pain had not only been unreasonably intense, but it was a reminder that her current human form was as fragile as glass. A seven-foot gargoyle with a hide so thick that it was impervious to harm could blunder around without concern. In fact, that was the fun of being such a solid creature. Why tiptoe your way around trouble when you could smash your way through it?

The fact that she had to be cautious was a never-ending source of annoyance to Bertha.

At last, the murk cleared, and Bertha glanced around her surroundings. Her brows arched as she caught sight of the white crystal floor that had been polished as smooth as glass. Like something out of a fairy-tale palace. The walls were chiseled out of the same crystal, but they had been left with sharp edges that threatened to slice open the unwary. The clear stone glowed a dull orange, reflecting the lava that flowed just behind them. It was the only light in the oblong-shaped space, giving it a creepy, horror-movie vibe.

Bertha's mood perked up.

She adored horror movies. It was the best thing humans had invented. Oh, except for honey buns. Warm honey buns with butter were the bomb.

Taking a step forward, she glanced toward the towering dais at the end of the room. She crossed her fingers, hoping for a hockey-masked villain to appear out of the gloom.

"Hello," she called out. "What's there?"

There was a stir of air, and suddenly she could make out a large male form, sprawled on a throne carved out of volcanic rock. He looked like a vampire. His features possessed an unearthly beauty, with a wide brow, a narrow nose, and chiseled cheekbones. His long hair was pale, with a metallic, platinum sheen that would be blinding in the daylight. His eyes, in contrast, were a deep, uncompromising ebony. Like dark pools of bottomless mystery. But he was larger than most vamps—even Styx, who was huge—and he held an off-the-charts power that thundered around him like a constant earthquake.

An unexpected, near cataclysmic awareness tingled through Bertha as she studied the stranger. Oh…my. The male was oozing with a potent, sensual charisma. It tugged at her with a gravitational force that was almost tangible, promising hours of searing hot sex and the sort of pleasure a female could happily drown in.

She flapped her transparent wings, trying to cool her blood, which was racing through her veins. This was nonsense. She was too old and wily for such nonsense, she sternly told herself. She hadn't had a lover since the Crusades. He'd been a massive orc who'd been sturdy enough for a gargoyle, but like all orcs, he'd proved to be a treacherous bastard. One night Bertha had awakened from her stone shape to discover he was trying to chip off her head. He said he just wanted a piece as a memento of their time together, but she'd known he was lying. Back then, many creatures believed that chunks of gargoyle flesh could heal those suffering from the demon-plague sweeping the world. He could have sold her head for a fortune on the black-market.

After that, she'd sworn off romance for all time. Sex wasn't worth losing her head over. Literally and figuratively.

The male on the throne smiled with smug satisfaction as he caught the scent of her awareness. Bertha sniffed. Gorgeous or not, he was a typical male.

Arrogant.

"You're not Jason," she said, not having to pretend her disappointment. She really had hoped it would be a hockey-masked villain.

The male blinked. "Jason?"

"I thought this might be a horror movie."

"Ah. Close." Fire danced over his naked chest as he slowly rose to his feet. He was wearing nothing more than a leather loincloth that barely covered his bits and pieces. "Welcome to the netherworld."

"The netherworld," she breathed, her brows drawing together. She'd been in the netherworld before. It had been hot and stinky and filled with the screams of souls being tortured. Or at least that was the version she'd visited. It was said the place was constantly evolving and changing. Like a lava lamp that flowed from one shape to another. "Land of illusion," she murmured, reminded of the warnings she'd heard over the centuries. "Are you real?"

"I'm very real, Bertha." He strolled toward her, the flames absorbed into his smooth skin as he spread his arms wide. "Touch me if you want to be sure."

She wanted to. But whether she wanted to run her fingers over the chiseled muscles or to throat-punch him for stirring sensations she didn't want stirred was the question.

Maybe both.

To avoid temptation, she placed her hands on her hips as she sent the stranger a stern frown.

"No thanks."

"A pity."

"Who are you?"

He strolled closer, bringing with him the fresh scent of cypress. Odd. He smelled like Greece.

"Don't you recognize me?" he asked.

"Should I?"

"We've been intimately connected for the past few weeks."

Intimately connected? Bertha shook her head in confusion. She was getting old, but that seemed like something she would remember. Then realization abruptly slapped her in the face.

"Oh. You're the voice in my head." She narrowed her gaze. "Do you have a name?"

There was a short pause. "You can call me Hades."

Bertha blinked. "The god?"

He shrugged. "To some."

"Not to me." Bertha sniffed. "You're an aggravating creature."

"Bertha." His power brushed over her with a delicious pressure. "Is that any way to talk to your partner?"

"I don't want to be your partner."

"There are benefits."

"Really?"

"You don't sound convinced." He allowed the flames to return, and they swirled over his body in a dazzling display. "Would you like me to reveal what I can offer?"

Hmm. Did she? Maybe. She'd never had a lover who was actually on fire. That had to add a whole new level of spice. But she'd given up on males, right? Plus, she couldn't forget he was responsible for her constant headaches.

"Not really."

The stranger blinked in shock. "You are the most unusual creature."

"Hey. That's not nice."

"Actually, it's the highest compliment I can offer," he argued, his gaze burning a path down the length of her body before returning to study her face with a blatant curiosity.

"Nonsense," she protested. "You could tell me that my smile is captivating."

"You haven't smiled."

"Or that my magic is astonishing."

"Again, you haven't used—"

"Or that my conversation is sparkling."

"You most certainly sparkle," he assured her, reaching out to trail his fingers over her barely-there wings. "These are exquisite."

She shrugged away his hand. The brief touch was enough to assure her that his fire was contagious. She felt as if she was burning from the inside out.

"If you actually want to please me, then you will tell me why you keep intruding into my brain. It's very rude, you know."

He shrugged. "All in good time."

"There is nothing 'good time' about it," she argued. "It's all very bad."

He continued to study her with blatant curiosity, as if she were a puzzle he couldn't figure out. Or maybe he was just trying to decide if she would be a tasty meal. Hard to say with a god.

"I mean you no harm," he finally assured her.

"No harm?" She clicked her tongue in annoyance. "You are pulling me about like a puppet on your strings. I… Wait." She glanced down at her slender body. Just how intrusive had this male been in her life? "Did you force me into this shape?"

"It's necessary."

She jerked her head up to glare into the compelling beauty of his face. "Necessary for whom?"

Hades considered his answer. "My world," he said. "And for your world. If a breach is opened, then all hell breaks loose."

"Literally or figuratively?"

"Both."

Bertha wasn't appeased. She wasn't a fan of hell breaking loose, but then again, she wasn't sure how she'd gotten involved.

"Why me?"

He blinked, as if surprised by her question. "You are one of the few creatures strong enough to survive the touch of my mind." He slowly smiled, his ebony eyes smoldering with a sensual promise. "And you fascinate me."

"Ah." Bertha nodded. She liked being called fascinating. She was, after all, intelligent, sophisticated, and cultured. A rare combination for gargoyles. But she really, really, really liked the thought that it was her power that attracted his attention. "Now, that is a compliment," she assured him.

His smile widened. "I'll keep that in mind."

"Keep it in mind for what?"

"The next time we meet in person."

Bertha's brief pleasure was squashed beneath her surge of irritation. The male might remind her of what it felt like to be young and passionate with nothing on her mind but sating her desires, but she was tired of the game he was forcing her to play.

"What if I don't want to meet again?" she demanded. "What if I want you to return me to my original shape and leave me alone?"

"You would condemn the world to a tidal wave of evil?"

The question hung in the air between them. Like the sword of Damocles.

"That's not fair," she at last protested. "I didn't volunteer to battle a tidal wave of anything."

"The price of power." Hades shrugged, holding her gaze as the silvery mist began to thicken. "We will speak again." His words were whispered through the gathering gloom. "Soon."

Chapter 6

Marco followed Satin down a narrow track that led into the shallow valley. They'd walked in silence for the past few hours. In part because Satin was obviously distracted as she used her powers to track the gargoyle. And in part because she was shaken by his confession that he'd lost interest in all other females after he'd caught sight of her.

It might not be the best time to reveal she had captivated him. She had more than a few things on her mind at the moment. But he wasn't sorry he'd told her. He wanted her to know the baby wasn't the only reason he was determined to keep her safe.

As they traveled through the darkness, Marco's gaze continued to scan their surroundings. The brush was thicker here with a few stunted trees. An old, wooden shack was perched near the narrow creek that cut through the rocky ground. The tin roof was rusted, and the front door hung open at a drunken angle. Marco assumed it had once belonged to a human searching for gold. Mortals were surprisingly resilient in their attempts to strike it rich.

A light breeze threaded its way through the valley, bringing with it a distinctive scent.

"I can smell dawn approaching. We need to find a place to rest for the day," he warned his companion.

Satin blinked, as if being brought out of a daze. Just another reminder that her powers put her in danger. He would have to make sure that he remained on constant guard until they managed to capture the gargoyle.

She glanced around, belatedly realizing just how much time had passed. "Yes, sooner rather than later."

They headed toward a wooden bridge that had been built across the creek. There was no obvious shelter nearby. Not unless you counted the shack, which he most certainly did not. Even from a distance, it looked like it was on the verge of utter collapse.

They would have to search the ridge above them for a cave.

As they stepped off the bridge, however, he reached out to grab Satin's arm, pulling her to a halt.

"Wait," he breathed.

"What's wrong?"

"I'm not sure." Marco sniffed the air. There was nothing unusual. Just the expected wildlife, mesquite, dirt, and the icy power that pulsed and eddied around Satin. A strange sensation, however, crawled over his skin, causing his inner wolf to howl in alarm. "It feels...hinky."

"Hinky?"

He struggled to find the right words. "I sense we're not alone, but I can't determine who is out there. It's as if their presence is being distorted, like a mirage."

"Magic?"

"That would be my guess."

Satin's features tightened with annoyance. "I hate magic. Can you tell what direction?"

Marco turned in a slow circle. There was a weird vibe that seeped through the valley, but the feeling of being watched came from a specific location. He pointed toward the miner shack.

"From that old building."

Satin frowned. Not in disbelief. She apparently trusted his ability to locate the hidden enemy. Instead, she appeared confused.

"It doesn't look big enough to hide more than a couple of demons," she muttered, only to hold up a slender hand as she tilted her head to the side.

"What is it?"

"There are tunnels beneath it."

Marco nodded. A vampire could sense a hole in the ground from miles away. A necessity for a creature who had a deadly allergy to the sun. The question was how large the tunnels were and how many demons were currently stuffed inside them.

"Stay here and I'll—"

"Stop right there," Satin snapped.

Marco shivered as the temperature dropped, but he determinedly pressed on. "Think about it, Satin. This might be a trap devised by the gargoyle."

She clenched her jaw, but, with a visible effort, she forced herself to squash her flare of anger.

"She's miles away from here."

"Perhaps she's physically miles away from here," he agreed, scrambling for an excuse to keep her off the front lines of danger. "But if she can sense you tracking her, then she might create an ambush so she can hide while you're distracted."

She sent him a wry glance. "That's a reach."

Busted. He shrugged. "Worth a try."

She flashed her fangs. "Don't treat me like I'm helpless."

"You said yourself that you've lost a portion of your strength."

"I can still destroy any demon who is stupid enough to challenge me." She released a blast of power that coated the nearby cacti in ice. "Including you."

Marco grimaced as the nearest cactus shattered into a pile of frozen shards. "Point taken," he muttered, grudgingly accepting he was doing more harm than good. Besides, she was right. Even if she wasn't at a hundred percent, she was still the top predator on the food chain. "You circle toward the back. I'll shift and go through the front door. That should herd them in your direction."

"I'll be waiting," she assured him, disappearing in a blur of motion.

Marco counted to one hundred, making sure Satin was in place before he closed his eyes and reached for his wolf. It was something he'd done a thousand times before. A million times. So, why did he suddenly have to struggle to change into his animal form? He could feel the heat and power of his wolf. And the tingles of his primitive power. But it was like he was stuck in the mud, spinning his wheels.

It had to have something to do with the mysterious cloaking spell the hidden demons were using, he silently reassured himself. It couldn't be that he was unable to perform under stress. That would be like admitting he was...impotent.

Unacceptable.

At last, he felt the familiar stretch and pull on his muscles as he started his shift. Thank the goddess, he silently breathed. He refused to consider what would have happened if he couldn't release his wolf.

Marco shuddered in bliss as the pleasurable pain torqued through him, popping bones and covering him in the familiar thick layer of fur. He tilted back his head to release a fierce howl. Then, barely waiting to complete the transformation, he was racing over the hard-packed ground and leaping onto the rickety porch. He didn't want to give the enemy the opportunity to realize that he'd sensed their presence.

It was the only means to take away the advantage of the waiting ambush.

Never slowing, Marco rammed into the door, easily smashing through the rotted wood. Once inside, he skidded to a halt, taking a quick glance around. There wasn't much to see. Just an open space that had once served as a living room, kitchen, and bedroom for the miner. Whatever furniture had been there was long gone, leaving it no more than a barren shell.

A good thing, Marco acknowledged. It made it easy to be confident there were no hidden attackers.

His attention focused on the three male vampires who were eyeing him with blatant contempt. They looked similar, with pale, narrow faces and long hair that was left to hang in tangles down their backs. Their clothing was surprisingly filthy, as if they'd been wearing it for several decades, and there was an unkempt negligence that hung in the air.

Marco wrinkled his snout in distaste. Most leeches were fastidious to the point of fanaticism. These creatures were nasty.

"I'll deal with the wolf." The tallest of the trio pointed toward a narrow door cut into the back of the shack. Marco guessed it had been added by the vampires after they'd taken over the place. "You two capture the female."

A leech with broad shoulders and weirdly red eyes released a laugh that sent a shiver of unease down Marco's spine. The creature looked as if he'd misplaced his sanity a long time ago.

"Don't damage her," Vampire Number One snapped. "We want top value when we barter for her return."

Marco had no idea why they would want to capture Satin, but he felt a small surge of relief. It would give her the advantage in any fight, even if it was two against one. He just had to make sure he dealt with the leader before they could outflank her.

"We know what we're doing," Red-Eyes growled.

"If you knew, then you wouldn't have ripped the head off our last prize," the leader reminded his companion, baring his massive fangs. Obviously, this male held a grudge.

"It wasn't my fault," the leech whined. "He tried to stick a stake through my heart."

"It was your stake, you moron. You let him take it away from you."

Marco crept closer as the two argued. If he wasn't so concerned about Satin, he might have enjoyed the live version of the Three Stooges. Instead, he was ready and eager to rip out their throats.

"I didn't *let* him do anything." Red-Eyes sulked.

"Just capture the female. I'll deal with the dog." With heavy steps, the vampires tromped out of the shack, leaving Marco alone with the leader. Perfect. Marco crouched low, his muscles clenched. Unaware he had signed his own death warrant, the vampire gazed down at him with a mocking smile. "You're a big one. Maybe I'll skin you and have your pelt made into a rug." He laughed at his own joke. "Would you like that, Fido? Becoming a nice fur rug for my floor?"

In answer, Marco launched himself at the male's face, his elongated fangs slashing through the male's mocking expression.

Screaming in pain, the vampire stumbled backward, his arms windmilling as he struggled to stay upright. At the same time, he released a bolt of ice that was sharp enough to slice through steel. Darting to the side, Marco avoided a killing blow, but he could feel a pain on his hind leg that warned he'd taken a glancing hit. It wasn't intensely painful, but it was deep enough to cause a wound.

Marco didn't hesitate. He was losing blood, which meant that his power was being drained. The quicker he could end the battle, the better.

Careful to avoid the swinging arms, Marco leaped forward, this time knocking the vampire onto his back. Then, with a savage growl, he perched on the male's chest. The leech snarled in fury, trying to release another bolt of ice. Marco parted his jaws, clamping them around the arm as it lifted in his direction.

There was an ear-piercing shriek as Marco's teeth crunched through the bone.

"No!" An acrid stench of fear blasted through the air as the vampire belatedly realized he was no match for Marco. "I submit. Release me, and I'll make sure you and the female can leave this place unharmed."

Marco's laugh came out as a harsh chuff. He lifted his head to savor the terror in the male's eyes. He didn't doubt for a second the male would attack if Marco was stupid enough to trust him.

It was that knowledge, along with the suspicion that the ragtag trio had been terrorizing travelers in this area for a very long time, that added an extra pleasure as his jaws once again parted. He was going to rip out the male's heart and eat it. Then he was going to track down the other two leeches and do the exact same thing to them.

It was a good night to be a wolf.

* * * *

Watching as Marco crashed through the door, Satin positioned herself in front of the towering cane cholla a few feet behind the shack. The cactus grew as tall as a tree with barbed spines that were painful enough to deter even demons. It was the only thing in the area that would protect her back. She didn't have long to wait before two vampires appeared, one of them thin with a pointed nose and the other short and broad with... were those red eyes?

Satin shrugged. Their physical size didn't matter. Even at a distance, she could sense that neither of the attackers could match her in sheer power. That didn't mean, however, that they weren't carrying a weapon. Or that there wasn't a hidden trap in the area. She would be an idiot to underestimate them.

The two moved cautiously forward, their heads swiveling from side to side. At last, the larger vampire pointed a finger in her direction.

"There she is." He swaggered to stand a few feet away from her. "You can't hide from us, female."

Satin held her ground, her lips curling at the sour stench that clung to the leech. This male had been drinking the blood of humans who were addicted to drugs or alcohol. It was the only way for a vampire to become intoxicated. And a quick trip to madness.

"Who's hiding?" She spread her arms. "I've been waiting for you."

"Ah." He tapped the end of one fang with his tongue. "A feisty one. I like 'em feisty."

Satin arched a brow. "Did you seriously just call me feisty?"

"You wanna do something about it, sweets?" He ran his gaze down the length of her body. "Let's dance."

"You're just one big cliché, aren't you?" She shook her head in disappointment. "But then, I suppose an original thought would be too much effort for you."

The male scowled, his bluster faltering. He knew he'd been insulted, he just didn't understand the joke.

"What's that mean?"

"Obviously you've been stuck in the middle of nowhere for too long. Or maybe that tainted blood you've been drinking has already rotted your brain." She raised a hand as if stifling a yawn. "Either way, you're a bore."

His hands curled into massive fists as he moved toward her. "Oh yeah?"

Satin widened her stance, preparing for his attack. She would have to deal with the vampire before his companion could join the fun.

"Yeah."

"Don't be an idiot, Tich!" Vampire Two called out. "She's trying to goad you into a fight."

"I'm not afraid of her," the red-eyed leech muttered, but he halted his approach, staying just out of reach.

Dammit.

"You should be afraid." The second male shook his head. "Can't you feel her power?"

"I don't care how powerful she is, there's no way she can take on two of us," the nearest vampire assured his companion.

"Of course, I can," Satin taunted, continuing to provoke the fool. She needed him concentrated on her, not listening to common sense from his friend. "I can destroy both of you in my sleep."

The male growled, but before he could attack, the second vampire moved to grab his arm.

"Tich, we're just supposed to capture her," he snapped. "If you let things get out of hand again, you can kiss your balls goodbye."

The red-eyed vamp hissed in fury. "At least I still have my balls. You lost yours a century ago."

Satin frowned in confusion. "Capture me for what?"

The nearest vamp snapped his fangs, a hunger burning in his weird eyes. "You best hope your chief is willing to pay top dollar for you, bitch. Otherwise, you become my new toy."

"Is that a joke?" Satin glanced from one male to the other before she abruptly burst out laughing.

It wasn't an attempt to aggravate her enemy. At least not entirely. She genuinely found the image of Styx conceding to blackmail by a pack of losers hilarious. But she wasn't disappointed when the nearest vamp shook a fist toward her face.

"Stop that."

"Styx is going to slice you into ribbons with his big-ass sword and then glue you back together so he can do it again," she informed them, her voice edged with anticipation. "And again. And again."

"Styx?" The second vampire had enough brains to be worried by her revelation that she was directly connected to the most powerful vampire in the world. Perhaps he wasn't her direct clan chief, but she was on a mission for him. Which meant he was going to take any interference very, very personally. "The Anasso?"

She nodded. "Your king."

"Not my king," the shorter male snarled.

"Actually, he is," Satin informed him. "Whether you like it or not."

"Never."

"Tich." The second vampire took a cautious step backward. "Maybe we should let her go."

The male jerked his head to the side, glaring at his companion. "Have you lost your mind?"

"It's one thing to piss off a clan chief, but I didn't sign up for a suicide mission."

"Stop being so dramatic."

"I'm being realistic. Only a fool would challenge the King of Vampires."

"Fine. Run away like a little bitch," the shorter vampire snarled, turning back to Satin to expose his fully extended fangs. "I intend to have some fun. And if it pisses off the king..." He stepped toward her, his foul stench tainting the air. "Bonus."

A strange rush of anticipation tingled through Satin. She was always ready to battle an opponent. She was a vampire. Vampires never walked away from a good fight. But this was something more. A hunger to cause pain that had nothing to do with being a trained warrior.

With a shake of her head, she forced herself to concentrate on the advancing male. Later she would worry about the bloodlust that was being stoked to a blazing fire.

"Styx isn't who you should be worried about," she whispered.

* * * *

Marco finished off the leech, not bothering to watch the creature turn to ash before he was charging out the back door. He could feel the brutal cold that was blasting through the air. A sure sign the vampires were in full battle mode.

Staying in his wolf form, Marco leaped off the back steps and landed on the hard ground. He caught a glimpse of Satin whirling through the air as she connected her foot against the side of her opponent's skull. The vamp staggered back, but with a snarl of fury, he regained his balance and charged toward Satin. Like a bull being baited by a matador.

On the point of launching an attack from behind, Marco caught sight of a movement out of the corner of his eye. It was the thinner vampire, who had been nearly hidden in the shadows of the surrounding cacti. Marco didn't know why the creature hadn't joined in the fight against Satin, and at the moment, he didn't care.

Veering to the right, Marco crouched as if intending to launch himself at the leech's head. The male predictably bent forward, putting him off-balance as Marco instead plowed directly into his legs. There was a loud curse as the vampire landed awkwardly on his face, but with a fluid strength, he was swiftly rolling to the side. He avoided the swipe from Marco's massive paws, but even as he tried to scramble away, Marco jumped onto his back, knocking him to the hard ground.

Ice crawled over the male, reaching Marco's paws and inching up his legs. The cold sank deep into his muscles and even into his bones. This was obviously the vampire's special power, but while it was painful, it wasn't any match for his raw, primitive strength.

Not when he was anxious to finish off the male so he could deal with the vampire currently attacking Satin. And putting his child at risk.

A growl wrenched from his throat, and with a savage strike, he had his jaws wrapped around the male's neck, his fangs sinking deep into the flesh. The vampire squirmed beneath him, trying to dislodge Marco and at the same time, spreading his ice until it coated Marco's fur in a thin layer.

The pain became a deep, throbbing ache as his body started to freeze, but Marco ignored the discomfort, pressing his fangs deeper and deeper. Slicing his way through the muscles and tendons, Marco hit bone. With a last, brutal clamp of his jaws, he snapped through the neck.

If he hadn't been a demon, he might have been disgusted by the sight of the head that gently rolled away from the body. Instead, he simply leaped to the side as the corpse paled to a creepy shade of gray and began to turn to ash.

Two down. One to go.

Marco turned, his muscles still stiff from the ice that was slowly melting. He intended to help Satin finish her fight, but he swiftly realized he was too late. Satin was already stepping over the dead vamp who was crumbling into a splotch of residue.

He sat on his haunches, his tongue hanging out. Being in his wolf form was more draining than his human shape. Not to mention the fact that he'd just battled two leeches. They might not have been top-tier vampires. In fact, he guessed they were scraping the bottom of the barrel, but any fight took a toll.

As Satin neared, a strange scent teased at his nose. A foul smell. Like rotten meat. A growl rumbled deep inside him as his wolf reacted to the stench. She halted directly in front of him, gazing down at him with eyes that blazed with a crimson fire. As if she were burning from the inside out.

Her mouth parted, her fangs extended as if she was preparing to strike, and Marco abruptly coiled his weary muscles.

He wasn't sure what was wrong with her, but it was obvious from her expression that she wasn't seeing a partner when she gazed down at him. There was a bloodlust twisting her features that warned he was currently on the menu.

Either he ran away, or he protected himself.

Or he died.

Trying to cause as little damage as possible, Marco leaped up to smash his heavy shoulder against Satin's skull. She surprisingly made no effort to avoid his attack, as if she were inwardly battling against her compulsion to hurt him.

With a grunt, she tumbled backward, hitting her head on a rock with enough force to knock her out. Shifting into his human form, Marco lurched forward, falling on his knees to gently scoop her into his arms.

Dios mio. What the hell was happening?

Chapter 7

Levet was feeling particularly peevish as he stood in the thick darkness. He'd only been trying to determine the source of the evil that was following Satin and Marco, but once again he'd been sucked into some unknown location. A location that was bound to be horrid. They always were.

It was so unfair. Why did bad things always happen to him? He was a demon with a heart of gold, was he not? A knight in shining armor, forever rushing to the rescue.

Perhaps that was the problem, a voice whispered in the back of his mind. In all the epic stories, the hero had a character arc that was supposed to transform him—or her—into a…well, he wasn't entirely sure what he was supposed to transform into, but the tales always included lots of suffering and betrayal and blah, blah, blah.

Eventually the world would recognize his brilliance, and he would be properly worshiped by his adoring masses.

"What is this place?"

Troy's question intruded into Levet's glorious daydream…wait, was it a nightdream if it took place at night? Either way, the imp had interrupted his very fine fantasy.

"How should I know?" He flapped his wings in annoyance.

Troy glared down at him. His cowboy hat was missing, and his arrogance wasn't quite as smug. "It was your rubbish magic that brought us here."

"My magic is not rubbish. It is awesome."

"You are a menace."

"Well, you are a…" Words failed Levet as he tried to think of a suitable insult.

"A what?"

"Poopy hand."

Troy frowned before heaving a resigned sigh. "Poopy head."

"*Oui.*" Levet paused, distracted by a sudden stench that filled the air. "Sulfur. Do you smell it?"

"How could I not?" Troy shuddered. "It's like a smack in the face."

Levet's snout curled in distaste. "It's familiar." He was attempting to determine where he'd smelled the foul odor when the darkness began to thin. Glancing around, Levet caught sight of the polished obsidian that surrounded them. Floors, walls, and ceiling. Just like standing in a black box. There were no recognizable features, but Levet suddenly recalled where he'd smelled that particular stench before. "Oh. The netherworld."

Troy's breath hissed between his clenched teeth. "Of course, you brought us to the pits of hell."

"*Non.*" Levet shook his head. "This is more like a waiting room."

"What's that mean?"

Levet cautiously moved forward, following the sound of water as it rushed over large boulders. They stepped through one of the walls that was nothing more than an illusion, then moved into a vast cavern that was split in two by the raging river. A thick mist swirled over their heads, giving the impression that anything might drop out of the fog. It wasn't the most pleasant sensation.

"We are between our world and the netherworld." He pointed toward the river. "You must cross the river to be fully in hell," Levet informed his companion.

Troy snorted, glaring down at Levet. "A lie. I can guarantee you that I am fully in hell."

Levet clicked his tongue. "Such a whiner."

"Gargoyle..." Troy apparently forgot what he was going to say when the ground shook beneath their feet.

In unison, they turned to watch an orc shuffle out of an opening on the far side of the cavern. He was big even for an orc, with bulging muscles that were on full display since he hadn't bothered to put on any clothes. He had, however, taken the time to grab a massive wooden club, which he dragged behind him as he tilted back his head to sniff the air.

Levet had devoted a large part of his life to avoiding the violent creatures. They were foul-tempered, selfish, untrustworthy demons who preyed on the vulnerable. Plus, they had a habit of forgetting to bathe. Sometimes for centuries. But he easily recognized this particular orc.

"Uh-oh," he muttered.

Troy kept a wary eye on the approaching demon. "An old friend?"

"*Non.*" Levet cleared his throat. He'd crossed paths with the orc nearly five hundred years ago in Nepal. Levet had been on the run from one of his numerous brothers who occasionally tried to kill him, and he'd hidden in a cave in the Himalayas. Unfortunately, it'd already been occupied by the orc, who'd taken a very unreasonable attitude toward Levet's trespassing. "He might blame me for killing him."

"I'm not remotely surprised," Troy drawled.

"It wasn't my fault."

The demon shambled his way to the edge of the river, lifting the club to point it directly at Levet.

"You chop off my head." The words were garbled. No surprise. It wasn't easy to talk with sharpened tusks sticking out of your lower jaw.

Troy, however, managed to decipher the mumbling. "You chopped off his head?" he demanded, sending Levet a shocked glance.

"It was more the mountain that collapsed on him that removed his head," Levet admitted.

"Impressive."

Levet fluttered his wings, attempting to appear humble. A difficult task, considering he had, indeed, used a magical spell that collapsed the mountain on top of the orc. Of course, there was no need to share that it had been an accident. And that he'd spent nearly a year trying to dig himself out from beneath the avalanche of stone.

"*Oui*...well..."

"Me smash you!" The orc's red eyes flashed with fury, his massive body quivering with rage.

Troy inched backward. "Can he get across the river?"

Levet wrinkled his snout. He'd been in various areas of the netherworld in the past. It was hard to determine the exact locations since they tended to change and move, as if the dimension itself flowed on a bed of hot lava. He'd never, however found himself on the opposite side of the river.

Thank the goddess.

"I do not think so," he said.

"You're not sure?"

There was a shrill whistle before a tall, powerful harpy with large wings dropped from the mist above. She landed next to the orc, her dark hair floating around her hauntingly beautiful face.

Levet had been traveling through the hillsides near Athens when Ozla decided that she wanted Levet as her new pet. Understandable. He was, after all, adorable. For a few years, Levet had endured being leashed and held hostage in the female's treehouse, but eventually he became bored with the game. Breaking out of his chains, he'd been headed out of the lair when Ozla tried to stop him. There'd been a battle that included a stray fireball that had set the tree on fire. Ozla had ridiculously tried to halt the flames that consumed her home despite his pleas to flee. It wasn't his fault she hadn't listened to him, was it?

"Levet!" She lifted the bow she carried in her hands. Obviously, the female didn't agree with his assessment that her death was her own fault. "I have waited an eon for your arrival."

"Perhaps we should move along." Levet tucked his wings tight against his body and scurried away from the river. And more importantly, away from the arrows currently flying in his direction. "Better safe than dead."

Troy used his over-long legs to easily catch up to Levet, the scent of plums thick in the air.

"For once we are in complete agreement, gargoyle," the imp muttered, clearly unnerved by their surroundings. "Which can only mean that hell is about to freeze over."

"Freeze over?" Levet frowned in confusion. "*Non.* It is growing warmer, not colder."

"I was...never mind." Troy made a sound of impatience, coming to a halt as they reached a solid wall. "How do we get out of here?"

Levet glanced around. All the openings in the cavern were on the opposite side of the river. A place he had no intention of going.

"How would I know?" he demanded.

"You were the one who brought us here."

"I didn't do it on purpose," Levet groused. Why was the creature obsessed with how they'd gotten there?

"You never do." Troy ducked just in time to avoid the arrow that pierced the stone wall with disturbing ease. "Just get us out of here."

Levet scratched one of his stunted horns, running through the various possibilities of how to escape from the netherworld.

"I suppose I could try—"

"Wait," Troy rudely interrupted. "Are you thinking about using your magic?"

"What else?"

Troy reached down to grab the top of Levet's wing, giving him a sharp shake.

"If I suspect for one second you intend to create a spell, I'll toss you across that river myself."

Chapter 8

Satin didn't know how much time had passed before she opened her eyes, but she could sense daylight pressing above her. Thankfully, there was a thick layer of earth between her and the deadly rays. But how had she gotten underground? The last thing she remembered was walking through the empty landscape with...

A sharp fear pierced her heart as she flowed to a seated position, her gaze scanning the thick darkness surrounding her. There wasn't much to see. She seemed to be in a narrow tunnel with a couple filthy mattresses thrown on the dirt floor and a pile of trash tossed in a shallow pit. On the plus side, she seemed to be alone. On the minus side, she seemed to be alone.

Instinctively touching the warm swell of her stomach, she called out. "Marco?"

There was the heavy sound of footsteps above her head, as if someone was walking across a wooden floor, then the scrape of a trapdoor being pulled open and someone landing in the tunnel just out of sight.

"I'm here." Marco appeared from an opening in the wall, hurrying to kneel next to her.

A shudder raced through her as his warmth wrapped around her body like a blanket. It was more than relief that he was alive and seemingly unharmed. It was a soul-deep comfort to have him nearby. As if a part of her had been missing when she didn't know where he was.

Satin fiercely slammed a mental door on her treacherous thoughts. They were temporary partners, united by a need to track down the gargoyle and discover what was happening to her. Nothing more. Right?

She brushed her hands together, trying to pretend she hadn't been on the edge of panic when she'd first awakened.

"What happened?" she asked.

Marco grimaced. "I suspect we walked into a trap."

A trap? Satin searched through the fog that clogged her brain. With an effort, she at last latched on to the image of walking into a valley and catching sight of an old, wooden shack. It had appeared abandoned until Marco had sensed a hidden enemy.

"Yes." She slowly nodded. "Two vampires came out of the back of the shack." She paused, visualizing the approaching leeches. One, weirdly, had red eyes. "They were trying to capture me," she abruptly recalled. "They intended to demand ransom from my clan chief."

"Bold." Marco's lips twisted into a humorless smile. "But mostly stupid."

Satin agreed with the stupid part. She could only assume that the kidnapping scheme was a recent business endeavor. Otherwise, the idiots would have been tracked down and disposed of a very long time ago.

"Renegades aren't famous for their intelligence," she told Marco in dry tones.

"Renegades." He said the word slowly, as if testing it on his tongue. "I thought they made peace with your king?"

It took her a second to realize what he meant. "Those were the Rebels."

"What's the difference?"

"The Rebels were banished five centuries ago by the former Anasso, when they began to suspect that he was destroying his mind with tainted blood. Chiron created a clan out of those who were exiled more out of necessity than any desire to be a leader," she explained. "When I visited him in Las Vegas, he seemed relieved to hand the duty back to Styx so he could concentrate on his chain of luxury resorts."

"And the renegades?"

Satin curled her lips in disgust. "They are the dregs of vampire society. They refuse the Anasso's authority, and worse, they survive by preying on other vampires. Most of them end up like the pathetic creatures who attacked us." She waved a hand toward the nearby trash pit. "Barely scraping by in the middle of nowhere."

"So we performed a public service?" Marco teased.

Satin nodded, then winced as a sharp pain sliced through her brain. She lifted a hand to touch her temple. Until the past few weeks, she'd never had a headache. Not unless she'd taken a severe wound that damaged her skull. Now she couldn't tell if she was injured or if her aches and pains had something to do with the baby.

"Did we destroy the vampires?" she asked, belatedly realizing she had no idea whether they were still in danger or not. What if she was in the tunnel because they were being held as prisoners?

"Yes," Marco quickly reassured her. "All three are tiny piles of ash."

"Good."

Marco studied her with a searching gaze. "You don't recall the battle?"

"The end is fuzzy." She kept her fingers pressed against her throbbing temple. "Did I take a blow to my head?"

"Something like that." He kept his answer vague as if he didn't really want to reveal the details. "What do you remember?"

She forced herself to genuinely consider the question. It was important to understand what had happened. Why? She wasn't sure. But there was a nagging certainty that there'd been something strange about the battle.

"I was standing behind the shack when two vampires came out." It wasn't hard to call up the image of their pale, hungry faces and the stench of burgeoning madness that clung to the red-eyed leech. "Neither of them was very powerful, but they mistakenly thought I would be an easy target. One attacked me and the other... Oh." She had a sudden memory of the second vampire turning away to confront a charging wolf. "He was distracted by you." Satin frowned as her memories became hazy. As if a mist were obscuring them. Was it because she'd taken a blow to the head? Another shudder raced through her. "I don't know what happened after that."

He reached out to touch her shoulder, a strange expression on his gorgeous features.

"It doesn't matter."

It did. Satin felt it in her bones that it mattered. But as hard as she tried, she couldn't force the memory. At last, she conceded defeat.

Instead, she studied their surroundings, a small shiver of disgust racing through her.

"Where are we?"

"The tunnels beneath the old shack."

Her nose curled. "That explains the rancid stench."

Marco grimaced, dusting his hands together as if attempting to wipe off the smell that hung heavy in the stagnant air.

"I knew the vamps would have made sure their lair was sun-proof, but I underestimated just how squalid it was going to be."

"They're a blight on my people."

Marco shrugged. "Vampires aren't the only ones who have to deal with defectors who prey on their own people."

"Curs?" she asked, referring to the humans who were infected by the bite of a Were. They weren't full werewolves, but they could shift into wolf form and were notoriously violent.

"That's expected." He shrugged. "They weren't born with their animal, so they never have control over their beast. Especially during a full moon. But purebloods have no excuse for giving in to their most feral instincts."

She studied the elegant perfection of his features. There was an edge in his voice that suggested this wasn't a casual comment.

"It sounds as if you're talking from personal experience."

His jaw tightened, as if he was clenching his teeth. "Renegades have one thing in common. A hatred against authority."

"Were you in authority?"

"*Dios*, no." He shuddered, as if horrified by the mere thought. "But I'm a cousin to the King. Most traitors were too cowardly to challenge Salvatore directly, but they were stupid enough to assume I would be an easier target."

Satin made a sound of disbelief. This male possessed a savage power that vibrated around him with a silent warning to anyone with a shred of intelligence. It made him a worthy opponent when they were playing, but she'd always known he would be a devastating enemy.

"That is stupid," she muttered.

"A compliment?" He arched his brows. "From you?"

She ignored his teasing. "What were they hoping to prove by attacking you?" she instead demanded.

For some unknown reason, it troubled her that he'd been forced to fight off gutless dogs.

"Some did it to harass Salvatore and make it seem he was an ineffective leader, some wanted to prove they were above the law, and a few were constantly looking for a fight." He lifted his hand to press it against the center of his chest, as if remembering a particularly painful wound. "It didn't matter who their opponent might be."

"Is that why you left Italy?"

He shook his head. "I was in search of a fresh start."

"Why?"

He paused, but she didn't think he was reluctant to answer her question. It was more an attempt to explain his emotional need to travel halfway around the world.

"We were isolated for centuries in our ancient hunting grounds," he said, thankfully not pointing out that the vampires had more or less kept them trapped in the remote location. At least until Styx and Salvatore had agreed to a peace treaty. "Few ever left the homeland, and since we struggled to have babies, our community started to stagnate."

Satin nodded. Vampires weren't isolated, but there were several clans who tried their best to avoid the progress of technology. As if ignoring the changing world would make it stay the same.

"They were stuck in the past?"

"Exactly," he agreed. "Ancient traditions became rigid duties that had to be precisely performed, as if ridiculous rituals could keep us safe, or increase our fading fertility. At the same time, packs were grimly trying to hold on to their social hierarchy by forcing children into matings that had nothing to do with genuine feelings or desire. It was all about manipulating others to try to grab power. Worse, any attempt at change could lead to bloodshed." He glanced away, as if lost in his memories. "I was suffocating."

She'd heard vague stories about the desperation of the Weres before Salvatore managed to destroy a demon lord who'd been leaching power from them.

"So you traveled to America to join your cousin?"

"Yes and no."

"That's not an answer."

Marco turned back, his expression impossible to read. "The reason I chose to immigrate to America was to be closer to my relative. We're pack animals at heart, and I've always considered Salvatore more of a brother than a cousin," he admitted. "But it was also to step out of Salvatore's shadow."

"Literally or figuratively?"

His lips twitched. "Figuratively," he clarified. "I've spent my entire life as the cousin to the King."

"Is that a bad thing?" she demanded. "You don't strike me as a male who wants to take over the throne."

"God, no." There was a fierceness in his response that made her wonder if he'd been pressed by others into challenging Salvatore. It would obviously improve the status of his parents and siblings for him to become the King. "I want to succeed on my own merits. Not because I happen to share DNA with Salvatore."

Satin could sympathize with his fierce need to prove his worth. How much of her life had she devoted to carving out a position of respect? Nothing had been more important to her.

"And opening your club offered you that success?"

"That's the beginning," he corrected.

"The beginning of what?"

"My world domination." He leaned toward her, his heat wrapping around her like an invitation to sin. "I intend to have the finest demon clubs and hunting grounds spread throughout every country."

She met his smoldering gaze, absorbing his rich musk. "Viper might have something to say about that," she warned. "He's convinced he's going to be master of the universe."

He leaned forward to brush his lips over hers. "Let the best male win."

His lingering kiss revealed that he wasn't just talking about surpassing Viper in business. He intended to claim Satin. She remained still, savoring the tingles of pleasure that chased away the strange sense of dread that lodged in the pit of her stomach.

Then, reluctantly, she pulled back. As much as she wanted to become lost in the pleasure that sizzled through her, now wasn't the time.

And it most certainly wasn't the place. Her nose wrinkled as a faint breeze stirred the nasty stench of rot.

"Marco..."

"Rest," he murmured, pulling her into his arms until she was snuggled against the broad strength of his chest. "As soon as night falls, we'll continue our journey."

* * * *

The sun had barely slipped behind the horizon when Marco and Satin scurried out of the tunnels, both anxious to be back on the trail of the gargoyle. Not to mention their gagging need for fresh air. Vampires might not need to breathe, but most of them were fastidious. She'd clearly been disturbed by the noxious filth that had surrounded them.

Once they were certain no other renegades were in the area, they continued their trek across the vast, empty landscape. They moved in silence, Satin concentrating on her invisible connection to their prey while he guarded her back.

The lack of conversation didn't bother Marco. It meant he wasn't distracted while his gaze searched the darkness for any hint of danger. And there was the added benefit of not having to answer any awkward questions.

Satin's memory of her battle with the renegade was obviously fragmented. But while she hadn't pressed for a detailed explanation of what had happened, he sensed that her inability to recall the fight was nagging at her. Eventually she was going to demand answers, and he didn't have a clue what he was going to tell her.

Mainly because he wasn't sure what the hell had happened.

After several hours, however, he started to worry that Satin's lack of conversation wasn't because she needed to focus on the gargoyle. Her pace had slowed, and her skin was more pale than usual in the silvery moonlight. Either using her powers had drained her more than she wanted to admit, or there was something else exhausting her.

Both possibilities were alarming.

"You're quiet," Marco at last broke the silence.

She shrugged. "I'm a female of few words."

"That's true," he readily agreed, carefully considering how to convince the stubborn female to admit she was weakened. His distraction meant he wasn't as tactful as he should have been. "I like that about you."

The temperature dropped as Satin sent him an icy glare. "You like that you don't have to listen to me talk?"

Oops. Marco cleared his throat and tried to recover. "You say more with your silence than any amount of chatter," he clarified, pointing at her when she reacted exactly as he'd expected. "There."

"What?"

"That lift of your brow," he said. "You were waiting for me to say something stupid so you could call me out."

The brow inched higher, and the air dropped another ten degrees. He was still in the doghouse.

"Am I so easy to read?"

"I'm a wolf." He lifted his hands in a gesture of peace. "I'm not subtle or diplomatic. Words can mean too many things and hide too many lies. I depend on body language to communicate. And your body language is telling me that you are tired."

She jerked, as if shocked he'd managed to pick up her weariness. "I'm fine," she swiftly assured him.

Marco shook his head. Someday she was going to tell him why she was so terrified to show vulnerability, but for now he was more concerned with easing her fatigue.

"Tell me what's wrong," he insisted.

Her jaw tightened, but she forced herself to answer. "I need to feed."

Marco blinked. He didn't know what he'd expected. A complaint that the baby was draining her of her strength. Or a mystery illness that could be related to the strange bloodlust that had consumed her after she'd battled the vampire. Or even a lingering weakness from the blow to her head.

Being hungry was remarkably...boring.

"That's an easy fix." He brushed a finger down the side of his neck. "I don't mind."

She hissed, as if shocked by his offer. "No."

Marco scowled, deeply offended by her sharp rejection. What the hell? He'd never once offered his vein to a leech. In fact, he would have fought to the death to prevent any vampire from sucking his blood.

But for Satin, he would not only offer a vein, but do it with a tingling sense of anticipation.

Instead, she'd shut him down as if he were some rabid hellhound who'd crawled out of the sewers.

"You have an aversion to Were blood?" The words came out as a low growl.

She kept her face averted, as if she didn't want him to see her expression. "I prefer bottled."

"Fine." Marco grimly refused to brood on her rebuff. He was obviously going to have to get used to thinking that Satin was beginning to trust him, only to have the proverbial door slammed in his face. He nodded toward the glow of lights that reflected off the night sky. "There's a human town over the next ridge. There should be a demon bar nearby."

She nodded, angling toward the lights even as she kept her face firmly turned away. Marco ground his teeth together, barely resisting the urge to stomp his feet like a petulant child. The female was going to drive him over the edge if he didn't take care.

They had just crested the ridgeline when Satin came to an abrupt halt. "I smell fairies."

Marco sniffed the air. He easily caught the scent of ripe apples and tart blueberries. There was also a hint of citrus that warned there was fey magic close by. Turning in a slow circle, he searched the darkness, at last catching sight of a telltale distortion of moonlight as it reflected off a potent spell. Like the sun rippling over a mirror.

"There's an illusion wrapped around that graveyard," he murmured, pointing toward the patch of ground that was framed by a weathered wooden fence and dotted with a handful of crumbling headstones. It was far enough from the distant town to avoid any unwanted interest from potential tourists, and yet it was an area that was considered consecrated by the humans. It meant the area wouldn't be bulldozed to put up a convenience store. A perfect spot for a demon bar. "I'll find a way in."

Without waiting for her response, Marco jogged forward. It wasn't that he was angry with Satin, although he was still…peevish. But a vampire couldn't sense magic. He was the only one capable of locating the opening.

Slowly circling the graveyard, Marco found the doorway. He carefully checked for any traps before spreading out his search to include the jagged dips and swells that crisscrossed the hard-packed earth. One of them might be big enough to hide an enemy.

When he was finally convinced that it was safe, he motioned for Satin to join him. She offered a jerky nod before she was striding forward, her body tense as if preparing for a fight. Probably not a bad idea, he wryly conceded. Most demon bars were sketchy as hell. Being ready for violence should be standing operating procedure.

Allowing Satin to step through the illusion first, Marco swept a last glance around the graveyard before he followed her inside. Immediately he was swallowed in a thick heat that came from the roaring flames in the stone fireplace. It wasn't to keep the place warm. Demons could regulate their own body temperature. It was to saturate the air with the milkweed plants piled on top of the logs. The smoke was a mild drug to the fey creatures that were crowded into the narrow space.

Marco wrinkled his nose. The smoke was bad enough, but there was an underlying scent of decay that spread through the building. As if it was rotting from the inside out.

He had a brief impression of a thatched roof and open beams overhead as well as wooden planks beneath his feet, but his attention was focused on the dozen or so demons who stopped what they were doing as Satin entered the bar.

Marco stepped beside her, wrapping a protective arm around her waist. There was nothing there that could hurt a vampire, but he didn't intend to take any chances.

"Fairies. A couple imps," he whispered, his gaze traveling over the cluster of tables before moving toward the long bar at the back. "The bartender is a brownie mongrel."

Satin kept her head tilted to an arrogant angle as the demons gawked at them with wary suspicion.

"There is an opening beneath our feet," she murmured, her steps steady as they moved toward the bar.

Marco was surprised. He would have sensed if there were fighting pits nearby. The feral savagery always pulsed through the air like the beat of a drum. And this didn't seem like an establishment that would offer private rooms for its guests.

"Crypts?" he at last guessed. The bar was built on top of a graveyard, after all.

Her brow furrowed, as if she was using her powers to explore the opening beneath their feet. "It's possible."

"Are they empty?"

She paused, then she sent him a warning glance. "I can't tell. The space must be protected by magic."

Unease feathered down Marco's spine. There was no reason to waste magic unless you had something to hide. It could be anything from an escape tunnel to a hoard of treasure to a pack of rabid hellhounds waiting to be released. He didn't intend to stay around long enough to find out.

"Let's get your blood and be on our way," he suggested.

"Agreed."

As they reached the back of the room, the bartender moved to take their order. Like all brownies, he had long earlobes that brushed his broad shoulders and roughly hewn features. His crimson eyes and pointed teeth, however, revealed that he had an orc relative somewhere in his family tree. He was wearing a leather vest and leather pants that revealed his thick muscles.

"What can I get you?" he asked, his gaze warily moving from Marco to Satin.

"Blood," she told him.

"Fresh? I have a wide selection."

He waved a hand toward a table where several female fairies were huddled together. They were wearing sheer gowns that revealed their slender forms, and their golden curls were braided to allow an unimpeded view of their necks. It was the air of misery shrouding them that captured Marco's attention. Were they blood-slaves? The mere thought caused Marco to growl in fury.

"Bottled," Satin snapped, tossing a gold coin on the bar.

The male shrugged, reaching beneath the bar to pull out a plastic bag. He slid it toward Satin.

"Suit yourself."

"I always do." Satin allowed a thin smile to curve her lips.

"True story," Marco muttered.

Satin lengthened her fangs, stabbing them through the plastic container to efficiently draw out the blood. A smart demon would have allowed her to drink in peace, but the brownie was clearly lacking in brains. He nodded toward the table on the opposite side of the room, and a flame-haired nymph jumped to her feet and scurried forward. By the time she'd reached the bar, she'd managed to paste a seductive expression on her pale face.

"Are you two interested in a party?" she asked huskily, running her hands down the black silk dress that clung to her gaunt frame.

Marco hid his grimace. The female's eyes were glazed by the milkweed smoke, and she looked as if it'd been days since she'd last had a decent meal.

"Not tonight, *piccolo*," he said in gentle tones.

"Pity." She licked her lips, casting a nervous glance toward the bartender. Was she expecting to be punished?

"It's late," he said, reaching into his pocket to pull out a wad of money. He shoved it in her slender hand. "Go home."

Her green eyes widened in shock, then with a tiny sob, she spun on her heel and raced toward the door.

"Hey." The brownie scurried toward the end of the bar, obviously intent on stopping the fleeing female.

Satin stepped to the side, blocking his path. "Leave her."

The male skidded to a halt, tilting his head back to glare at Satin. "She doesn't go home until I say she goes home," he groused.

Marco folded his arms over his chest, shaking his head at the man's suicidal tendencies. Couldn't he see the ice that was crawling over the wooden floor and up the edges of the wall?

"Is she your slave?" Satin demanded.

The brownie hesitated, belatedly realizing he was pissing off a very powerful vampire. At the same time, he wasn't willing to back down. Not when every creature in the place was regarding the exchange with avid curiosity.

Marco had met his type a million times before. He was a bully who ruled the place with brute intimidation. If he backed down, he would lose his most potent weapon.

Fear.

"This is my bar," he stubbornly insisted.

Satin peered down at the creature, her lips curling with disdain. "That can be changed."

"It's not for sale."

She tapped her tongue against the tip of one fully extended fang. "Did I say I was going to pay for it?"

The bartender paled, but even as his lips parted to dig his own grave, there was an unexpected shudder beneath their feet. The wooden boards rippled, like they were standing on the deck of a ship during a violent storm.

Marco widened his stance, struggling to keep his balance. The brownie didn't even try. Instead, he grabbed the edge of the bar and held on as if his life depended on it.

"Shit," he rasped, genuine fear burning in the crimson eyes as he glared at Satin. "You woke her."

"Woke who?" Marco demanded.

"Me."

The voice came from the direction of the fireplace. Marco cautiously turned, expecting one of the fey creatures to be speaking. Instead, the flames spewed outward, spinning in a vortex that sent sparks flying.

Was it a demon? Or a spirit? Maybe a spell?

His thoughts were shattered when the customers screamed in terror, jumping from their seats as they tried to escape the fiery tornado. None of them managed to get more than a few steps. There was a blast of magic that resonated through the bar with the force of an exploding bomb, freezing them in place.

Including Marco.

Chapter 9

Troy adjusted his long strides to stay a step behind Levet. He was arrogant, but he wasn't going to risk stumbling into a nasty surprise. He'd let the gargoyle trigger any hidden traps. Besides, if he was being completely honest, he'd admit he'd become lost in the maze of tunnels long ago.

Not his fault, he silently assured himself. It all looked the same. Same rock, same weird, muted glow in the air, and the same stench. On occasion, they would step out of a tunnel to discover they were near the river, and each time they hurried away from the water and the increasing crowd of angry demons who were howling for revenge.

And not just revenge for Levet.

More than one of Troy's ancient enemies had made an appearance as they traveled through the underworld. One of them was his younger brother, who'd tried to kill him to become the next in line for the throne. Idiot. Troy had never had any interest in ruling the imps. And if by some unfortunate set of circumstances, he would have become the king, he would have paid someone to take the crown away from him.

Instead, he'd been forced to kill the overly ambitious sibling. That was only one of many reasons he'd walked away from his family.

They were currently hiking through a passageway narrow enough that the walls brushed his shoulders and low enough that he was in constant danger of smacking his head. He was at the point of claiming they were walking in circles when they rounded a corner to discover a large chamber with crystals that shimmered in the rough granite.

Well, this was new. Troy tilted back his head to examine the coved ceiling that soared above them. For the first time in what felt like hours, he could stand upright without fear of banging his skull.

Levet halted, clicking his tongue at the solid wall ahead of them. "Dead end. We must go back."

Troy resisted the urge to reach out and throttle the creature. What good would it do? Okay, it might ease a portion of his frustration, but it wouldn't create an exit out of this hellhole. Reluctantly turning, Troy muttered a curse, his gaze desperately searching for the tunnel they'd stepped out of mere seconds ago.

It was gone.

Rushing forward, Troy pressed his hands flat against the wall. He had a vague hope that it was some sort of trapdoor. And that if he pushed hard enough, it would swing back open. Waste of time, of course. There was nothing there. Not the smallest indication that there had ever been an opening in the thick stone.

Clenching his hands at his side, Troy whirled around to glare at his companion. "Now what?"

Levet stomped his foot, his ugly features set in a petulant expression. "Stop asking that question."

"Be happy I still hope that you can get us out of this mess," Troy snapped. "That's the only reason you aren't currently floating down the river."

Levet stuck out his tongue in a rude gesture. Did anything frighten the ridiculous pest?

"Do not get your panties in a twister," he chided.

Troy squeezed his eyes shut, wondering if this was some huge cosmic punishment for his numerous sins.

"I have died, and this is my hell," he muttered.

"Fah. You should be so lucky as to be trapped with me for all eternity."

Troy's eyes snapped open. An eternity. Trapped with Levet? No, no, no, no. He pressed a hand to his thumping heart.

"I'm going to have a panic attack."

"Oh." Levet lifted his hand, pointing a claw toward Troy. "I have a spell that will help."

"Just concentrate on a way to get us out of here. And do it over there," Troy hastily ordered, waving Levet away from him. The only thing that would make the situation worse would be to be the victim of the gargoyle's volatile magic. He'd probably be turned into a frog. "I'll concentrate over here."

The gargoyle sniffed, turning to waddle across the chamber. "As you wish."

Troy grimaced. What he wished was that he was back at the Hunting Grounds, enjoying a very fine glass of bourbon and counting his money.

Or spending the evening with a lovely ice sprite. The things they could do with frost on his bare skin was pure magic.

Then again, if that's what he truly wanted, why had he volunteered to track down Marco? It wasn't his job. The male Were might have become a friend, as well as his current employer, but Troy had lots of friends. He wasn't going to drop everything and chase after them every time one of them wandered off. And he most certainly wasn't going to endure the company of Levet. He didn't like anyone that much.

But a part of him was no longer satisfied with his old life, he ruefully acknowledged. It took more than money, or sex, or even power to stir his interest. He craved...excitement. Adventure.

Like he was once again a youngling, drenched in constant stimulation, not an aging prince who should be ready to settle down and enjoy his substantial treasure.

He blamed Levet. Until the gargoyle had started dragging him from one crazy escapade to another, he'd been perfectly content with his existence. Now...

"There is a crack," Levet called out, thankfully intruding into Troy's dark thoughts.

Troy didn't hesitate as he hurried across the space to stand next to the miniature demon. He was an imp. He had no talent for seeking out tunnels or comprehending the difference between the various types of rock. Hell, he didn't even know if the pointy formations growing from the ceiling were stalagmites or stalactites. But then again...did anyone?

Gargoyles, on the other hand, preferred dark, cramped places. And they had the added bonus of possessing a kinship with the stone. Probably because they became chunks of granite during the daylight.

Staring at the rough stone wall, Troy tried to locate the crack. He leaned close, his nose nearly touching one of the crystals that shimmered from the inside, as if it was alive. At long last, he managed to make out the hairline fracture that ran from the floor up toward the ceiling.

"That's not a crack," he protested. "That's a fissure."

Levet sent him an impatient glance. "What are you? The geologist police?"

Troy blinked in shock. The creature had actually managed an insult without mangling the English language.

"Nice."

Levet looked smug. "But, of course. I am *trés* clever."

"Don't push it," Troy warned before returning his attention to the fissure. "How is this supposed to help us?"

"We need to widen it."

Levet lifted his hand, and Troy reached down to grab his wrist. "No fireballs."

"You are just jealous of my magnificent balls."

Troy rolled his eyes. "The last time you tossed around your magnificent balls, they bounced off the walls and singed my man-bun." Troy reached up to touch his flowing crimson hair. "I had to use extensions until the missing patches grew back in."

Levet widened his eyes. "It is not real?" He reached up as if intending to touch Troy's hair.

"Don't even think about it," Troy warned, swatting away the tiny hand.

Levet sniffed, turning to lay his palm flat against the rock. "I have more important matters to attend to."

Troy frowned, watching as the gargoyle slowly dug his claw into the fissure.

"Can you manipulate the stone?" he asked. A few gargoyles had the magic to soften the rock. Some could even turn it to a soft clay.

"I can, but it is not without risk," Levet said, his gaze never leaving the wall in front of him. "Being stuck in here is annoying, but several tons of stone crashing down on our heads would be worse."

With a grimace, Troy glanced up at the stalagmite hanging over his head. Or was it stalactite? Either way, he wasn't eager to be impaled by the thing.

"No shit," he muttered. Then he grimaced. "Unfortunately, we have to try something."

"*Oui.*"

Levet lifted his other hand and pressed it against the stone. His brow furrowed as he concentrated on his magic, the scent of granite thick in the stale air. Troy watched in silence, not wanting to distract the creature. Not when a slip might trigger a cave-in.

The minutes ticked past, the air heating as if Levet was trying to melt the stone. Nothing seemed to be happening. Not unless you counted the sweat that was coating Troy's face. Then, without warning, the thin fracture began to widen, as if the wall was being split in half.

Troy glanced down at Levet, easily seeing the strain on his face. It was taking everything the tiny demon possessed to create the potential escape route.

"What do I need to do to help?" he asked.

Levet's wings drooped as he struggled to battle against the rigid stone. "I will continue to soften the wall," he gasped. "You try to pull it apart."

"Got it."

Troy reached over Levet, wedging his hands into the fracture. He wasn't sure what he'd expected, but it wasn't the weird, spongy texture that squished beneath his fingers. Shuddering at the strange sensation, Troy forced himself to concentrate on wrenching open the crack. It widened, but even with his considerable strength, it was a battle for each precious inch. As if the rock was trying to fight against Levet's magic.

Grunting at the effort, Troy wrestled to widen the fracture, managing to create a narrow space before the stone refused to budge another inch.

"I think that is as far as it's going to go," he hissed between clenched teeth.

"*Oui*," Levet agreed, his voice reedy, as if it was a struggle to speak. "I will squeeze through first and make sure it opens on the other side."

An unexpected dread clenched Troy's heart at the thought of Levet disappearing into the crack. He would be left alone in a strange cavern with no guarantee of escape.

"Don't forget I'm here," he rasped before he could halt the plea.

Levet stilled, sending him a questioning glance. Annoyed at his display of vulnerability, Troy folded his arms over his chest. He wasn't about to admit that he'd had a flashback to his early years at his parents' castle when they tried to cure his habit of running off by locking him in his rooms. It wasn't a prison. Just the opposite. It would be hard to discover a more luxurious place to be secluded. But for Troy, it'd felt like an elegant trap that was ruthlessly crushing his spirit.

"I would never do that." Levet's voice was oddly gentle, as if he could sympathize with Troy's surge of horror. And probably he could. The creature had been terrorized by his own family since the day he was born. "But I might need to use my magic to widen the other side before you can fit through."

The words made sense. Troy forced himself to nod. "Okay. Let's do this."

Levet tucked his wings tight against his body and wriggled his way into the crack. Troy winced at the sound of his tough hide being scraped against the narrow walls. He was much wider than the gargoyle, which meant he was going to be flayed by the time he reached the other side. A sacrifice he was willing to make, he acknowledged, as Levet disappeared into the darkness.

Time seemed to come to a stop as Troy impatiently waited for some sign that Levet had reached the other side.

"Come on, come on, come on," he muttered, shifting his weight from foot to foot.

After what felt like an eternity, he at last heard Levet's voice echoing through the thick air.

"It's open."

"Thank the goddess."

Troy turned sideways, grimly forcing his way through the constricted space. It was perhaps one of the most difficult things he'd ever done. Not only because he had a genuine fear of being crushed between the two stone walls, but also because he was still plagued with an irrational sense of being utterly alone.

An unbearable torture.

Refusing to panic, Troy focused on shuffling forward. It took nearly a half hour to push and prod his way through the crack, the painful process ruining his chaps and taking off the top layer of skin, but Troy didn't allow himself to falter. Each step was taking him closer to his goal.

At long last, he wriggled out the opening on the other side, stepping into a cramped tunnel and sagging against the wall. A shudder raced through him as he struggled to keep his knees from collapsing.

"Success!" Levet cried out, his expression smug. "I never doubted my magic for a moment."

Troy wasn't nearly as excited. Sure, he was relieved not to spend the rest of eternity trapped in the chamber with an aggravating gargoyle. Epically relieved. But their misery appeared to be far from over.

"We're still in the netherworld." He pointed out the obvious.

Levet shrugged. "*Oui*, but we overcame the challenge."

"Challenge?" Troy straightened, slowly turning to face the crack that was already closing.

"Fah. That is the correct word," Levet groused. "I am weary of being forever told I am saying things wrong."

"Hush, I'm thinking," Troy muttered. The word had triggered a suspicion in his mind.

"Obviously a difficult task," Levet mocked, then hastily lifted his hands in a gesture of peace when Troy glared at him. "Think away."

Troy ignored the tiny pest, trying to sort through his tangled thoughts. Over his very long life, he'd done his best to avoid the netherworld. It wasn't a place that any sane demon was eager to visit. But like every fey creature, he'd grown up reading stories about noble heroes who'd been trapped by some evil villain and climbed their way out of hell. There'd always been various obstacles put in their way that were designed to test their darkest fears.

"Was it a random challenge we had to overcome?" he spoke his hypothesis out loud. "Or a deliberate one?"

Levet blinked, staring at him as if he'd taken a serious blow to the head. "You believe the stone was deliberately challenging you?"

"Not just the stone." Troy spread his arms, indicating their surroundings. "I think it came from the netherworld."

"Ah." Levet's eyes widened. "I understand. It is to test whether or not we are worthy heroes."

Troy's lips twisted into a humorless smile. "Or whether we'll kill each other before we manage to escape hell."

Levet grimaced. "I do not like our odds."

"Me either."

* * * *

Satin frowned in confusion. One second the crowd was jumping to their feet to flee the firestorm, and the next they appeared to be frozen in place, except for their eyes, which were darting back and forth in horror. Including Marco's.

Obviously, it was some sort of inertia spell. Magic that would prevent a demon from moving but allow them to see and hear what was happening around them.

So why hadn't she gotten caught in the spell?

Did it have something to do with her being a vampire? Or was there another purpose?

Satin had a feeling she was about to find out, as the twirling flames swirled across the floor, headed directly for her. Holding out her hand, she released a blast of ice. She didn't know what or who was controlling the fire, but it was the one certain way for her to die. She wasn't going to wait and see what happened.

There was a loud sizzle as her powers smacked into the flames. A thick layer of smoke rose between her and the advancing creature, momentarily obscuring the entire bar. With a hiss, Satin leaped to the side, expecting to be blindsided by an attack. Oddly, nothing happened.

Instead, the fog began to dissipate as a lavender scent flowed through the room. Satin warily stepped back, watching the mist coalesce into a human shape. First feet and legs appeared, followed by a slender torso and arms that were draped in a flowing black gown with silver stars. Finally, a narrow face with strong features formed out of the smoke. She had a bold nose, wide lips, and a cloud of soft black curls that tumbled down her back. There was something ancient etched into her features, but it was her eyes that revealed her true identity. They were completely white, with swirls of gray. Like a thick bank of fog rolling off the ocean.

"Elemental," Satin muttered, belatedly realizing how the entire bar was frozen in place.

It wasn't a spell. Elementals were capable of manipulating the world around them. The wind, water, fire, and earth. This creature had obviously wrapped the customers in bands of air.

The female pressed a hand over her heart in a formal gesture. "I am Zephyr," she introduced herself. "Who are you?"

"Satin."

The demon frowned. "I don't recognize you. Why have you intruded into my lair?"

Satin warily studied the female's face. Was she unstable? Elementals were mercurial under the best of circumstances. There was no telling how dangerous they might be if they became confused or unbalanced.

"Are you lost?" she cautiously demanded.

"Of course, I'm not lost," Zephyr snapped. "I was hibernating in my bed just below your feet before you disturbed me."

That explained the spell to disguise what was hidden, Satin silently acknowledged. When a demon went into hibernation, they were utterly vulnerable. They closed off all entrances to their lair so nothing could reach them, or they used magic to create a protective shield. The fact that this elemental had been so deeply asleep might also explain her confusion.

"I had no intention of waking you," Satin cautiously assured her companion. Any creature powerful enough to freeze a room full of demons deserved respect. "I was in need of sustenance, and this was the most convenient location to purchase a bottle of blood."

The female frowned. "Why would you assume my lair would have blood?"

Satin hesitated. Was this a trick? Some devious way to claim that she was trespassing on the demon's private property? It seemed a stretch. The female didn't need a reason to attack Satin, if that was what she wanted.

"Most demon bars offer blood for vampires."

"Bar?" Zephyr blinked, as if confused by the word. Then with an eerily liquid grace, she turned in a slow circle. "What is happening here? Why are all these creatures in my home?"

Satin arched her brows. Perhaps the bar had been built after the female went to sleep. "I don't know how long you've been hibernating, but this place has a beacon to invite demons." She waved her hand around the crowded room, her gaze lingering on Marco. His grim expression and the beads of sweat on his brow revealed he was frantically fighting against the invisible bands that held him. Hurriedly, she moved her attention to the rest of the crowd. If this female was plotting some sort of retaliation for them trespassing into her territory, she didn't want Marco to be blamed. "I can't sense the beacon, but the scent of fey creatures led me here." She deliberately turned to point at the brownie, who was looking wild-eyed with fear. "That male is in charge."

Zephyr turned, her eyes narrowing as she studied the brownie. "Where is Fyfe?"

"Who?" Satin demanded.

"The brownie I put in charge of protecting the opening to my lair."

The elemental pointed a finger at the male, who was trembling in fear. "Who are you?"

"Sean," the brownie croaked as the invisible bonds that covered his mouth were seemingly removed. "Fyfe's son. I took his place after he had an unfortunate encounter with a troll a few years ago."

The scent of lavender blasted through the air. "Why didn't you wake me to tell me of his death?"

Satin took a cautious step backward, suddenly sensing that she could use the female's annoyance to her advantage. She knew very little about elementals. They were rare, elusive creatures. But she didn't need to be an expert to realize the Zephyr had bartered with Sean's father to keep an eye on the opening to her hidden lair and that she was less than pleased that the place had since become a seedy bar.

The trick was finding a way to convince the female to willingly release Marco and allow them to escape. The last thing she wanted was another unnecessary battle.

"I can tell you why he didn't wake you," Satin drawled. "Obviously he's an enterprising brownie. While you were unconscious, he created a side business to make some extra cash. Who knows how many creatures have been just a few feet from where you were lying...completely vulnerable."

Zephyr's lips curled. "Traitor."

Satin ignored the brownie's scent of terror, which tainted the air. Sean had preyed on lesser demons. Now he would pay for his greed.

"No! I swear—" Sean's words were cut short when Zephyr gave a wave of her hand, as if returning the invisible gag to his mouth.

"He was not only a traitor to you, but to the poor fey creatures in the area," Satin pressed her advantage. She nodded toward the fairies, who'd remained huddled together as they'd tried to flee. "He enslaved them to use as fresh blood or sex for his paying customers."

Genuine shock rippled over the elemental's face. "Slaves?" She waited for Satin's emphatic nod before she released a burst of power that lifted the horrified brownie off his feet and pinned him to the wall. "You will pay for this treachery, Sean."

Satin stepped to the side, closer to Marco. "While you deal with the trash, I will be on my way. If you'll just release…."

"No." Without warning, Zephyr whirled to face Satin, her eyes swirling with thunderclouds. "There's a reason you woke me."

Satin snapped her fangs together, her patience worn raw. She had many skills, including being diplomatic when necessary, but she was done. She could sense the gargoyle moving farther away.

"I'm just passing through." She allowed her powers to lower the temperature in the room. "And now I'm leaving."

The elemental ignored the subtle warning, her gown brushing the floorboards as she moved toward Satin.

"Your arrival here shouldn't have intruded into my hibernation. Not unless my senses warned me that you were a threat." The scent of lavender filled the air. "What are you?"

"Obviously I'm a vampire," Satin snapped. Was the female playing games?

Zephyr shook her head. "There's something more."

About to demand that Zephyr release Marco so she could leave, Satin abruptly realized what the elemental had said. Was it possible that the creature had recognized the evil presence that Bertha had claimed was shrouded around her? And just as importantly, could she tell Satin how to get rid of it?

"More?" she prompted.

There was a long silence, as if the elemental was trying to determine exactly what she was sensing. Or maybe she was trying to accept that it was real and not just a figment of her imagination. Then she shuddered, her body briefly turning to mist before she managed to regain command of her emotions.

"Elwha," she spit out, her voice harsh.

Satin felt a sharp fear clench her stomach. The female's intense reaction only heightened her suspicion that the presence was a danger. And not only to her.

"I don't know what 'Elwha' means," she said between clenched teeth.

"Not what." Zephyr reached out her hand. "Who."

Satin hissed as the female's fingers aimed toward the gentle swell of her belly. Without hesitation, she knocked the approaching hand to the side, tossing caution to the wind. Literally, since the elemental could use her ability to manipulate the air to crush Satin.

"Harm my baby, and I'll rip out your heart and feed it to the vultures," she said, each word encased in ice. It wasn't a threat. It was a promise.

The stormy eyes widened in shock. "A child? How..." Zephyr gave a shake of her head, visibly dismissing her astonishment. "That isn't what I sense." She paused, tilting her head to the side as she studied Satin. "Although there is a connection."

Satin didn't allow herself to accept the implication the child she was carrying was a part of the darkness. One nightmare at a time.

"Tell me what it is."

"My enemy." The elemental drifted to the side, slowly circling Satin. "Or at least the spirit of my enemy."

Satin warily turned to face her companion. "Another elemental?"

Her features twisted with a surge of fury. "No. He was death to my people. Including my parents."

An ominous pressure began to build in the room. As if a lightning storm was forming over her head. Satin shivered, but she refused to be intimidated. This was too important.

"Tell me about Elwha," she insisted.

"He is pure evil." Zephyr glared at Satin as if she'd personally destroyed her family. "A blight on our world."

"'Evil' is a little vague." Satin tried to hide her festering impatience. She'd already had to deal with a gargoyle who'd mumbled about ambiguous shadows that were attached or haunting or maybe possessing Satin. She needed a clear, logical description. How else could she battle it? "Is it a spirit?"

The elemental appeared to consider the question. "Perhaps now. But it wasn't a spirit when it stalked my people."

"Then what was it?"

"An ifrit."

Satin was braced for anything. Dark magic. A haunting. A possession by some unknown creature. But she was more confused than alarmed by the mention of a species of demons who had been banished several millennium ago.

"I thought they were trapped in the underworld," she said.

"Not all." The air continued to thicken, sizzling with an unmistakable threat. "The oldest and most cunning ifrit managed to escape and hide in the deepest bowels of the earth, crawling out only to capture one of my people and suck the life from them."

Satin stepped back, preparing to battle the creature. It was obvious the elemental held her personally responsible for whatever sins the ifrit had committed. At the same time, she continued to probe for information.

"Where is he now?"

"We combined our strength and banished him back to the pits of hell. It nearly destroyed me. That's why I'm forced to hibernate for centuries at a time. I will never have my full powers again."

Satin frowned at the explanation. Okay. Either the elemental was confused, or the evil clinging to her was trapped in another dimension. Which surely meant that it couldn't hurt her or anyone else, right?

"Then why do you claim it has something to do with me?"

A sudden wind ripped through the room, picking up the wooden chairs and smashing them against the walls. Satin held her arms over her head, as much to keep her hair out of her eyes as to prevent the splinters from impaling her face.

"Because you carry the stench of the beast." The female stepped closer. "It has somehow managed to infect you. It is once again up to me to end this threat."

Satin pulled back her lips, her fangs fully extended as she prepared to send a blast of ice toward the female. It might not hurt an elemental, but it would distract her long enough for Satin to rip out her throat.

Or at least that was the plan until she felt a surge of heat. Satin dodged to the side, keeping her gaze locked on Zephyr. She'd already seen the fire tornado the female could create. As a highly flammable creature, she preferred to avoid getting caught in the flames.

It wasn't until a familiar musk scented the air that she realized that it wasn't Zephyr creating the heat. It was an infuriated Were. Out of the corner of her eye, she caught a blur of movement.

Somehow Marco had broken free of the magic that had been holding him captive, and he was now prepared to have his revenge. The air shimmered around him as he started to shift and Satin muttered a curse. She didn't know if an elemental could be harmed by claws and teeth. Hell, she didn't know if they could be harmed by anything. And she wasn't willing to allow Marco to put himself in danger.

"Marco, no! She has the answers I need," Satin called out.

She had no idea if the female had answers or if her grief was causing her to see phantoms that didn't exist, but she was willing to say whatever was necessary to protect Marco.

Chapter 10

Marco was a typical Were. He was quick-tempered, impulsive, and ready and willing to respond with violence when necessary. And that was under the best of circumstances. So, being held hostage by invisible bands of air and forced to watch as a strange female threatened Satin was guaranteed to drive him into a mindless fury.

Struggling against the magic that held him captive, Marco released a primitive burst of power that came directly from his wolf. Heat sizzled through the air, hot enough to slice through the bonds wrapped around him. Freedom! Marco leaped forward, on the verge of shifting. His animal was stronger and faster than his human half. A pure killing machine.

Before he could call his wolf, however, he heard Satin's demand to stop. A command he would have happily ignored if she hadn't added the reminder that Zephyr appeared to have answers they needed.

With a snarl of pure frustration, he leashed his wolf and instead moved to stand next to Satin, breathing deeply of her cool scent to soothe the fury pulsing through him.

As if sensing the effort it was taking him not to rip out the female's throat, Satin reached to touch his hand. It was a light, fleeting brush of her fingers, but it helped to calm his enraged beast.

"I didn't destroy your parents or prey on your people," Satin informed the female. "Until this moment, I've never even encountered an elemental."

Zephyr shook her head, her dark curls swirling around her shoulders as if they were floating on a soft breeze. It added to the sense that the creature wasn't quite solid. As if she might disappear at any moment.

Not that it made her any less dangerous, he sternly reminded himself, glancing around at the numerous demons who were still being held hostage. He'd been caught off-guard once. It wasn't going to happen again.

"Then why do you carry his presence?" Zephyr demanded, glaring at Satin.

"I don't know, but I very much want to find out," Satin assured the female. "Are you willing to tell me about Elwha?"

Zephyr paused, as if silently deciding whether to simply destroy Satin along with the evil that was connected to her. Then she abruptly stepped back, her expression tight with frustration. Did she have her own questions she wanted answered?

"Not here," she said, lifting her hand. "We'll go to my private lair." Marco wasn't sure if the female intended to whisk Satin away with her magic or physically force her to follow her, but neither was going to happen. Not on his watch. With a low growl, he pounced to stand between the two females. He'd barely landed when those bands of air were once again wrapping around him. This time they didn't cover his mouth, but instead lifted him off his feet so he was dangling in midair. "Don't be a fool," she snapped. "If I wanted to hurt you or the leech, I would already have disposed of you."

Marco bared his fangs, struggling against the magic. "Release me."

Zephyr circled his tightly clenched body, studying him as if she was baffled by what she was seeing. Had she never seen a werewolf before? Or was she wondering if he'd gone feral? It usually happened to curs, but purebloods could sometimes become consumed by their most primitive cravings. At last, she came to a halt directly in front of him. "Is he yours?" she asked Satin.

Satin shrugged. "For now."

"I haven't had a wolf. He is..." Zephyr pursed her lips, her brow furrowed. "What is the word?"

"Yummy," Satin supplied.

"Yummy." The female considered the term before giving a nod of her head. "That will do."

Marco ignored the elemental, his gaze locked on Satin. "Did you just call me yummy?"

Her expression gave nothing away. "I've called you worse."

"True." He sighed at the fuzzy warmth that sizzled through him. Once upon a time, he'd laughed at idiots who'd twisted themselves into knots to earn the smile of a particular female. Now he understood with painful clarity. He grimly returned his attention to the elemental. "Are you going to release me?"

"If you promise to behave."

Satin snorted, but Marco kept his gaze on Zephyr. He didn't trust the mysterious demon, but he had to concede she could have hurt them at any point. Not that he couldn't do his own damage if she tried. And Satin could flatten the place if she was truly pissed off.

For now, he was willing to offer a temporary truce.

"I won't attack as long as you don't," he muttered.

With a flick of her hand, the elemental lowered him to the ground and removed the magic holding him captive. Her strange eyes swirled with warning as she waited for him to break his word. When he simply placed a protective arm around Satin's shoulders, she turned toward the brownie, who was still plastered against the wall.

"Don't think I've forgotten about you," she warned the bartender. "I'll let you wait here and consider the numerous ways I intend to torture you for your treachery." The male's eyes bulged with terror, but Zephyr smoothly turned toward the fey, who were frozen in place. "Go."

She waved her hand, and with squeaks of fear, the creatures scuttled toward the door, the tang of citrus thick in the air. Marco watched them leave with a stab of satisfaction. He trusted that the elemental would make good on her threat to return and punish the brownie. If she didn't, he would rid the world of the nasty creature.

There was nothing he hated more than a bully.

Once the room had cleared, Zephyr floated toward the fireplace. She spoke an unfamiliar word, and the stones rippled before they appeared to melt to create an opening. He watched Satin grimace before she rigidly followed behind the female. Vampires hated magic. And for once, he was fully onboard with her wariness. He didn't know enough about elementals or their powers to be prepared for what might be waiting for them.

Cautiously approaching the narrow space in the wall, Marco sniffed the air. Lavender and ambrosia. A welcoming scent, and it helped to ease his suspicion as he stepped into the stairwell that led to the darkness below. If there was a threat nearby, he should be able to smell it.

Of course, he hadn't sensed the elemental before she'd appeared and wrapped him up like a damn mummy, he wryly reminded himself.

Waiting for the two females to reach the bottom of the stairs, Marco made sure there was no one behind them before he leaped off the top step to land lightly on the hard-packed earth. He cast a quick glance around, surprised to discover he wasn't in a crypt. Instead, it was a large, natural cavern that had been created by water running through the soft limestone.

In the center of the space was a pile of satin pillows that he assumed had been used as a bed for the elemental and a wooden chest that was piled high with leather-bound books. His attention, however, was captured by the water droplets that floated near the low ceiling. They appeared to be suspended in midair, but even as he watched, they floated together to create an intricate design. It shimmered with an inner fire, like diamonds catching the light. A second later, they pulled apart and danced around the room before they swirled together to repeat the performance.

Fascinated, Marco walked toward the droplets. "Is this your magic?"

"No, my mother created the droplets when I was born. She said they were the only thing that would keep me occupied when she wanted a few moments of peace."

"Exquisite," he murmured, recalling that his own mother had to build an obstacle course in the center of the village to keep him from constantly destroying her furniture.

"You said the ifrit killed her." He turned the conversation back to the reason they were standing in the cavern.

"She was traveling with my father and my brother to Siberia."

Satin made a strangled sound. "Why Siberia?"

"That was the only location we could gather the vita berries that we need to survive." Zephyr shrugged. "They're grown by the frost sprites in the Altai Mountains."

Marco glanced toward Satin. Her expression was as icily composed as always, but he could sense she was deeply disturbed by the female's explanation.

Why? A question for later.

"They were attacked by the ifrit?" he instead asked the elemental.

She nodded. "If my brother hadn't managed to escape, we would never have known what happened."

"You said the creature fed on elementals," Satin said in a tight voice, as if she was struggling to speak.

Zephyr sent her a strange glance. "They're like a vampire. Only he drained them of their fire, not their blood."

Marco frowned in confusion. "Why bother with elementals? Why not create his own fire to snack on? Or live in a volcano? There would be plenty of fire there."

Zephyr arched her brows, as if astonished that he'd stumbled on the obvious question.

"That was what my father wondered as well," she admitted. "He devoted his life to discovering the habits and weaknesses of the creature."

Satin stepped toward the female, her hands clenched into tight fists. "What did he discover?"

"Much remained shadowed in mystery, but after years of study, he determined that Elwha had some sort of anchor that kept him from being sucked back into the underworld and he needed the magic in our fire to maintain his hold on the anchor."

Marco considered the explanation. The ifrit was a creature of hell, so it made sense he would be able to manipulate fire.

"Like a tether?"

"That's the exact word," Zephyr told him, something that might have been approval in her tone.

"What was the anchor?" Satin asked.

Frustration rippled over Zephyr's face. "We could never find out what it was or where he kept it hidden."

Satin's jaw tightened. No doubt she was fighting back the urge to keep probing for answers the elemental didn't have. Marco didn't blame her. For one thing they discovered about the mysterious ifrit, there were a dozen more unknowns.

Could he feed on other demons, or did it specifically have to be elementals? Had he roamed the world or remained hidden in his location? Was the anchor an object or another demon? How the hell had he attached himself to Satin?

With an obvious effort, Satin concentrated on what information the female could offer.

"So how did you banish him?"

"We gathered all the elementals together and traveled to Siberia," Zephyr said. "We hoped that Elwha would still be lurking near the area where the sprite fairies tended to the vita berries."

Marco nodded. Any predator would know to wait near the feeding grounds of its prey. Like a lion stalking a gazelle.

"That's what I would have done."

The clouds in the elemental's eyes swirled, a hint of lightning flashing through them. Was she recalling the loss of her family? For an immortal, the wound would be eternal.

"Unfortunately, we had no way to pinpoint his exact location, so we devised a trap to draw out the ifrit."

"How?" Satin asked.

"I traveled our ancient route to gather our food."

The words were said without emotion, but Marco could imagine how hard it must have been for her not only to walk the same path her parents had taken, but to do so knowing she was putting her life in genuine danger.

"Alone?" he demanded.

"Alone, but with the knowledge my people were nearby." She shrugged. "It gave me the courage I needed."

"Along with your thirst for revenge," Satin murmured.

The female nodded, her eyes still filled with storm clouds. "That, too. I would have done whatever was necessary to track down the beast."

"I assume Elwha took the bait?" Marco asked.

"He did. A lone elemental was too tempting to resist for the beast."

Marco nodded. The one downfall of many predators was their arrogance. It was impossible for them to imagine that superior intelligence could overcome brute strength. A mistake he'd made when he was just a pup tracking down a wood nymph. Certain he was about to capture the delicate creature, he instead stepped on an invisible trip wire and found himself wrapped in a net that was impossible to escape.

Salvatore insisted that he be left in the stupid thing for hours while his pack mates walked by laughing at his predicament. The older male claimed it was a lesson in what happened when you underestimated an opponent. He was right. Marco never forgot.

"Did he have a corporal form?" Satin asked, her expression intent.

"At the time he appeared human," Zephyr told her, speaking slowly as if trying to recall her encounter with the ifrit. "I'm not sure if he chose to take that shape or if he'd invaded the body of a mortal."

Marco tried to dredge up any information he had on ifrits. He had nothing. There were enough demons to worry about without adding in creatures who were supposedly stuck in the netherworld.

"What are his powers?" he asked.

The elemental glanced in his direction. "He can trap you in his smoke."

"Smoke?" Marco blinked. "That's it?"

She arched a brow, as if unable to believe he could ask such a stupid question.

"Once encased in his magic, you can never escape," she informed him. "No one knows if you're placed in another dimension, or if you're sucked into the netherworld, but you wander, lost in the mist forever. It's rumored that when you are close enough to the ifrit, you can hear the screams of the demons who've gone mad. Is that enough?"

Marco grimaced. There might be worse ways to spend eternity, but it was hard to imagine one.

"Yeah, it's enough."

"How did you return him to hell?" Satin asked, seemingly more interested in how to defeat the creature than the potential danger in confronting him. Typical.

"That wasn't intentional," the elemental admitted. "When he attacked me, the hidden elementals rushed forward to encircle him. Then we combined our powers to try to draw the fire out of him. We hoped it would sever his connection to his powers so we could destroy him, but he managed to avoid his fate by returning to the netherworld." The female glared at Satin. "Until now."

Marco stepped toward Satin, sensing the elemental was at the end of her patience. Satin, however, seemed impervious to the scent of scorched lavender.

"How can you be so certain it is Elwha that you sense?" Satin demanded.

The droplets seemed to shatter as they were swept toward the corners of the cavern. Were they affected by Zephyr's mood? Or was she carefully protecting them in case things between her and Satin went south?

Both were plausible explanations.

"Do you think I could forget the stench of the beast who destroyed my parents?" Zephyr hissed.

Ice formed around Satin's feet, spreading outward in a visible warning. "Stench?"

Zephyr leaned toward the vampire, sniffing the air. "It clings to you. Like a shroud."

Satin made a sound of impatience, blithely indifferent to her danger. "I've never had any dealings with an ifrit, and I've never been to the underworld. How could one have"—she wrinkled her slender nose—"infected me?"

The elemental floated forward. "I don't know. And I don't care. I just want it gone."

Marco smoothly stepped between the two women, his wolf poised to explode into action if necessary.

"No more than we do," he insisted.

Satin stepped to the side, her gaze locked on Zephyr. Marco swallowed a sigh. Stubborn female. Why wouldn't she allow him to protect her?

"How do I get rid of it?" she asked the elemental, ignoring his glare of frustration.

"You die," Zephyr said.

Marco growled. "Not happening."

The stormy eyes turned in his direction. "You think you're a match for me?"

"Not now," Satin snapped. A frigid wind whipped through the cavern, nearly knocking Marco off his feet.

The elemental appeared outraged, clearly unused to being told what to do. "Excuse me?"

"We all want the same thing," Satin pointed out in clipped tones. "The demon out of this world."

"Not out of this world." Lightning flashed through her eyes. "Dead."

Marco crouched, preparing for the inevitable battle, but Satin held up a slender hand, her expression stern.

"Destroying me might satisfy your need for revenge, but it's no guarantee that the ifrit won't be able to find another demon to possess. Perhaps one he will be able to control," she calmly pointed out. "We have to find a way to be certain he is destroyed. Or banished."

Zephyr stared at Satin, torn between her need to strike at the demon who'd destroyed her family and the fear that Satin might be right. It was possible the ifrit might have a means of attaching himself to someone or something else if Satin became a pile of ash.

"We spent centuries attempting to discover how to destroy the creature. What do you intend to do?"

Satin flashed a cold smile. "Go back to the beginning."

Chapter 11

Satin was acutely aware of the violence that sizzled in the air. Not just from Zephyr, who hungered for the death of her enemy, but from Marco, who was preparing to protect her. Even if it meant destroying the best means they had of discovering what was infecting her and how to get rid of it.

She had to act quickly to prevent disaster.

"The beginning of what?" Zephyr demanded, her expression suspicious.

Satin considered her answer. She'd been shocked when the elemental had revealed her parents had been killed in Siberia. It wasn't that she didn't think a violent demon hiding from the netherworld wouldn't choose such a remote, ruggedly brutal location. It was the perfect spot. But because that had been her homeland for centuries.

There had to be a connection.

Didn't there?

Still, she didn't want to give away everything to Zephyr. The female was eager to destroy the ifrit. Even if it meant obliterating Satin in the process. She needed to persuade the female to let her deal with the evil spirit. And the only way to do that was to convince her that she had some sort of plan.

"The beginning of when it was possible that I crossed paths with Elwha," Satin at last confessed. "Can you open a portal to Siberia?"

The female sucked in a sharp breath, her hair floating on an unseen wind. "Crossed paths with him? You claimed you didn't know the creature."

"I don't. But I did spend several centuries in the area." Satin pretended she didn't notice the lightning flashing in the female's eyes or the scent of lavender that drenched the air. "If he left behind a portion of his residue before he was banished, it might have infected me."

Zephyr frowned. She didn't appear to be mollified by Satin's explanation, but she was no longer on the verge of releasing her enormous powers. Satin was going to take that as a temporary win.

"Even if that's true, how will it help to travel back there?"

An excellent question. One that was gnawing at the back of her mind. She couldn't explain the vague premonition that was driving her to return.

"There have to be demons in the area who will remember him," Satin smoothly offered the only excuse that might satisfy the elemental. "Some might even have interacted with the creature. Any information we can gather will help to defeat it."

"Or more likely, you desire to escape so you can continue to spread your evil," Zephyr countered, abruptly moving forward to brush her fingers down Satin's cheek. "There."

Marco growled, but before he could attack, Satin gave a sharp shake of her head. As satisfying as it would be to punish the elemental for putting her hands on her, she didn't dare. Not only couldn't she risk a potential injury when they were at the mercy of this female, but she needed a way to travel to Siberia. Immediately.

She reached up to touch her cheek. "What did you do?"

"A simple tracing spell." Zephyr floated backward. Not out of fear, but as if she'd finished her business. "You have until the full moon to destroy Elwha. Or I will—"

Focused on the elemental, Satin nearly missed the blur of movement as Marco launched himself forward. Obviously, he didn't like her being threatened. Satin hissed, reaching out to grasp his arm before he could attack.

"No, Marco," she snapped, trembling at the effort of keeping him from attacking the female. If she hadn't been a vampire with above-average power, she never would have been able to stop him. "Create the portal," she commanded through clenched fangs. Then her brows snapped together as she realized it would still be sunlight on the other side of the world. "Wait. I need the opening to be located in a place that's protected from the sun."

Zephyr lifted her arm to wave her hand in an intricate gesture, at the same time keeping a wary eye on the male struggling to reach her. The female claimed she wasn't afraid of a vampire or a werewolf, but there was no doubt she wasn't eager to tangle with Marco in his current mood.

Which proved she wasn't stupid.

"It's open," Zephyr told Satin, her eyes stormy as she delivered a parting warning. "Just remember…you fail and I will find you. Now, I have business to take care of."

There was a blast of air as the elemental unexpectedly turned into a whirlwind of smoke. A moment later, she was spinning toward the stairs that led to the upper floors. Marco growled as he watched his prey escape, but with a visible effort, he regained command of his temper.

"I'll go through the portal first to make sure there's no light to make you crispy," he muttered.

Satin nodded her agreement. Not only was she unwilling to trust Zephyr, but she wanted out of the cavern. There was an oppressive heaviness in the air that warned the elemental was about to release her powers. It seemed wise to be someplace else when that happened.

Marco stepped forward, disappearing from the cavern as he entered the portal. Seconds later, she heard his disembodied voice calling out.

"You can come through."

Satin grimaced as she forced herself to follow in Marco's exact footsteps. She couldn't feel the magic, but in the blink of an eye, she had gone from the underground cavern into an open cave on top of a mountain. It was shadowed where she was standing, but she could see the glow of sunlight that streamed through a narrow opening at the far end of the space. Behind her she could hear the shrill screams coming from the brownie as Zephyr made good on her promise to punish the male who was supposed to be protecting her.

"I never encountered an elemental before." Marco wrinkled his nose as the cries for mercy were abruptly cut off as the portal closed. "Once was enough."

Satin glanced around the cave. It looked the same as any other. Lots of smooth stone worn away by the years and a few bats hidden in the fissures that ran the length of the low ceiling. There was an icy bite in the air that was a relief after the smothering heat of the demon bar.

Satin lifted a hand to touch her cheek. She didn't doubt for a moment that she carried Zephyr's mark. "If she ever touches me again, I'll rip out her heart," she said, meaning every word. Then she shrugged. "But I don't blame her hunger for revenge. And to be honest, I like a strong female who can take care of her business."

The tension eased from Marco's features. "No surprise there."

"You have a problem with strong females?"

"Obviously not." His gaze deliberately ran down the length of her body before returning to her face. "But if the female tries to harm you, I'll kill her without a second thought."

A tingle of pleasure raced through Satin. As if she was pleased by his macho promise of protection. Idiotic. She was perfectly capable of taking care of herself. Even if she was carrying around a baby and a mysterious evil spirit. Right?

With a shake of her head, she moved toward the back of the cave. With one fluid motion, she lowered herself to the ground, leaning her back against the hard stone wall. She didn't need a watch to know the exact time. A vampire could sense the precise rhythm of day and night no matter where they were in the world.

"We have a couple hours to wait until sunset."

"Good." Marco settled next to her, his warm musk brushing against her like a gentle caress. "You can tell me your plan."

"I don't really have a plan."

His brows drew together as he studied her in confusion. "Then why are we here?" He held up his hand as she prepared to repeat what she'd said before. "I know what you told the elemental about finding demons who might remember the ifrit. I want the *real* reason."

Satin glanced away from his demanding gaze. There was a part of her that resented his question. She'd spent her very-long life keeping others at a distance, and she never answered to anyone. Not even Viper, unless she was in the mood. But Marco was different. He wasn't another male trying to control her because he was an alpha. Or because he was intimidated by her power. He truly cared. And more than that, he was risking everything to stand at her side.

He deserved the truth.

She kept her eyes locked on the distant glow of sunlight that kept her effectively trapped in the cave.

"Like most vampires, I woke with no idea of who or what I was," she said, referring to the fact that her species had no memory of the time when they were a human. "Thankfully, I was lucky enough to be taken in by the local clan, who taught me how to survive." She didn't need to add that most vampires perished within hours of being created.

"They became your family?" Marco asked.

She shrugged. "For a while."

Marco tilted his head to the side, able to sense that the mention of her first clan was a painful subject.

"What happened?"

Satin allowed her thoughts to return to the dark place she tried so hard to forget.

"We were traveling away from Moscow," she said, her voice a mere whisper. "The local khan was being driven from his territory, along with the Golden Horde."

She could feel Marco's curious gaze. "What did human politics have to do with you?"

"In those days an army always put the torch to a town they were pillaging. Vampires prefer to avoid open flames. Not to mention the fact that there were hundreds of wooden arrows being launched through the air. It seemed a good time to relocate."

"That makes sense, I suppose," he murmured. "Did you escape?"

"We thought so." A shiver raced through her body as she recalled the flight through the darkness. They'd been concentrating on the humans who were engaged in violent clashes, along with the spreading fires. None of them had considered the possibility they were fleeing into an ambush. Not until it was too late. "A rival clan arrived with the new warlord. They were waiting for us just outside the city. Before we realized what was happening, they'd managed to kill my chief and took us hostage."

Heat sizzled around her as Marco scooted closer to her stiff body. "What do you mean by hostage?" he asked. "Were you enslaved?"

"Not exactly. I wasn't locked in a cell or kept in chains, but I was the weakest in the clan," she admitted, a layer of ice beginning to form on the ground. A sure indication that she was battling strong emotions. "It meant I was expected to take on the duties that no one else wanted."

There was a short silence as Marco waited for her to continue. "And?" he at last prompted.

"And submit to the will of my clansmen."

He hissed at her blunt confession, the ice around her abruptly melting as his fury blasted through the air.

"You were abused?"

Satin didn't want to talk about the brutality she endured. Nothing could change the endless years that she'd been forced to satisfy the desires of whatever clansman happened to be her master. Or the savage punishment she faced when her chief decided she wasn't performing her duties as quickly or efficiently as he expected.

Putting the nightmare behind her was the only way she could exist without drowning in bitterness and anger.

"I was weak."

She heard a growl rumbling in his chest, but he was wise enough not to demand details.

"I assume you escaped?"

Her lips twisted. In retrospect, it was impossible to recall why she hadn't simply walked away. At the time, however, she'd been so vulnerable that the mere thought of trying to survive on her own was enough to put her into a panic. It was easier to stay than to venture into the vast, scary unknown.

"As the years passed, it became unbearable to remain with the clan."

Her hands clenched as she recalled her breaking point. It'd been a feast night, and the chief had invited a rival clan to join in their celebrations. She'd been hiding in the shadows watching the others pass around the fairies who had been captured for the meal, when she'd heard one of the males demand a trial to the death to determine which clan was superior. An immediate battle had erupted, the clash between the vampires so violent that the aging fortress they'd taken as their lair threatened to collapse on their heads.

Satin had suddenly had enough. Did it really matter what was out there? It couldn't be any worse than her current existence.

She'd slipped away and never looked back.

"Where did you go?" Marco asked, thankfully diverting her grim memories.

"I roamed through Siberia, hiding in caves and avoiding any contact with demons."

"How long did you wander?"

"Time became a blur," she admitted. Being alone was less stressful, but it meant that the nights slid into meaninglessness. "All I remember is that I was constantly afraid. It gnawed at me like a cancer."

Marco reached out to grab her hand, giving her fingers a soft squeeze. "I'm sorry."

She surprised herself by leaning toward him, as if savoring his searing heat. Or was it the rich scent of his musk that she wanted wrapped around her? Maybe both. No, not maybe. Definitely both. A delicate shiver raced through her body, but this time it wasn't from the painful memories. It was all about Marco and her awareness of his hard, male body.

She forced herself to return her attention to their conversation. "I suppose I would have spent the rest of eternity hiding if I hadn't come into my powers."

"How did it happen?"

Satin shrugged. "For most vampires, it's a slow increase in strength that begins when they're created and lasts for several centuries."

"You were different?"

"Yes. I'd assumed since I wasn't acquiring more power that I was as strong as I was ever going to get. But then one night—"

Marco squeezed her fingers as she cut off her words. "Tell me."

Satin grimaced. She'd already revealed her years of being a defenseless victim. So why was it so hard to reveal how she'd become a strong, ruthless female who could kick the ass of anyone stupid enough to challenge her? She knew why. She just didn't want to dredge up her ancient fear.

"It hit like a bolt of lightning," she finally told him. "One second I was as weak as a dew fairy, and the next I was filled with so much power I thought I might burst. To be honest, I was afraid it was going to destroy me."

Marco studied her, as if baffled by her lack of excitement in acquiring such an enormous gift. "Were you injured?"

Satin's lips twisted in a wry smile. "No, but I was sore for days. I had to sleep in a stack of hay until the cramps in my muscles eased."

"Have you ever heard of any other vampire acquiring their power in one blast?"

She slowly turned her head to meet his gaze. A tingle of excitement inched down her spine as she caught sight of the wolf lurking in the dark depths. She hadn't realized his animal was so close to the surface.

She...liked it. A lot.

"I've never asked," she admitted.

"Why not?"

"At first I was simply too ecstatic to care why it'd happened the way it did. For the first time in my existence, I found the courage to leave my cave and walk alone through the countryside." She didn't admit that it'd taken her nearly a month to build up the courage to take that midnight stroll. "Suddenly the lesser demons were scurrying away in fear as I moved through their territory, and even the local troll went out of his way to avoid me. It was intoxicating."

"Yeah, there's nothing like going from an awkward pup to a badass," he murmured, as if hoping to ease her tension.

It worked. Her lips twitched as she studied him in disbelief. "You were awkward?"

"I was a gawky wolf who tripped over my feet, fell into whatever water happened to be close by, and singed my tail in the kitchen fireplace when I tried to sneak a bite of the chicken my mother was roasting." He chuckled at the memory. "My father was convinced I was never going to survive long enough to grow out of my clumsy stage."

It was almost impossible to image the male as anything but lethally graceful. "But you did."

"Eventually."

"And then you were a badass?" she teased.

His eyes smoldered with a sudden heat. "I'll let you decide."

"Hmm." Satin pretended to ponder the question. They both knew she'd already decided. He was without a doubt a badass. Thankfully, he was a true alpha who used his superior strength to offer protection, not to abuse those weaker than him.

Marco turned until he was fully facing her. "Why are we here, Satin?"

Her brief amusement faded as he cut straight to the heart of why she'd never questioned the strange powers that surged through her. Or why she'd fled her homeland as soon as she was certain she had the ability to survive without a clan.

"I want to return to the caves where I was staying when my powers first appeared," she told him, the words a mere whisper.

"Why?"

She held his gaze. She was slowly beginning to understand why she'd felt compelled to return to Siberia.

"I have to know if the power belongs to me." There was a long, painful pause. "Or the ifrit."

His eyes darkened, as if abruptly realizing what she was saying. Surprisingly, he didn't flee in terror. Not that she would have blamed him if he had. Who would want to be with a female infested with a creature from hell?

Marco, however, in typical Marco fashion, was more concerned than horrified by her revelation.

"You think you'll find the answers in that cave if you go back?"

Did she? Satin shook her head. She didn't know what she was searching for, or even where to look. She just knew she had to go back.

"I don't know."

Marco wrapped his arm around her waist and gently tugged her against his warm body. "We'll go as soon as the sun sets," he promised. "But first, you need to rest."

"I'm fine." The words were an automatic defense against appearing weak.

"Okay, I need to rest," he murmured.

With an effort, Satin forced herself to lay her head against his shoulder. Just for once, she wasn't going to battle against his offer of comfort. Not when the sensation of his warm embrace was banishing the grinding dread that was gnawing at her soul.

They would be trapped in the cave until sundown. Why not let down her guard and relax?

"We'll both rest."

"All three of us," he softly corrected, his hand moving to hover over the swell of her belly. "May I?"

Satin stiffened. She never truly forgot about the baby. There was a bundle of awareness in the back of her mind that constantly monitored the child, ensuring that it was continuing to thrive. But until she'd rid herself of the evil presence, she couldn't allow herself to fully focus on the changes in her body. One epic problem at a time.

At last, she nodded.

"So warm," Marco murmured, his fingers lightly pressed against her belly. "Like a Were."

Satin snuggled closer to the hard muscles of his body. The feel of his hand was creating all sorts of chaos. A chaos that had nothing to do with the baby and everything to do with an aching desire to feel this man's touch.

"The heat was the first thing I noticed," she admitted. "Along with my strength being drained."

His fingers lightly skimmed toward the deep vee of her red leather vest. The soft caress seared against her skin, sending jolts of pleasure through her.

"Are you still angry?"

Satin genuinely considered the question. She'd been furious when she'd realized what was happening. And eager to blame Marco. Not exactly a reasonable reaction, but she wasn't really feeling reasonable at the time. Now she was still overwhelmed with emotions, but they'd transformed since Marco had arrived to stand at her side.

"I'm confused." She paused, the words threatening to become stuck in her throat. "And scared."

"Me too," he readily admitted. "But we're going to figure this out."

"You sound very sure of yourself."

"Together we're fairly formidable. A true power couple."

She arched a brow. "Couple?"

"Why not?"

Blindsided by his casual words, she stared at him in disbelief. Was this some sort of a joke? Yes. It had to be. Demons weren't like humans. They changed lovers on a regular basis. Being a couple implied something more permanent. Like a mating...

"To start with, I'm a vampire, and you're a werewolf. Natural enemies."

He shrugged. "A mixed mating works just fine for your Anasso and Darcy."

She studied his handsome features, unable to discover any hint of teasing. There was nothing. In fact, he'd never looked more serious.

Satin, on the other hand, felt like the world was out of focus. As if the profound changes occurring in her life were too much to absorb. Or maybe she was stubbornly trying to cling to a life that was no longer possible, she wistfully acknowledged.

Not that things had been perfect. But she'd created a place for herself in Chicago that offered a sense of peace. Something she'd desperately needed, even if it was occasionally boring.

"We're also complete opposites," she stubbornly insisted.

"Not really." His fingers skimmed up the curve of her throat before he cupped her cheek in the warmth of his palm. "We both manage demon clubs. We both enjoy an exciting game of chase. And we are both determined to protect our baby."

"You have an answer for everything."

"I'm trying." He bent his head to brush his mouth over lips before he urged her head to lie against his shoulder. "Rest."

For once, Satin didn't argue. Not only was she tired, but she understood she was going to need her strength to search for any signs of the ifrit.

She closed her eyes and slept.

Chapter 12

The sun had dipped over the horizon when Marco opened his eyes to discover Satin burrowed in his arms. Inside, his wolf growled in smug satisfaction.

Yes. This was how he was supposed to awaken. With Satin's head on his shoulder and her arms wrapped tightly around his waist. The only thing that would make it more perfect was if they were safely tucked in his bed, not in a remote cave in Siberia.

Oh, and if she were naked.

A smile curved his lips as he stroked his fingers through the dark strands of her hair that he'd released from her braid. He marveled at the sensation. The strands felt as soft and sleek as the lotus silk his mother used to import from Myanmar. Was it any wonder he'd spent so many hours recalling how delicious it felt spilling over his bare chest as she straddled him?

His fingers moved to the cool skin of her cheek, which was just as silky smooth. Another growl rumbled in his chest. His wolf desperately wanted to rub against that skin, coating her in his musk. Marco blinked, caught off-guard by the intensity of his need to mark her. When had that happened? Desire was one thing, but this…

Could it be because of the baby? Weres were desperate for children. Was it affecting his primitive instincts to claim his pup?

No. He lightly traced the outline of her lips, studying the delicate features that haunted his dreams. This had nothing to do with becoming a father. The baby filled his heart with joy, but this need was a fierce, primitive hunger that was all a male's need for a female. And not just any female.

This female.

And no other.

Marco should have been shaken by the absolute certainty that settled in the center of his soul. This was big. Life-altering, never-be-the-same-again big. But instead, there was a strange sense of peace. As if the puzzle pieces that made up who he was meant to be had clicked into place.

Dramatic, but true.

The astonishing realization was still fresh when Satin slowly lifted her lashes to reveal those extraordinary cognac eyes. She appeared momentarily confused as she stared into his face, which was only inches away. Then her eyes darkened with a primitive awareness she couldn't disguise, her hand reaching up to touch his cheek.

Marco tightened his arms around her, squeezing her so tight she would have shattered if she'd been a human. At the same time his head lowered. He had to taste her. It wasn't a desire. It was a necessity. As if he'd starve without the taste of her on his lips.

Before he could claim her mouth, Satin pressed her hand flat against his chest.

"The sun has set," she murmured.

His gaze seared over her delicate features, lingering on her lips that remained temptingly out of reach.

"Yes," he murmured.

"We should go."

Marco's fingers drifted down her throat and through the valley between her breasts, at last reaching the black laces that held her red leather vest together.

"Is there any need to hurry?"

She shivered, a hint of fang peeking between her parted lips and her sweet arousal, which scented the air.

"Besides the fact that Zephyr threatened to track me down if I don't destroy the ifrit by the full moon?"

Marco snorted, not believing for a second that she was actually scared of the elemental.

"Next time I'll be ready for her," he promised, lowering his head to nuzzle a spot just below her ear. She made a choked sound, her nails digging into his chest. Marco chuckled; during her visits to the Hunting Grounds, he'd discovered each and every one of this female's erogenous zones. "She won't have a chance of getting close to you."

A hiss of pleasure escaped between her clenched teeth as he nibbled a path to the tender spot at the base of her throat.

"I still need to find the gargoyle and return her to Styx," she muttered, the words distracted, as if she was having trouble concentrating.

Good.

He nipped her collarbone. "Styx can find someone else to track her."

"Not your decision," she informed him, even as her hand stroked down the length of his chest to the clenched muscles of his abdomen.

It wasn't, of course. Even if she was his mate, Satin would do whatever she wanted to do. All vampires possessed an independent streak that would rebel against any attempt to control them. And Satin was more stubborn than most.

Thankfully, or perhaps unfortunately, Marco was equally stubborn.

Their future together was destined to be...explosive.

"Hmm. We'll see."

He abruptly tugged on the lace, watching as the vest parted to reveal her breasts, which were crested with dark pink nipples. His breath caught in his throat as he reached to cup the soft mound in the palm of his hand.

It wasn't anything he hadn't seen before. On numerous occasions. But as he gazed down at her, Marco felt as if he was seeing her for the first time. Or maybe with a new understanding.

This wasn't another lover.

This was the female whom fate had chosen for him.

And nothing could make him happier.

Heat prickled through him as he leaned down to flick his tongue over her nipple, the rough stroke wrenching a groan from her lips.

Still, she struggled against the passion that was swiftly spiraling out of control. As if sensing that this wasn't the same as their previous sexual encounters.

This time it mattered.

"I thought you were in a hurry to return to Chicago?"

He slid his hand down her body, briefly lingering over the bundle of warmth he could feel in her belly before he was slipping his fingers beneath the stretchy material of her yoga pants. With one smooth tug, he had them pulled down her legs and was tossing them aside. At the same time, he tugged off her shoes, leaving her fully exposed.

"I want you away from danger," he murmured, allowing his hands to sweep up her naked body as need pulsed through him.

Her hips arched upward in silent invitation. "This feels plenty dangerous."

He chuckled, shedding his clothes with jerky motions. Right now, he wasn't worried about appearing overeager. He wanted her to know she had his wolf hot and bothered.

"Good dangerous or bad dangerous?" he demanded, settling his back against the wall of the cave, and stretching out his legs.

It was a silent invitation. As eager as he might be to seduce this female, whatever happened between them had to be a mutual decision. This was no longer a game of chasing his prey. Or being the one hunted down and subdued. As much fun as those nights had been, this wasn't sex. It was a bonding.

As if realizing what he needed from her, Satin flowed to her feet. He tilted back his head to admire the elegant lines of her body. She possessed the long, sleek muscles of a jungle cat. A lethal predator who would destroy without mercy.

"Wicked dangerous," she answered his question, tossing her long black curls as she turned to face him.

"That's the best kind," Marco assured him, his wolf starting to pant as she stepped across him so she had a foot on each side of his hips. He might even have drooled a little. Who wouldn't? She was sexy as hell.

"You would think that."

"Because I'm wicked."

"Yes."

He reached out to run the tips of his fingers up the back of her legs in a soft caress.

"Good wicked or bad wicked?"

"Wicked wicked," she informed him as she slowly lowered herself until she was straddling his lap.

Dios. Marco groaned, his back arching as her cool flesh pressed against his thickening erection. His hands cupped the curve of her hips, his fingers digging into her flesh as the pleasure battered through him. Like a tidal wave of sheer bliss. He struggled against the fierce urge to rub himself against the moist cleft. Or better yet, to lift her high enough to shove his aching cock into the welcoming sweetness of her body.

For now, he was going to let her set the pace.

And trust that he had the self-control not to embarrass himself.

His wolf snarled in frustration, but the hunger that was twisting his gut into a painful knot was eased as he caught sight of the smug amusement that smoldered in her beautiful eyes. She knew exactly what she was doing—savoring her power over him.

Marco leaned forward to brush his lips over her mouth. "I miss that."

"Miss what?"

He nipped the lush softness of her bottom lip before pulling back to meet her curious gaze.

"That fierce confidence. As if you walk through the world with the absolute certainty that you're invincible," he explained. "It's what I first noticed about you. I've never seen anyone with such a bold style as when you walked into the Hunting Grounds and silently dared anyone to challenge you. The light in your eyes has dulled since you began tracking the gargoyle."

Her lips twisted. "I've had a lot on my mind."

That was perhaps the biggest understatement that Marco had ever heard. In the past month, Satin had discovered she was pregnant despite the fact that vampires couldn't have babies. She'd gone on the hunt for a gargoyle, only to discover she was infected by an evil spirit. And now she was struggling with the fear that her powers weren't actually her powers, but the taint of an ifrit who was reaching out from hell.

It was…a lot.

"*Si.* I have not forgotten," he agreed in gentle tones, holding her gaze. "But your burden would be lighter if you shared it with me."

She held his gaze, her expression suddenly impossible to read. "I'm not sure I can do that."

Marco flinched. Okay, he probably should have been prepared for the less-than-subtle rejection. While he'd been busy shuffling through his tangled emotions to discover that this female was destined to be his mate, she'd been overwhelmed with the shocking upheavals in her life. She hadn't had the opportunity to consider the future. Especially not a future with him.

"Because I'm a Were?" he forced himself to ask.

She was shaking her head before he finished speaking. "It's not that." She paused, trying to find the words to explain her reluctance. "I'm not sure I know how to open myself up to someone else. I've been alone for a very long time."

"Ah." Relief shuddered through him. He couldn't change being a Were if that was what was bothering her. Everything else was negotiable. He leaned forward to lap his tongue over the tip of her breast. "We can start here." He moved to the other breast, teasing it to a tight point. "And here."

She grasped his shoulders, her nails biting into his flesh hard enough to draw blood. Marco growled in pleasure. A little pain was always fun for a werewolf.

"I think we've already tried this approach." She reminded him of the savage couplings that had left them deliciously sated.

Marco tilted his hips upward, stroking his cock against the precise spot that always made her scream in pleasure.

"Practice makes perfect," he assured her.

"True." With a smile of sensual temptation, Satin lifted her hips before lowering herself directly onto his throbbing arousal.

"Satin." The breath was wrenched from Marco's lungs as desire exploded through him. His entire body vibrated with the need to grind himself against her, thrusting them toward the looming orgasm. But just as urgent was his primitive need to claim her as his mate. "I want you," he rasped between clenched teeth.

She leaned her head down to press her forehead against his, her nose flaring as if savoring his musk, which was heating the air.

"If you haven't noticed, you have me."

His hands skimmed upward to caress her breasts, his thumbs lightly circling her nipples. "I have your body," he agreed. "I want all of you."

Ice began to creep over the floor of the cave. A sure sign that Satin was struggling to control her emotions.

"You're a very persistent wolf," she muttered.

"It's part of my charm."

She scraped her fangs down his cheek, her fingers tangling in his hair. At the same time, she began to ride him with a slow, ruthless rhythm. "Being a stubborn hound?"

Marco grunted, his thoughts threatening to shatter as desire thundered through him. He lifted his hips off the floor to meet her thrust for thrust.

"Being a male who knows what he desires and does whatever necessary to claim it for his own," he managed to mutter.

She jerked at his blunt confession. "'Claim' is a dangerous word."

Marco refused to back down. It was only fair that she understood she was never getting rid of him. Not ever.

"It doesn't change what I intend to do."

She lifted her head to gaze at him with passion-darkened eyes. "You are either very brave or very stupid."

"Probably both," Marco readily agreed, reaching up to frame her face in his hands.

Then, tugging down her head, he kissed her with a pent-up hunger that refused to be denied. Satin moaned in approval, her fangs pressing against his lips as she returned the kiss with her own searing need.

"No more talking," she informed him.

Marco agreed. They could continue the discussion later. For now, nothing mattered but fulfilling their driving desire.

Surging together, the heat of his wolf clashed with her icy power, creating a mist that swirled through the cave. It was as beautiful and mysterious as the female he held tightly in his arms.

Tilting back his head, Marco bayed at the moon as she rode him to paradise.

Chapter 13

Levet's enthusiasm at having escaped the cavern waned quickly as they trudged through the endless spiderweb of tunnels. He was relieved not to be stuck. That hadn't been any fun at all. But it wasn't much better to wander in an aimless pattern through the weird orangey glow of the netherworld.

He wanted to be back with Inga in her underwater castle. Or sneaking into the cellar beneath the Viper Pit to enjoy an expensive bottle of tequila. Or even hanging around Styx's mansion, teasing the oversized vampire until he stomped away in fury.

Ah…good times.

"Admit it." Troy's sharp words intruded into Levet's lovely daydreams.

He turned his head to scowl at the imp, who was glancing around the narrow cave they'd just entered with a sour expression.

"*Excusez-moi?*"

"Admit that we're going in circles," Troy commanded.

Levet stiffened in outrage. Typical. The arrogant male put Levet in charge of escaping the bowels of hell and then complained when he didn't think it was happening fast enough. Did he assume that Levet was deliberately avoiding the exit? As if he wanted to remain trapped in the smelly place with the distant screams of his enemies on constant replay.

"Of course, we are not going in circles," he protested. "Why would we do that?" Levet hesitated as he was struck by a sudden thought. "Unless we were on a carousel. There was one near our lair when I was just a baby. Do you not adore them? The tiny painted horses and the poopy music." He shook his head. "*Non.* Not poopy. Peppy. Peppy music. But they go 'round and 'round."

Troy heaved a harsh sigh, pointing toward a pile of stones that were leaning at a wonky angle.

"We have walked past this rock formation a dozen times."

"Fah. How can you tell?" Levet moved toward the stones. Had he seen the thing before? Possibly. He shrugged. "All rock formations appear the same."

"This one looks like you."

"Have you gone blind?" Levet demanded in confusion. "It looks nothing like me."

"It's squat, lumpy, and gray."

"Squat? I am not squat." Levet glanced down at his non-squat body. The imp truly must have lost his sight. "I am delightfully diminutive."

"You're a lump of stone."

Levet came to an abrupt halt. Why hadn't he left the ungrateful imp trapped in the cavern?

"That is not nice," he groused.

Troy wrinkled his nose, almost as if he regretted his harsh words. "Look. I'm tired, I'm hungry, and I'm bored out of my ever-loving mind. Three things that tend to make me a tad fussy."

Levet scowled, but he allowed his annoyance to fade. The male was a selfish pain in the derrière, but Levet could sympathize with his foul mood. This place would make any demon cantankerous. Including himself.

"*Oui.*" Levet pressed a hand against his empty stomach. "My belly is growly."

Troy nodded toward the stack of stones. "And we're going in circles."

"We are..." Levet's protest dried on his lips as a faint breeze wafted past his face. "Wait."

"You aren't going to distract me with some bizarre story about your childhood in Paris or the time you saved the world with one of your stupid fireballs. We've been through this cave a dozen times."

Levet impatiently waved away the imp's accusation. "Sniff the air," he commanded.

"Why?" Troy placed a hand over his face, his eyes narrowing. "Is there something vile?"

Levet rolled his eyes. As if the air was not already vile. "Beyond the stench of hell?"

"Yeah, beyond the stench of hell."

"*Non.*" Levet tilted back his head and sucked in a deep breath. "Just the opposite."

"What do you smell?"

"Freedom."

Troy stilled, eyeing him with a lingering suspicion. "Don't screw with me, gargoyle. I'm not in the mood."

Levet snapped his wings. "You are never in the mood."

"Not true," Troy predictably argued. "I'm often in the mood, just never when you're around."

Levet made a choked sound of annoyance. The imp was nearly as aggravating as a leech. And that was saying something.

"Just smell."

With obvious reluctance, Troy sniffed the air. Then he sniffed again. Deeper this time.

"Cactus," he at last murmured. "I smell cactus. And desert air."

Levet touched his snout with the tip of one claw. "*Précisément.*"

Troy abruptly twisted his head from side to side. "Which direction?"

Levet closed his eyes, attempting to pinpoint from where the breeze was originating. Once he was confident that he knew where to go, he opened his eyes and turned to hurry toward an opening across the cave.

"This way."

He waddled across the smooth stone floor, entering the wide tunnel that curved in one direction and then another. Expecting to reach an opening that would lead out of the underworld, Levet's steps began to slow. Was this yet another trick? Were they indeed going in circles that were leading nowhere? Or worse, were they headed even deeper into the netherworld?

The sense of dread only intensified as the tunnel began to narrow. As if it was going to squeeze so tight they would be stuck. Not a very pleasant thought. Especially with the imp literally breathing down his neck.

"Are you sure this is the right way?" Troy at last snapped.

"Of course, I am sure," Levet readily lied, picking up his pace with more confidence than he felt. "It isn't much farther." They rounded yet another curve, but this time there was an opening at the end. "There, you see?"

"Does that lead us out of here?"

Levet scurried through the carved doorway and into the wide cavern with a low ceiling. It looked remarkably similar to the cavern they'd been trapped in earlier, only it wasn't a dead end. Thank the goddess. On the opposite wall was a wide set of stairs leading upward. And even better, the light that spilled out of the opening wasn't the sickening orange glow. It was an untainted sliver of moonlight.

"See?" Levet sent his companion a smug smile. "All we have to do is cross the cavern and head up the stairs."

The words had barely left his lips when a weird, whooshing sound filled their ears. As if the air was being sucked from the space. Then, without warning, the stone floor cracked open and a line of fire spewed out. The inferno sizzled with enough heat to drive both Levet and Troy back as it expanded from side to side as well as upward to touch the ceiling.

"Easy, right?" Troy growled in frustration. "Just across the cavern through the massive wall of flames."

"*Oui.*" Levet's wings drooped. "Through the massive wall of flames."

* * * *

Bertha had no idea where she was going to be when she stepped out of the portal. After her strange encounter with the creature from the underworld, she'd wandered through the desert until her feet had grown tired and she was parched with thirst. At last, she'd opened a portal, intending to travel to Hong Kong. Why not? She'd been there several months ago, and she'd loved the hustle and bustle of the city. Just what she needed to forget the relentless voice in her head. And prove to both of them she wasn't some mindless slave he could use and abuse.

But instead of arriving in a street crowded with humans and the smell of stewing fish balls, she'd been in the middle of a desert. Obviously, Hades was capable of disrupting her magic. The...horse patootie.

Grimly she tried again. And again. This was her third try.

She hoped it would be the charm, but honestly, she was prepared for disappointment. Moving forward, she glanced around. Her heart sank. All she could see was a barren landscape occasionally dotted with jagged rock.

Mon Dieu.

Desert. Again.

Then her nose twitched. What was that smell? Humans? Yes. And a lot of them.

Barely daring to breathe, she turned to discover the sky reflecting the glow of thousands of distant lights. She leaned forward, her gaze eagerly searching for any hint that would reveal the identity of her location. It was at last the tip of the Eiffel Tower that gave it away.

Not the real Eiffel Tower, of course. But that didn't matter.

"Vegas," she breathed, excitement tingling through her. "Now we're talking."

"Don't get distracted," Hades warned, his voice echoing through her mind.

"Go away," Bertha muttered, hiking up her dress as she sprinted across the hard ground. The last thing she wanted was to have the flimsy material trip her.

"Why do you keep saying that?" There was a hint of amusement in the seductive tones. "You must realize you're not getting rid of me."

Bertha ground her teeth as a familiar annoyance seared through her. She was an ancient gargoyle who'd spent several thousand years doing exactly what she wanted, when she wanted, and how she wanted. The mere idea that anyone could turn her into their puppet was rubbing her nerves raw.

"A challenge?" she growled.

A warmth swirled through her. Like a caress. "A promise."

"Bah." Bertha ignored the tingles of pleasure as she hit the outskirts of the city and headed straight for the strip. Moving easily through the crowded streets, she passed by the massive hotels until her roaming eye caught sight of a brightly painted one that had been built in the shape of a medieval castle. Ah, yes. Perfect. Using the front door, she entered the casino and sucked in a deep breath. "Mmm. I adore the smell of Chanel and greed. It reminds me of Paris."

Nearly skipping in pleasure, Bertha weaved her way through the tightly packed slot-machines that blasted music and sirens and whistles that were meant to attract the gamblers who strolled past. Overhead, the massive chandeliers spilled a muted light over the guests, and on the walls, fake stained-glass windows glowed with hidden lamps. Having actually stayed in medieval castles before, she noted that this one wasn't very realistic, but she accepted that it wasn't meant to be.

After all, who wanted to spend time in a cold, inevitably damp room with straw on the floor and smoke from the fires choking the air? That didn't even include the stench of the nearby latrines and unwashed humans.

She much preferred modern amenities and the scent of the buffet wafting through the air.

Angling toward the tables covered with a green baize, she debated whether or not to join one of the games. She was an excellent poker player. Then again, that buffet was calling her name.

As if on cue, the voice intruded into her lovely thoughts. "Why are there so many flashing lights?" Hades groused. "It's very chaotic."

Bertha came to a sharp halt. "You can see what I see?"

"Of course."

Bertha didn't know why the realization bothered her. She'd been aware she was carrying a hitchhiker in her brain. But somehow the knowledge that it was more than a whisper of awareness, that he could actually use her eyes to view the world and maybe even take full control of her body, was infuriating.

"How would you like it if I was rummaging around in your head?" she snapped, speaking out loud despite the fact that the male could obviously read her mind.

"An interesting possibility." There was a pause, as if Hades was considering her question. "I'm not sure if you would survive. Would you like to try?"

"No, I would not like to try," she snapped. "It's rude."

"Necessary," he corrected.

"For what?"

"You'll see."

"Argh." Bertha threw her hands up in disgust.

"Can I help you?"

It took a second for Bertha to realize that the question had come from the man standing in front of her and not the voice in her head. She blinked, studying the human, who was wearing a Polo shirt and khaki slacks. His blond hair was cut short and combed to the side, and his face was freshly shaved. He looked to be thirty in mortal years, with a cocky smile that Bertha didn't like. It made her want to slap it off his face.

"Help me with what?" she demanded, annoyed by the interruption.

"Whatever you need."

"Doubtful."

"Let me try."

"Fine." Bertha planted her hands on her hips. "I would like you to evict a denizen of hell from my mind and return me to my original form."

The cocky smile widened, as if the man assumed Bertha was teasing him. "There's nothing wrong with your form. In fact…" The man reached out his hand as if intending to touch Bertha. With a muttered curse, she prepared to step back. She wasn't in the mood to deal with the idiot.

Before she could move, however, she felt a blast of energy travel through her. It wasn't the familiar, earthy sensation of her own magic. This was exotic and hot and thunderous. Like lava spilling through a volcano.

Wondering what the hell was happening, she watched in confusion as the man in front of her abruptly jumped backward, cradling his hand against his chest as if it'd been injured.

"Ow!" he screeched, loud enough to attract the attention of nearby guests. "What did you do to me?"

Bertha scowled. "Stop that," she told her inner companion.

"Crazy bitch," the man in front of her snarled, his eyes snapping with outrage. He'd seemingly expected her to melt with pleasure at being accosted in the middle of a busy casino; instead, he'd had his fingers burnt to a crisp. Exactly what he deserved, even if she was pissed at how it'd happened.

"Oh...go away," she muttered.

"We've already discussed this," Hades reminded her.

"I'm not talking to you." She pointed toward the human. "I'm talking to you."

"Christ." The man warily backed toward the nearby exit. "I don't know what's wrong with you, but you need to be locked away."

She took a sudden step in his direction, and with a shrill cry of alarm, he turned on his heel and dashed toward the door. Bertha rolled her eyes, returning her attention to the male in her head who was ruining everything.

"And as for you. Why did you do that?"

"I didn't want him touching you."

Bertha stiffened, puzzled by his blunt confession. "Why not?"

"A good question."

Bertha waited for him continue. Predictably, he left her hanging.

"Yeah, I'm full of them," she informed him. "A damn shame you don't have any answers."

"Are you always this peevish?"

"Peevish? I am not—" Bertha bit off her words and forced herself to suck in a deep breath. "Enough. I'm going to enjoy myself."

Squaring her shoulders, Bertha continued her journey through the casino. She ignored the card tables, sensing that she was too distracted to gamble. What she needed was some mindless entertainment.

"Where are you going?" Hades asked.

She ignored him, threading her way past the lobby and into a new section of the hotel. The truth was, she didn't know where she was going. Not until she caught sight of a life-sized poster with six half-naked men gazing down at her in wicked invitation.

Male dancers? Yes, please.

Veering toward the nearby theater, Bertha used her magic to hide herself from the uniformed humans who were taking tickets from the customers standing in a neat line. She darted inside the theater, pausing long enough to scope out the room before heading toward the VIP section at the front. Close enough to the elevated stage to have an unimpeded view. She was settled in her seat with a fruity drink in front of her when the lights at last went down and the music started pumping.

Seconds later, the men made a flamboyant entrance, dancing and smoothing their hands over their bare chests with the sort of energy that had the room screaming in approval. Bertha sipped her drink.

Paradise.

"No!" the voice cried in the back of her mind.

Chapter 14

Marco leaned against the wall of the cave, his arms folded across his chest as he watched Satin pull on her stretchy pants and lace up her leather vest. She was stunningly beautiful with her glossy black hair spilling down her back and her eyes darkened to an antique gold from their recent bout of lovemaking. But it was her effortless grace and the power in her lean body that made his wolf growl in appreciation.

His warrior female. Precisely what he desired in his mate...

Stepping into her boots, Satin sent him a puzzled frown. "Aren't you going to get dressed?"

Marco pushed away from the wall, strolling forward. "I'm enjoying the view."

Satin rolled her eyes. "Sometimes you're such a male."

"Just sometimes?"

"Yes." She smiled. "Thankfully."

"Hmm. Why do I feel as if I was just insulted?"

"You weren't. I promise."

Marco reached out to tuck a raven curl behind her ear. "Is there a reason you dislike males?"

She blinked, as if confused by his question. "It's not males in general," she corrected him. "It's the ones who have no appreciation for an independent female."

Marco studied her defensive expression, sensing the wounds that had not entirely healed.

"Or those who abuse the vulnerable?"

"Yes." Her lips twisted. "Though, to be fair, plenty of females are willing to be bullies."

His hand cupped her cheek, his thumb rubbing against the soft fullness of her lower lip.

"Wolves choose a mate who is also their partner," he assured her. "They work together as equals."

She abruptly stepped back, eyeing him with blatant suspicion. "Speaking of wolves, why do I smell like your animal?"

"We did just spend some quality time rubbing against each other." Marco hid his smile. He wondered when she would notice that his wolf was busy claiming her as his own as he held her in his arms. And not for the first time. His gaze lowered to her hip, where he could see the narrow silver lines that marred her skin. They had to be the scratch marks he'd inadvertently given her months ago. The fact that they were still visible— at least to him—meant his animal had already made its decision. "Very quality time."

She narrowed her eyes. "Your scent might cling to my skin, but your musk is deeper." She lifted her arm to press it against her nose. "Like it's inside me."

Ah. Obviously, she wasn't going to be satisfied with his flippant answer. Marco turned away, grabbing his clothes off the ground and methodically pulling them on. He needed a second to gather his thoughts. This wasn't going to be an easy conversation.

Once he was fully clothed, he turned back to catch Satin eyeing him with an unmistakable appreciation. A growl rumbled in his chest. But before he could take advantage of her smoldering awareness, she was giving a sharp shake of her head.

"Tell me why I carry your musk."

Marco swallowed a sigh. "Do you want the truth?"

She stiffened as if she sensed his answer was going to be complicated. "Is it going to piss me off?"

"Probably."

There was a long pause. Was she wondering whether or not to let it go? Probably. After all, ignorance truly could be bliss.

A minute ticked past, then she squared her shoulders. "Tell me."

"It's my mark," Marco bluntly admitted.

She stared at him, as if waiting for him to continue. "Mark?"

"To warn other werewolves that you're my mate," he clarified, making sure she couldn't pretend to be confused.

It wasn't the time or place for the conversation, but the sooner she knew the truth, the sooner she could accept that she could always depend on him. No matter what happened in the future.

Unfortunately, at the moment she didn't appear overjoyed at the thought of becoming eternally bound together. In fact, she was stepping back as if in dire need of space.

"I'm not your mate."

"My wolf would disagree," he insisted. There was no going back now. No matter how brutally his pride might get trampled.

"Marco."

"It's out of my control, *cara*." He held her gaze. "Destiny has chosen you for me."

"And what if I don't choose you?"

Marco battled back his stab of disappointment. What had he expected? Overwhelming joy? Screams of delight? A confession that she'd been hoping to hear those very words?

No. He hadn't hoped for any of those things. But it might have been nice if she hadn't looked quite so horrified.

"Then I will accept your decision," he assured her, his voice carefully devoid of emotion.

"Just like that?"

Marco chose his words with care. He wanted to assure her that he would never try to force his presence on her. Not if she didn't want him around. Then again, there was no way he was going to walk away from the child she was carrying.

"I hope to be a father to my pup, but I can't force you..." Marco's words dried on his lips as he was struck by a sudden realization.

He hadn't paid much attention to his father's lectures on becoming a mature male. There'd been warnings about controlling his wolf as he hit puberty and learning his place in the pack. He'd also droned on for hours about the changes that would happen once Marco had discovered his true mate. At the time Marco had barely listened. He'd known it might be centuries before he found the female destined to become his partner. Why bother to fill his head with stuff that wasn't going to matter until the event finally occurred? He had, however, maintained a distant memory about the physical transformation that a male could expect to endure. Probably because he'd been outraged by the mere thought.

"Traditionally a male wolf who has chosen his partner but hasn't completed his mating begins to weaken," he admitted.

"Why?"

It was the same question he'd asked all those years ago. "To prevent a male from forcing himself on a potential mate."

"Oh." She studied him with a curious gaze. "You don't feel weaker?"

Marco shook his head, taking a swift inventory of the energy that pulsed through him. It felt as he was bursting with a tidal wave of power. Odd.

"No." He shook his head in confusion. "In fact, I've never felt stronger."

"Then obviously you're mistaken." Something flashed through her eyes. Marco's chest squeezed. He could have sworn it was disappointment. "I'm not your mate."

He stepped closer, but he was wise enough not to try to touch her. She was on edge, and bad things could happen when you startled a vampire. It usually included broken bones and lots of blood.

"There's no mistake. I've never been more certain of anything in my very long life. I think my wolf has known from the moment you stepped into the Hunting Grounds that you were mine."

She was shaking her head before he finished speaking. "But some part of you must not accept the mating."

"It's not that." He ignored her determination to deny the mating. Eventually she would accept it was real. At least that's what he was telling himself. Instead, he concentrated on the energy that was humming through him. There was only one reasonable explanation. "I assume it has something to do with the baby."

Her hand moved to cradle her stomach. "Why do you say that?"

"It makes sense that my instincts wouldn't allow me to be at my weakest when you're pregnant," he spoke his thoughts out loud. "Even if you haven't accepted me as a mate, my duty is to protect you and the baby."

She considered his words, then planted her hands on her hips. Stubborn to the end.

"Perhaps the baby is the reason you think we're mates. The goddess knows that it's screwing up my instincts."

Marco heaved a heavy sigh. He was trying to be patient. He truly was. "Is it the general idea of a mate that you oppose? Or specifically me as a mate?"

She glanced away. "It's a complication I can't deal with. Not now."

The words were sharp, but Marco didn't miss the hint of vulnerability in her voice.

"There's no complication." He brushed a light hand over her shoulder. "Just you and me fighting evil together."

She glanced back, a reluctant smile hovering on her lips. "Fighting evil together? You really know how to sweet-talk a girl."

"I used to, but you have me off my game," he admitted, stepping close enough to catch the scent of his musk clinging tenaciously to her skin. His wolf howled in silent satisfaction. Primitive? Maybe. But while he might look human, he was an animal at heart. His hand moved to trace the curve of her throat. "Or maybe what is happening between us is too important for games."

Their gazes clashed, both of them acutely aware that nothing was ever going to be the same again.

Then, with a toss of her head, Satin turned toward the entrance of the cave. "We need to go."

"Lead the way."

* * * *

Satin followed the narrow trail that wound along the base of the towering mountains. Eventually she would have to climb toward the upper slopes, but she preferred to wait until they were closer to the cave she'd once used as her hidden lair. The jagged rocks were coated in a thin layer of frost that would make the hike treacherous. Even for demons.

Especially when she was too distracted to properly concentrate.

Threading their way through the Siberian larch trees, Satin shivered as Marco's heat brushed against her back. Not that she needed his heat to remind her that he was only inches behind her. The sense of him was a constant pulse deep inside her. As if he was embedded into her soul.

The knowledge should have terrified her. It was one thing to have him tell her that his wolf had chosen her as his partner. He'd sworn he wouldn't press her to complete the mating, and she trusted he would keep his word. This acute awareness, however, had nothing to do with Marco's claim. She could still smell his musk on her skin, but her sizzling connection to the male was a primitive need that came from deep inside her.

Oddly, the realization wasn't nearly as unnerving as it should have been. In fact, there were renegade tingles of excitement that were doing nothing to help her focus on the frigid darkness that surrounded them. Which might explain why she didn't detect the danger approaching from behind. Not until Marco reached out to grab her elbow.

"We're being followed," he warned in low tones.

Coming to an abrupt halt, Satin tilted back her head, absorbing the breeze that whipped around them.

There were dozens of smells. Fir trees, granite coated with moss, a snow leopard prowling on the cliffs above them, and a tribe of approaching fey creatures.

"Sprites," she murmured.

Marco moved to stand at her side. "This must be their territory."

Satin frowned. It wasn't uncommon to travel through the homeland of dozens of creatures. But they weren't foolish enough to confront a vampire. Or a pure-blooded Were.

"So why aren't they hiding until we pass through?" She spoke her thoughts out loud.

"They must be protecting something."

It had to be something of vital importance for the sprites to risk a confrontation with two of the most powerful demons in the entire world. Which meant that they might very well be willing to engage in a battle.

Satin wrinkled her nose. "I prefer to avoid a fight."

"Yeah, me too," Marco agreed. "But I don't like the feeling that we're being herded."

Satin sent him a startled glance. If he feared they were being steered into a trap, then he must have been aware of the sprites long before he'd brought them to her attention. Which was just embarrassing. What kind of apex predator was completely oblivious to being stalked?

Hoping Marco didn't mention her lapse to Viper or Styx, Satin glanced around, considering their limited options. To one side was a sheer cliff face, and to the other side was a thickly wooded area that surrounded a large lake. The path, however, was wider at this spot and reasonably flat.

"We can head up the mountain and hope they don't follow," she said. "Or stand our ground."

Marco didn't hesitate. "I vote for stand our ground. We have space to fight if necessary and there's limited opportunity for anyone to sneak up on us." He took a step to the side, his heat prickling through the air as he prepared to shift.

"Show yourself," he called out.

There was a soft tread of footsteps before the sprites stepped out of the surrounding trees. Satin counted six warriors who were wearing dark robes that allowed them to blend in with the night. They all had the long silvery hair of frost sprites and the sort of delicate features that made it easy to underestimate them. Or at least it would be easy to underestimate them if they weren't pointing wooden arrows directly at her heart. Not to mention the fact that there were probably a dozen more hidden out of sight.

The largest of the warriors stepped forward. He was as tall as Satin with eyes that looked like faceted diamonds that caught and reflected the moonlight. His pale face was flawlessly smooth, but Satin could sense he was old. Even older than her. And he wore a golden crown on his head. An indication that he was a member of fey royalty.

His age and bloodline warned Satin that he was far more powerful than an ordinary sprite.

It also meant that he possessed an arrogance that allowed him to glare at Marco in blatant disdain.

"This is our territory, wolf," he drawled. "You don't give orders here."

Marco stepped forward, the air sizzling as his eyes glowed with a golden fire. "I give orders anywhere I damn well please."

"Very diplomatic," Satin muttered, preparing for the inevitable battle.

Marco shrugged. "I don't like his attitude."

The sprite waved a slender hand, not nearly as scared as he should be. "We have no quarrel with you, wolf. You are free to go."

Satin narrowed her gaze. "That implies you have a quarrel with me."

The sprite slowly turned his head to meet her gaze. "We have long memories." His expression tightened with a fierce emotion, the air suddenly laced with the scent of bitter raspberries. "Very long."

Satin studied the male in confusion. She'd encountered thousands of demons over the long years of her life. It wouldn't be strange not to recognize the majority of them centuries later. Why would she remember them all?

But she sensed he was implying they'd had more than a passing encounter. Something he'd seemingly brooded on for a very long time.

"Who are you?" she demanded.

He held out his hand, as if expecting her to kiss the topaz-studded ring. "I am Cosma. King of the Frost Sprites."

Marco flowed forward, smacking away the sprite's arm with enough force to make the male grunt in pain.

"Stay back," Marco warned.

Cosmo scowled toward the Were. "I said we have no wish to involve you."

"Oh, I'm involved," Marco assured him, his fangs flashing in the moonlight. "One hundred percent."

Satin smoothly stepped in front of the furious werewolf. Not only because she was beginning to suspect that whatever had happened between her and the sprite was important, but also because she wasn't going to allow the stubborn wolf to be injured. Not when she needed him.

A wry smile curved her lips. There. She'd admitted it. If only to herself.

"You haven't explained why you're following me," she firmly distracted Cosma's attention back to her.

The male's jaw tightened, but with a visible effort, he resisted the urge to do something foolish. With a deliberate motion, he smoothed his hands down his robe, which was threaded with gold. Sparks of magic danced around his fingers, snapping with power. A less-than-subtle reminder that while he might be fey, he wasn't helpless.

"We were tracking you because you were driven from these lands centuries ago and warned never to return," he informed her in stiff tones. "The punishment of disobeying that order is death."

Satin made a sound of annoyance. If she'd been banished by this male, she most certainly would have remembered. She wasn't universally loved. Far from it. But until the last few days, she'd never been threatened on a regular basis... Oh.

She wasn't the one who had been threatened. It was the evil spirit she carried.

"Are you talking about the ifrit?" she asked.

There was a rustle of unease from the nearby warriors. As if the mere mention of the creature was enough to frighten them. Cosma, however, gave a sharp shake of his head.

"That devil was returned to hell, where he belongs." He pointed a finger in Satin's direction. "You were warned to leave and never return."

Satin curled her hands into tight fists. She'd tried to be patient, but she was done with his vague accusations.

"You've made a mistake, sprite," she informed him in an icy voice that should have sent him scurrying. "Now I suggest you leave before I allow my pissed-off companion to rip you into tiny pieces."

Marco released a loud growl to add to the threat, but astonishingly, the male stood his ground. Did he have a death wish?

"There is no mistake." Cosma ran a hard gaze down the length of her body. "You might have become a vampire since we last met, but I would recognize you anywhere."

Satin jerked. It hadn't occurred to her that he was referring to her existence before she'd been turned. Probably because that life had nothing to do with her. They were two separate beings.

"You knew me when I was a human?" she pressed. She needed to be sure there was no misunderstanding.

Cosma curled his lips in disgust. "Unfortunately."

Chapter 15

Satin wavered. What was the purpose in arguing about what had happened when she was a human? It had nothing to do with her, despite the fact they shared a body. Then again, the frost sprite had obviously had dealings with Elwha. She needed to discover if they had some idea how he could have infected her with his evil spirit.

And more importantly, how the hell she could get rid of it.

"If our encounter happened when I was a mortal, then you must realize I have no memory of that meeting." She grudgingly gave in to the inevitable.

The creature wasn't going to be satisfied until he'd been allowed to vent his grievances.

The diamond eyes flared with self-righteous fury. "That doesn't erase the crime."

Satin tried not to look bored. She genuinely had no interest in what atrocities the human had committed.

"What crime?"

"Luring fey creatures to their doom."

Satin sent the male an impatient frown. "I might not remember being mortal, but I do know that most humans have no idea demons even exist. And even if I did, I would have been far too weak to have caused any harm."

Cosma shrugged. "That was my thought, as well. At least in the beginning. It was too late by the time I realized your full treachery."

"How?"

"You wish to know?"

Satin made a sharp sound of impatience. Time was wasting, and this idiot was playing games.

"Just tell me," she snapped.

"I have a better suggestion," Cosma drawled, sliding his hand into a hidden pocket of his robe. A second later he was pulling out a thin vial that held a dark blue liquid. "I'll show you."

"What's that?"

"A simple memory spell. I prepared it when I sensed you entered my territory."

Satin studied the vial, the temperature dropping as she prepared to lash out with her powers. This suddenly felt like a trap.

"I don't understand."

The male offered the vial, as if it held the answer to her unspoken questions. "I could tell you about the past, or you could simply relive it."

Relive it? Was he implying that he could conjure the memories of the human who had died centuries ago?

"That's impossible," she bit out.

Cosma's nose flared, as if annoyed by her refusal to blindly accept his crazy promises. Then his gaze slowly lowered to the bump visible beneath her pants.

"You're carrying a child," he pointed out, as if she'd failed to notice the baby growing inside her. "Obviously nothing is impossible." He shoved the vial into her hand. "Drink."

"No, Satin." With a swirl of sizzling heat, Marco was standing beside her, his fingers gripping her arm as if to keep her from raising the vial to her lips. "It's a trick."

"There's no trick, wolf," Cosma snapped.

Satin kept her gaze locked on the sprite. "A vampire doesn't possess the memories of the human it takes as a host."

"They're there," the male argued. "You just have to access them."

Satin glanced back down at the blue liquid. She'd never heard of a vampire retrieving memories. Then again, she'd never heard of a vampire being pregnant. Or toting around evil spirits. Or any of the other weird-ass things that were suddenly happening to her.

She shook the vial, watching the bubbles form. "And this will let me...." She tried to recall the word that Cosma had used. "Access them?"

"For a brief time. Once the spell ends, they will be erased again."

Hmm. It still sounded sketchy to Satin. "How do I know that what I see will be true? You could be planting anything you want in my mind."

The sprite lifted his hands. "You will have to trust me."

"Screw that," Marco snarled, his fingers tightening on her arm. "Satin, these must be the frost sprites who helped Zephyr and her people."

Satin nodded. That had been her thought, as well. How many tribes of frost sprites could there be in the area?

Cosma made a sound of shock. "How do you know Zephyr?"

Satin silently dismissed the possibility that the elemental and these sprites were working together. His surprise was too genuine to be faked.

"Our paths recently crossed." Satin kept her answer vague. "She was the one who sent me here."

The sprite scowled. "Why would she send *you* here?"

"For answers."

Cosma appeared to consider her words before giving a slow shake of his head. "I suppose she wouldn't know that you were our enemy. The ifrit hunted the elementals without your assistance."

Satin flinched, as if she'd taken a physical blow. And that was exactly how it felt. The creature was implying that she wasn't a victim of Elwha. Just the opposite. That she'd somehow been an accomplice.

"What did I do?" she demanded.

Cosma nodded toward the vial she clutched in her fingers. "Drink and find out."

"No," Marco rasped, his features tight with fear. "Please, Satin, let's leave this place."

Satin understood his unease. She didn't trust the sprite any more than he did. But how could she walk away when Cosma offered her the answers she desperately needed? It was the reason she'd commanded Zephyr to open a portal to this place. And the reason she wasn't safely tucked in her private rooms beneath the Viper Pit.

Besides, what was the alternative? Roaming through Siberia on the vague hope that there was some other creature who might have information to rid her of the ifrit's spirit?

No, this was the opportunity she'd been seeking, even if it wasn't exactly what she'd expected.

First, however, she had to make sure the potion wasn't dangerous. She would happily risk herself, but she couldn't take a chance with her child.

"Will this endanger my baby?"

"No," the sprite swiftly assured her. "It is perfectly harmless."

"Bullshit," Marco growled, glaring at the male. "The fey are notorious for punishing their enemies. If they believe you are guilty of some sin, they will most certainly do everything in their power to hurt you." He clenched his jaw, visibly struggling against his urge to toss her over his shoulder and simply leave. "And the baby."

"True enough," Cosma intruded into the conversation. "But to enjoy my revenge fully, she must first understand why she needs to be punished. Otherwise, what's the point?"

Satin ignored the sprite, holding Marco's smoldering gaze. "I have to know. It's the only way to protect our future." She deliberately cupped her hand over her stomach.

They both understood the true danger to their child was the darkness that shrouded her in evil.

Marco hissed in frustration. "I don't like this."

"Shocker," she tried to tease, reaching out to grasp his hand. "Don't..." The words stuck in her throat.

"Don't what?"

"Don't leave me."

He stepped closer, wrapping her in the protection of his arms. "Never."

Reassured that he would watch her back, Satin lifted the vial and poured the spell into her mouth.

* * * *

Troy hastily backed away from the blazing barrier. It didn't matter that there was no heat coming from the hellfire. That didn't mean it was harmless. Just the opposite. The magical flames were almost guaranteed to sear the flesh from his bones. A particularly unpleasant prospect. And one he preferred to avoid.

At all costs.

Standing at his side, Levet appeared equally reluctant to enter the swirling flames. He cleared his throat, his twitching tail revealing his unease.

"Do you wish to go first?" he asked.

Troy snorted at the ridiculous question. "In case you haven't noticed, I am a highly flammable creature."

Levet shrugged. "You have magic to protect yourself."

It was true. All fey creatures had some ability to control the temperature around them. They could avoid frostbite during the winter, and even walk through lava if necessary. And as an imp with royal blood, Troy had more talent than other creatures in manipulating his environment. That didn't mean, however, there was no danger. If this was another test from the netherworld, then anything could be hiding behind the flames.

"Perhaps, but I just had a very expensive spa treatment a few days ago," Troy murmured. "My skin is as soft as a dew fairy's butt. I'm not about to damage it with those nasty flames. Not even with my magic protecting me."

Levet widened his eyes. "Truly? As soft as a dew fairy's butt?" Levet reached out his hand, as if he had to discover for himself. "Can I feel?"

Troy leaned down, turning his face in invitation. "Knock yourself out."

Levet laid his palm against Troy's cheek. "Oh. It is soft," he breathed. Then, lowering his arm, he glared at Troy with obvious annoyance. "Why did you not invite *moi*? I adore a spa day. How am I expected to get properly exfoliated if I never get a professional body scrub? So rude."

Troy arched a brow, studying the leathery gray creature who regularly turned into a lump of granite.

"You go to a spa with that skin?"

Levet was instantly offended. "What's wrong with my skin?"

"Nothing. It is perfect—for a gargoyle." A cunning smile touched Troy's lips. "And no doubt exactly what is needed to walk through a wall of hellfire."

"Bah. You are attempting to trick me into going first."

"Is it working?"

Levet sniffed, his wings drooping. "I thought we were partners? Like Batman and Robin."

Troy knew he was being manipulated. A rare event. He was usually the one doing the manipulating. But there was no doubt that the aggravating creature had proved to be a handy companion. And if Troy was being honest with himself, he'd admit that he didn't want to be left behind. Being alone in this place seemed like a bad thing.

Even worse than being stuck with Levet.

Which was saying something.

"Fine," he grudgingly muttered. "We are partners. But not like Batman and Robin."

Levet cocked his head to the side. "Thelma and Louise?"

"Didn't they die at the end?"

"*Oui*." Levet turned toward the wall of flames. "Are you ready?"

Troy rolled his eyes. "No, but that never stopped me before."

Levet squared his shoulders and tromped forward with a courage that Troy couldn't help but admire. There weren't many creatures who would walk straight into a wall of flames without some hesitation. Unfortunately, that meant he had to match the creature stride for stride, his chin held high. Okay, he might be marching toward his death, but by the goddess, he wasn't going to be outdone by a three-foot-tall gargoyle.

Reaching the flames, Troy conjured his magic, wrapping himself in a protective bubble. If it was thick enough to survive a nuclear blast, surely it was also effective against the magical hellfire. Only one way to find out.

Clenching his teeth, Troy stepped forward, entering the flames. Braced for the blazing inferno to press against his spell, Troy stumbled forward when it instead parted before him.

Warily glancing around, Troy watched the fire dance in eerie silence, encircling him and the gargoyle but remaining several feet away. As if they were standing in the center of the storm.

"This is not so bad," Levet muttered.

Troy grimaced. "Speak for yourself, gargoyle," he retorted, his mouth dry with fear. There was nothing normal about the fire. There was no *snap, crackle,* or *pop* as the flames swirled around them. No searing heat. No smell of charred flesh. He might have suspected it was nothing more than an illusion if he hadn't been able to see the black soot that marred the floor of the cavern. "Let's just get out of here."

Levet nodded, cautiously inching forward. The circle of calm went with the gargoyle, and Troy hurried to walk at his side. He didn't know what the deal was with the flames, but he didn't want them touching him. Or the shield of magic around him.

Intent on keeping as close as possible to the gargoyle, Troy lost track of time. At least until he felt a cramp in his calf. They'd spent endless hours wandering through the underworld, and they were *still* roaming. Only now, they couldn't even see where they were headed.

"We should be through the barrier," he groused.

"*Oui*," Levet agreed.

Troy heaved a harsh sigh. "We are lost again, aren't we?"

The predicable scowl furrowed the gargoyle's brow. "We are not lost. We are discovering an alternate route."

"Discovering an alternate route?" Troy clenched his hands. It was that or reaching out to shake the idiot until the rocks in his brain rattled. "Sometimes, gargoyle..." Troy's words were forgotten as he felt a sharp tug. As if someone had wrapped an invisible rope around his waist and was pulling him backward. Troy spread his legs, struggling to maintain his balance. "Argh."

Levet's scowl deepened. "What is wrong now?"

There was another tug, and Troy felt his feet slide across the stone floor. He was being hauled into the nearby flames.

"Levet!" he rasped, desperately trying to grab hold of the gargoyle. The mini-demon might not be full-sized, but he weighed a ton.

His fingertips stretched out, but he was already too late. Before he could grasp anything but air, he was flying backward with a speed that made his eyes water.

Crap.

"Troy. Come back!" he heard Levet call out. "Come back this instant."

Troy closed his eyes, concentrating on keeping his bubble of magic tightly wrapped around him.

He had the feeling he was going to need it.

Chapter 16

Satin could feel the liquid slide down her throat and spread through her body. It wasn't as intense as she'd expected. In fact, she was beginning to suspect it was no more than colored water when the world started to recede like she was being sucked into another dimension. Or traveling through a portal. She didn't fight the sensation. This had to mean the spell was working, right? And she would soon be tapping in to the human's memories.

She waited, expecting the images to start flickering through her mind, but there was nothing. Instead, a strange sensation tingled through her. A slow, disturbing realization that she was no longer alone in her own body.

What the hell? She was herself, but not herself. As if she'd been shoved into the back of her mind so another presence could take control.

She might have panicked if it hadn't been for the warm scent of Marco's musk. It was a reminder that whatever was happening wasn't real. And that she was safely tucked in the protection of his arms.

Perhaps determined to test her courage, the darkness began to fade as an early morning light seemed to spread its rosy glow over the landscape. Satin instinctively flinched, but there was no searing pain. No turning to ash. The rays did nothing but warm her chilled flesh.

A miracle.

No, a voice whispered in the back of her mind. *Magic.*

Battling back her instinctive need to stay in control, Satin forced herself to enter the thoughts of the human who was currently sharing her body.

It was surprisingly easy, and before she was fully prepared, Satin was sinking into the mind of a young woman. Shuffling through her memories, she could quickly determine that her name was Mila, and that she was the pampered only child of a wealthy baron who lived near

Moscow. She couldn't establish the exact year, but judging by the lavish gown and embroidered cloak she was wearing, she was guessing it was the mid-fifteenth century. About the same time, she was turned into a vampire. Interesting.

With a grudging effort, she forced herself to sink deeper, briefly merging herself with the human so she actually became Mila.

At the moment, she was standing on top of a turret at the corner of a massive stone fortress. It was mid-morning, and despite the bright sunlight, there was a sharp chill in the breeze. Mila was glancing over the low balustrade at the vast forest that seemed to spread as far as the eye could see.

It was a beautiful view, but she wasn't impressed. The sight inspired nothing more than a sharp stab of frustration. It churned through her like poison. She had been pacing the turret since the crack of dawn, waiting for an important announcement. How much longer would she be forced to waste her time?

Minutes passed, then the soft tread of footsteps disturbed the silence. Mila whirled to watch her mother, the Baroness Nadia, walking toward her. The older woman was wrapped in a heavy green cloak trimmed with fur, and a hood was pulled over her braided silver hair. Her round face was pale, but there was a shimmer of tears in her dark eyes.

She was crying.

Mila lifted her hand to touch the golden medallion dangling from a delicate chain beneath her cloak, joy replacing her frustration.

At last!

This was the moment she'd been anticipating since her father had collapsed during a battle with the raiders nearly six months ago. He should have died then. He was *meant* to die then. That had been her bargain when she'd led the stupid men past her father's guards and into the fortress. But he'd lingered in his bed day after day, stubbornly refusing to give in to the inevitable.

Last night, however, the healers had been hastily summoned along with a priest. Certain signs that the end was finally here.

"Well?" she demanded as her mother came to a halt. "Is he gone?"

Nadia's lips curled into a shaky smile. "Nay. He is awake. And even sitting up in bed to eat his breakfast." She blinked back the tears that Mila belatedly realized were caused by happiness, not sorrow. "It is a miracle."

Mila struggled to accept what she was hearing. "He will live?"

The older woman beamed at her, completely unaware of Mila's tumultuous emotions.

"He will not only live, but there is now hope for a full recovery. Is that not marvelous news?"

Mila clenched her teeth, holding back the raw scream of disbelief. "I do not understand. You told me the healers claimed he would never see the dawn."

Nadia waved away her words. "They underestimated the power of my prayers. I spent the evening in the chapel, beseeching God to spare your father's life. He is too dear to all of us to be taken."

"You are certain?" Mila pressed. "There is no chance of a relapse?"

Her mother gave an emphatic shake of her head. "There will be no relapse. It is truly a blessing," she insisted. "I fed him breakfast, and then I came to find you. I knew you would want to see him as soon as possible."

"Did you?" Mila ground out. She'd been willing to allow nature to take its course. Even if it wasn't happening as swiftly as she desired. But fate had snatched away her victory. It was obvious she would have to provide destiny a helping hand.

"Of course." Her mother's smile faltered. "I realize you disliked visiting your father when he was on his deathbed, but now that he is on the mend, I do feel you should spend some time at his side."

"You are right, I should go see him," Mila agreed, yanking her hands out of her mother's grasp.

The unexpected jerk knocked the older woman off-balance, and she stumbled forward. Pretending she was reaching out to catch her mother, Mila instead put her hands against the woman's chest and shoved with all her might. Nadia's eyes widened in confusion, too late realizing that the enemy they'd always feared wasn't the Golden Horde or random raiders. It was her own flesh and blood.

With a wail of despair, the older woman fell backward, hitting the balustrade with enough force to flip head over heels as she toppled off the turret. Mila stepped forward, watching the woman who'd loved and nurtured her for twenty-three years flail her arms in an effort to halt her lethal plunge. It was futile, of course. With a satisfying thud, the woman hit the frozen ground and lay still.

Mila smiled. There was no doubt the baroness was dead. The cloak fanned over her like a death shroud, hiding her broken body, but her head was tilted to an angle that was only possible if her neck had snapped. Oddly, her eyes were wide open, staring sightlessly at the daughter who'd just betrayed her.

Another woman might have been disturbed by those accusing eyes, but not Mila. With a toss of her raven curls, she turned away from the balustrade and headed toward the nearby door her mother had left open.

She descended the spiral staircase that led her to the private apartments. Unlike the forbidding starkness of the outer fortress, the living area was lushly decorated.

Rich tapestries covered the walls, and woven rugs were strewn across the floor. The furniture had been hand-carved by local craftsmen and upholstered with crimson and gold material. Hung over the large fireplace was an ancient shield that was painted with the family crest.

Mila passed through the outer chamber and stepped into the bedroom. It was even more lavishly decorated with fur rugs, silver candelabras, and treasure chests filled with priceless gems. In the center of the room was a massive four-poster bed, where her father was propped up on a pile of satin pillows.

Vlad, the current baron, had once been a large, jovial man with rosy cheeks and eyes that twinkled with humor. The sort of man who was beloved by his numerous servants and even tolerated by the serfs, who accepted he was a better master than most noblemen.

Over the past months, however, he'd become a shrunken version of himself. The festering wound had sapped his strength until he couldn't even feed himself. And for the moment, he was as weak as a kitten. But Mila wasn't stupid. His current vulnerability would swiftly pass if the wound was truly purged. She had to act decisively or all would be lost. An unacceptable delay to her plans.

Raising her hand, she sent the maid who was bathing her father's face with a damp cloth scurrying from the room. The servants had discovered she didn't possess her parents' kind heart. They obeyed swiftly or she would have them beaten. Or worse.

The older man offered her a smile of pleasure as she approached the bed.

"Mila," he murmured in a voice that was rusty from the days he'd been too weak to speak. "I am so happy you have come to visit. Have you heard the glad tidings? I am no longer on death's door."

"I would not be so certain, Father," Mila warned, halting next to the bed.

His smile faltered, his gaze sweeping over her face. "Have you spoken with the healers?"

"There was no need." Mila smoothed the heavy coverlet that was spread over her father's frail body before perching on the edge of the bed. "Do you remember when I was just a child, Father?"

The unease vanished from the baron's expression as he gazed fondly at his only child. "Of course, I remember. You were a lovely baby." Something that might have been regret flickered in his dark eyes. "Perhaps a bit overindulged, but we had been so desperate for a child we were overjoyed when you were finally born."

Mila ignored the implication that she was spoiled. She had been, of course. It had been inevitable. She was not only astonishingly beautiful, but she was also clever. The combination had ensured that she was capable of manipulating those around her.

Especially her parents.

"I used to love to walk in the forest," she reminded him. "I thought it was enchanted."

He nodded. "You said there were fairies who danced on the frost."

"There were." Her voice hardened. She'd been fascinated by the exquisite creatures she'd glimpsed skipping and whirling through the trees. But each time she'd tried to get close enough to join them, they'd disappeared in a puff of mist. "You insisted they were figments of my imagination."

"All children are fanciful. And you had no playmates. It was no doubt inevitable you would allow your fantasies to run wild."

"That is not what you said at the time," she reminded Vlad in sharp tones. "In fact, you forbid me to walk alone in the forest."

The baron's features settled into defensive lines. "Your mother insisted that your obsession with the imaginary creatures was unhealthy. We were only thinking of your welfare."

Mila rolled her eyes. "You were not worried. You were embarrassed that I insisted on believing the fairies were real."

Vlad glanced away as the truth of her words slammed into him. "We only did what we thought best for you."

"Oh, it was," she assured him in mocking tones, her hands still smoothing over the embroidered coverlet. "I lost interest in the fairies. Not because of anything you or Mother did. I would have slipped out the window to visit them if I'd desired." A cold smile twisted her lips at the mere thought of the baron and baroness attempting to control her. Fools. "Instead, I began to listen to the voice that whispered to me from the flames. He was far more interesting than any mysterious creatures dancing among the trees." Mila paused, then gave a small shrug. "At least I assume it is a man. I have never actually seen him before."

The baron frowned. "Voice in the fire? What are you talking about?"

"At first he came to me in my dreams," she told the older man, recalling the precise moment when she'd become aware of the voice. She'd been sound asleep, but she'd known instinctively that the whispers weren't a part of her dream. They assured her that she was special. And that her ability to see the fairies meant that she was destined for far greater things than being bartered off to a rich nobleman to fatten her father's coffers. Mila had eagerly believed each and every promise the voice offered her. "Later, he spoke to me directly from the flames in my fireplace."

Vlad licked his lips, clearly troubled by her revelation. "My dearest, it was your imagination—"

"Shut up!" she cut off his words, a fierce anger surging through her. "For once in your life, you will listen to me."

The older man flushed, but as if sensing he was currently too weak to enforce his will on her, he slowly nodded.

"Very well."

"He revealed that I had a rare talent for seeing beyond the mortal realm," Mila continued, oddly relieved to finally confess the truth. She'd kept it a secret for so very long. "It was a gift that came with enormous rewards."

"Rewards?"

Mila smiled. "Power. And not just becoming the chattel of some disgusting nobleman. Real power, that is mine alone." Her smile widened. "And riches beyond my wildest fantasy."

Vlad cleared his throat. "Mila, you must put these childish notions behind you. Soon you will be married with children of your own—"

"Never." Mila surged to her feet, her hands clenched at her side. "I am destined to rule, not to be oppressed by a husband or burdened with squalling babies. The voice promised this to me."

The baron shook his head. "What can a voice do?"

It was a question Mila couldn't answer. She'd been given hope for a glorious future, but no precise details as to how it was going to be achieved. Nothing beyond the fact that she needed to take command of the fortress by ridding herself of her meddlesome parents, and that her power would ultimately come from the fairies she alone could see.

Annoyed that her father had forced her to consider the possibility of failure, Mila reached out to grab one of the pillows.

"My future is no longer your concern, Father. I am willing to believe, even if you are too blind to see."

He shook his head, genuine fear in his dark eyes as he realized he'd underestimated the depths of her ambition.

"What are you doing, Mila?"

"Goodbye, Father. Don't wait for me at heaven's gate. I have another destination in mind."

"Please…"

The wheezing voice was cut off as Mila leaned forward and placed the pillow over the baron's face.

At first the older man sat in rigid shock, as if he thought it might be some sort of tasteless joke. But as Mila pressed the pillow even tighter, Vlad began to thrash in earnest. Mila spread her legs, gaining leverage as she continued to smother the man who'd given her life, a home, and his love.

In her mind, she owed him nothing.

Baron Vlad was nothing more than a barrier standing in the path of her glorious future. He had to be eliminated. One way or another.

Ignoring the hands that blindly reached up to try to grab her, along with the desperate grunts, she concentrated on keeping her arms straight. They were already starting to tremble from the strain. Suffocating a man, even one weakened by injury, wasn't as easy as she assumed it would be. And worse, it was taking far longer than she'd expected. There was always the risk that one of the numerous servants would stroll into the room. Or find her mother's body and raise the alarm.

A sudden fear blasted through her. Why would the stupid man not die? His days were over. It was her time to rule. And not just a small duchy in the middle of a forest, she assured herself. She had been promised the world. But to claim her future, she had to rid herself of her past.

After what felt like an eternity, her father's hands fell away, and his body went limp. Still, Mila continued to hold the pillow tight against his face. She wasn't going to risk failure. Not when her dreams were about to come true.

Counting to one hundred, Mila at last relaxed her trembling arms and stepped back. She counted again, watching her father's body for the smallest twitch. There was nothing.

He was dead.

Tossing the pillow onto the floor, Mila turned away from the bed and headed toward the door. She didn't bother to turn around for one last glance. Her father had been a necessary sacrifice. Just like her mother.

Once in the outer room, she reached to tug one of the ropes that were attached to the various servants' rooms.

The minutes ticked past before a middle-aged man in heavy fur robes hurried into the room. Seneschal Yuri was bald except for a silver fringe that circled his head like a crown, and he wore a thick gold medallion around his neck. A symbol of authority as her father's chief steward.

He was eagerly headed to the bedroom when he caught sight of Mila standing next to the stone fireplace. The smile faded from his chubby face as he came to a reluctant halt. He'd never been deceived by Mila's pretty face and practiced charm.

"I was summoned by the baron. Is he awake?"

"No, I summoned you."

The man pinched his lips, struggling to contain his annoyance. "I do hope your need is important. I am quite busy."

"I would say the death of my father is very important. Would you not agree?"

"His death?" The man's eyes widened in shock. "That is impossible. The healers—"

"Were mistaken," she coldly interrupted. "Not for the first time."

"You are sure?"

Mila waved a careless hand toward the connecting door. "You are welcome to check if you wish."

Yuri shook his head, looking as if he might be sick as he tried to process the news. Or, more likely, he was attempting to calculate the potential change in his position.

"Where is the baroness?" he at last demanded, his eyes darting from side to side. "She will need my assistance during these difficult times."

Mila folded her arms over her waist. The man was already calculating how he could manipulate her mother to his advantage. She admired his ambition, even as she intended to crush it.

"My mother is also dead," she bluntly informed her companion. "In her grief at losing her beloved husband, she threw herself off the top of the fortress." Mila tilted back her head, pretending to glance toward heaven. "May she rest in peace."

There was a long silence as the man struggled to speak. "Both the baron and baroness are dead?"

"That is what I just told you." Mila lowered her gaze to send the man a stern frown. "Which means that I am now in charge of the household."

The steward studied her with a wary expression. "You do understand that the land and title will go to your cousin, Boris?"

Mila shrugged. Her distant cousin was hundreds of miles away. It would take months before a message could reach him and he could gather his belongings to make the long journey. By then she intended to be in full control.

"In the meantime, we need to prepare a proper burial for my parents. I will leave the details to you."

He jerked as if stunned by her offhand words. "Surely you wish to personally—"

"You heard what I said, did you not?"

Yuri's jaw tightened. "Yes."

"Then go do it." She shooed him away.

With a stiff bow, the steward marched out of the room, his shoulders set to a rigid angle beneath his cloak. Sooner or later, he would have to die, but for now she needed him to deal with the pesky details of running such a large household. Eventually she would be living in a grand palace and this cold, damp fortress could rot, but for now she wanted to ensure she had servants prepared to tend to her every need.

Dismissing the steward from her mind, Mila turned toward the roaring fire and sank to her knees. At the same time, she reached beneath her cloak to touch the medallion nestled between her breasts.

"It is done," she said out loud.

The flames flickered, as if there was someone inside the fire. She'd never seen who or what the presence was, but the voice was crystal clear as it echoed through the room.

"You have taken control?"

"Yes." Mila leaned close enough to feel the heat against her skin. "Now I desire the power and riches you promised me."

A hollow chuckle floated out of the flames. *"So rash. Like all mortals."*

"I have waited too long." Her voice was petulant. "Soon I will be too old and gray to appreciate my good fortune."

"Perhaps we can discuss the gift of immortality. If you prove worthy."

Mila's breath caught in her throat. Immortality? "I will live forever?"

"As I said, if you can offer me what I need."

Mila's heart missed a beat. This was even better than she'd dreamed possible. "What must I do?"

"Come closer."

Chapter 17

Marco was honest enough to admit that he was a mess.

It didn't make sense, of course. He was holding Satin tightly in his arms, making sure that nothing could harm her. Not without going through him first.

So, why did he feel as if she was slipping away?

Perhaps it was the spell that had been given to her by Cosma. He hated the thought of Satin being at the mercy of fairy magic he didn't fully understand. Especially when a dozen warriors still circled them with expressions of ancient hatred. Or maybe it was the sour smell of human that unexpectedly coated Satin's skin. It was as if a foreign invader was attempting to take over her body.

Was it just the return of the memories that was causing the smell? Or had the magic conjured the dead human?

Either way, he didn't like it.

He wanted Satin's icy scent filling his senses. And her cognac eyes wide open and smoldering with power. He wanted his female as she was meant to be. A gloriously confident vampire who didn't take shit from anyone.

"How long does the spell last?" he at last demanded.

Cosma shrugged, his aloof expression impossible to read. "The leech is free to bring an end to the memories whenever she wants."

Marco frowned. Did he trust the fairy? Not for a second. But Satin had made her choice. As much as he longed to interfere, he couldn't risk destroying this opportunity. Not when it offered the potential to get rid of the clinging evil.

"You claimed she lured your people to their deaths," he said between clenched teeth. He needed a distraction before he did something stupid. "What did she supposedly do?"

The diamond eyes sparkled with ancient fury. "There is no 'supposedly' about it."

"Tell me."

Cosma sucked in a deep, calming breath, his hands smoothing down his robe as he struggled to leash his emotions.

"Her forefathers owned the land in our territory, but unlike other humans, they didn't indulge in constant warfare or taint the forests with their human waste," he at last said, glancing around the area as if reassuring himself that it remained unspoiled. "We lived in harmony for years. Until their descendant, Mila, gained control of the estate."

"I assume she wasn't as careful in protecting the land?"

The male's lips curled with disgust. "Worse. She was born a pradictus."

Marco hissed in surprise. He'd heard of mortals who possessed the ability to detect demons, but he'd always imagined they were a myth. Like leprechauns. Certainly, he'd never met one.

"She could see you?"

Cosma nodded. "Once we discovered her ability, we considered abandoning our homeland. Mortals are weak, but they pose a danger to any demon."

That was true enough. Especially as their technology became more advanced.

"Why did you stay?" he asked.

"At first, she did nothing with her gift beyond spying on us in the forest," Cosma explained. "And even that stopped as she matured. We assumed she'd convinced herself that we were no more than figments of her imagination."

"But she hadn't?"

"No." His lips twisted into a humorless smile. "She'd merely been distracted by another demon."

Another demon? It took Marco a second to realize what creature must have been lurking in the area.

"Oh. A vampire."

Cosma shook his head. "The ifrit."

Marco grunted, feeling as if he'd taken a blow to the gut. They'd been so focused on discovering how Satin might have been infected that they hadn't considered the possibility it'd happened before she was turned. After all, it made sense to infect a vampire. They were one of the most lethal demons in the world. Not to mention the fact that they were immortal. But a human?

He shook his head in disbelief. "She encountered the creature when she was still mortal?"

"Of course." The frost fairy appeared confused by the question. "I doubt he could have so easily manipulated a demon."

Marco grimaced. That was true enough. There were few creatures more stubborn than a vampire. As he was painfully aware.

A human was much easier to infect. Plus, the fact that she was a pradictus would make her even more vulnerable to the influence of the ifrit. Still, it seemed a risky move for the demon. Humans were extraordinarily fragile.

"How did he contact her?"

Cosma waved a slender hand. "There's no way of knowing for sure, but he must have some means to maintain a connection to this world."

The words echoed what the elemental had said when she'd spoken about the enemy of her people.

"An anchor," he murmured.

"Exactly."

Marco considered what was involved in an anchor. Was it a mystical mooring or something more tangible? An object of power? Or a specific place?

His own magic was a primitive alchemy that came directly from nature. It couldn't be manipulated or corrupted by others. But demons who used spells and enchantments were at risk of having their powers disrupted.

Was it possible to locate the anchor and destroy the thing?

That seemed to be the most efficient means of getting rid of the ifrit's connection to this world. And, more importantly, the taint that was infecting Satin.

"Where is it?" he demanded.

Frustration twisted the male's features. "We've never managed to figure out what it was or where it was hidden."

Marco's brief hope was efficiently squashed. He didn't doubt the fairies had searched far and wide. He would need outrageous luck to simply stumble across it.

And luck was the one thing he never depended on.

He returned his attention to how the creature had managed to infect Satin's body.

"How can you be sure the human was working with the ifrit, or even aware of its presence?"

Cosma shuddered, as if recoiling from a painful memory. "We had sensed a darkness beginning to creep through our territory. We didn't know at first what it was, and honestly, we'd become so complacent after decades of isolated peace that we didn't pay as much attention to the threat as we should have. I suppose we thought it would simply disappear. It wasn't until we were awakened to discover our hidden lairs were encircled by a ring of fire that we recognized the danger."

Marco studied the male in confusion. "You're frost fairies. Surely you can quench a few flames?"

"It was hellfire," the male clarified, his hands clenching and unclenching as he struggled against a sudden surge of emotions. "We have magic to protect ourselves, but only for a limited time. It was imperative that we escape."

Ah. That made sense. Marco had never encountered hellfire, but he didn't doubt it would be a nasty way to die. Anything that originated in the underworld was best avoided, as far as he was concerned.

"What does this have to do with Satin?"

The moonlight hit the diamond eyes and reflected with jagged sparks. "*Mila*," Cosma stressed the human name, "stepped through the flames looking like an angel and called for us to follow her to safety."

Marco snorted. What demon would ever trust a human? Especially one who had revealed she could see fey creatures.

"And you did?"

Cosma looked embarrassed, as if he wished he hadn't shared his impulsive decision to give in to the mortal's promise of safety. Then he stuck out his chin to a defensive angle.

"We were in a panic," he snapped. "We had no way of knowing who had created the hellfire or if they were enemies lurking in the fortress."

Marco didn't press the issue. Could he really claim that he'd never made a rash decision he later regretted?

Besides, he was more concerned with the rising anger he could sense coming from the gathered warriors as they recalled Satin's supposed betrayal. He smoothed his hands down her back, instinctively comforting her despite the fact that she was unaware of the gathering danger.

"What happened?" he asked, knowing it was best to keep the male talking. At least until Satin was fully conscious.

As far as he was concerned, they had all the answers the frost fairies could give them. It was time to go.

The sooner, the better.

"Over half my tribe followed Mila inside the fortress before I realized it was a trap," Cosma revealed in bleak tones.

Marco hissed in shock. "Half?"

"Yes."

A genuine stab of pity sliced through Marco's heart. No wonder the male was anxious to have his revenge. The loss of any member of his tribe would be painful, but to lose half? That was a brutal cost for a leader to bear.

"Did you see them again?" He asked the question already knowing the answer.

"Never," Cosma rasped, his pain still raw. "They simply disappeared. It wasn't until later we discovered that they'd been fed to the ifrit."

Marco studied the male in confusion. "Fed? As in dinner?"

"He didn't eat their flesh, but their magic was drained until they could no longer survive."

"The elemental told us the ifrit absorbed the fire of her people," Marco said, recalling his conversation with Zephyr. "Why would he need frost fairies?"

"The elementals determined that their fire was how he kept his connection to this world," Cosma explained. "He consumed the magic of other fey creatures to increase his powers."

"You believe that Satin…" Marco grimaced. Whoever had sacrificed the frost fairies to the ifrit, it wasn't the vampire he held in his arms. "Mila," he corrected himself, "was aware of what she was doing when she led your people to the fortress? She might have been under the compulsion of the demon."

The male's diamond gaze rested on Satin, his hatred a palpable force that pulsed in the air.

"She is still guilty."

"No. Mila is long gone. Satin—"

Marco bit off his words as the vampire in his arms suddenly stiffened. Was she waking? He glanced down, but before he could catch sight of her face, she was lifting her hands to push herself out of his tight grasp.

Caught off-guard by the violent shove, Marco stumbled backward. At the same time, the surrounding warriors abruptly stepped forward, their expression taut with fury.

"The ifrit," Cosma rasped. "She's returned the beast."

"What?" Marco started to turn toward the frost fairy when he belatedly caught the stench of sulfur. Shit. He whirled back toward Satin, realizing that her stunning cognac eyes were now swirling with crimson flames, her pale face devoid of expression.

"Kill her!" Cosma commanded.

Marco leaped to stand directly in front of Satin, his arms spread wide. "No."

Cosma lifted his arm, and the warriors drew back their bows, prepared to destroy Satin. Marco snarled, preparing to shift even as he accepted there was no way he was going to be able to halt every arrow. It would only take one to go through Satin's heart and kill her.

Intent on the fey, Marco did the unthinkable. He forgot the enemy at his back. Not that he could ever consider Satin his enemy. She would always be the female whom he would protect to the bitter end, no matter what happened.

Proving that the bitter end might be closer than he anticipated, Marco was lifted off his feet and tossed toward the nearby trees as if he were no more than a leaf caught on a breeze. Marco hissed in pain as he hit the trunk of a massive oak with bone-shattering force.

Around him, he could hear the various moans and groans that indicated the fey warriors had been caught in the same blast of air. And that they'd suffered the same humiliating fate.

Indifferent to the muttered curses of the fey and their desperate scramble to regain their weapons, Marco leaped to his feet and turned to discover that Satin had disappeared.

His heart halted mid-beat, terror twisting his stomach into a hard knot. Had she run off while he was slamming into the tree? Or had she been whisked away by magic? He took a deep, desperate sniff of the chilled night air. There was no hint of his vampire, but the odor of sulfur was tainting the breeze. It seemed to come from the trail leading into the nearby mountains.

"Satin!" he bellowed, preparing to shift.

Without warning, Cosma was standing directly in front of him, a trail of blood trickling from a wound at his temple and his crown tilted to a funky angle.

"She's no longer your vampire, wolf," he snapped in sharp tones. "She's Mila. A vessel for the ifrit."

Marco snapped out his hand to grasp the creature's robe, hauling him forward until they were nose to nose.

"You did this," he growled.

The diamond eyes flared. "The ifrit was banished. The only one capable of returning it to this world is Mila."

"It was your magic—"

"It was a memory spell, nothing more," Cosma interrupted. "Certainly it couldn't conjure a powerful demon from the bowels of hell."

Marco battled back his urgent need to deny that Satin had any connection to the evil creature. He was wasting precious time.

"Where is the ifrit's lair?" he demanded, assuming that was where Satin was headed.

Cosma shrugged. "The old fortress."

"Where?"

Cosma pointed toward the nearest mountain. "At the top of that peak."

Marco nodded, tightening his hold on the male's robe as he glared at him in warning.

"If you try to hurt Satin again, I will hunt you down and destroy you," he snarled.

The fairy gave a sharp shake of his head as his warriors lifted their weapons, but his gaze never wavered from Marco's hard expression.

"You can threaten me all you want, wolf. I won't let that creature return to harm my tribe. Not again."

A growl rumbled in Marco's throat, but releasing his grip on the male's robe, he stepped away. Satin was collecting enemies at an alarming rate. He needed to get her to safety before anything could happen to her.

Releasing the power of his animal, Marco shuddered as the primitive magic raced through him. He was vaguely aware of the fairies hastily stepping away as he transformed, but he'd already put them from his mind. The wooden arrows might hurt, but they posed no danger to a pureblood Were. Especially when he was in his wolf form.

He tilted back his head, and a howl ripped from his throat as his muscles were twisted and stretched. Then, barely waiting until he'd solidified into his wolf, he was leaping forward, hot on the trail of his female.

* * * *

Levet stomped his foot as Troy was snatched away by the flames. What was wrong with the ridiculous imp? This was no time to be flying around like a honeymoon. Wait. Was that right? Looney tune? Levet made a sound of impatience. It didn't matter.

"Troy!" He turned around. There was nothing to see. Nothing beyond the roaring fire that continued to encircle him. "I am going to leave you here. Do you hear me?"

He waited. And waited. All he heard was the heavy silence that pressed against him like a shroud.

"*Sacrebleu.*" Levet gave another stomp of his foot. "I will come and find you, but I will not be happy. Indeed, I intend to be quite annoyed."

Levet cautiously moved forward in the direction that Troy had disappeared, an icky feeling in the pit of his stomach as the fire moved with him. It was like he was standing in the center of a spotlight that followed his every move. He didn't want to be engulfed in flames. No matter what the imp claimed, a gargoyle wasn't created to endure hellfire. It was certain to chafe his skin. But it troubled him that the space around him seemed to know where he was going. Was it magic? Or was someone... or something...spying on him?

Either thought was disturbing.

With a shake of his head, Levet forced one foot in front of the other. He wanted to locate Troy so they could get out of this awful place.

"*Leave him,*" a voice whispered.

Levet's wings snapped in fear, his eyes wide as he turned his head from side to side. He couldn't see anyone, but there had to be a creature skulking in the fire.

"Show yourself," he commanded, trying to sound more courageous than he felt.

"*Leave him,*" the voice repeated in a low hiss.

Levet wrinkled his snout. "Leave him what?"

"*Abandon the imp and save yourself.*"

"Oh." Levet blinked in surprise. It hadn't occurred to him to abandon Troy. "Why would I do that?"

"*Because he would never search for you.*"

Levet wrinkled his snout. That was true enough. The imp would no doubt do whatever was necessary to save his own spa-treated, fairy-butt-softened skin. Still, Levet held himself to a higher standard.

"I am a knight in shining armor," he announced, proudly pushing out his chest. "I do not flee from danger. I flee to danger..." Levet realized he was not being entirely honest. "Well, I do not precisely flee. At the moment, it is more of a cautious shuffle. But I am not going to leave without my friend."

The fire seemed to freeze in place, as if baffled by his response. Or perhaps it was running out of juice. Hope briefly lightened Levet's mood before he heaved a resigned sigh. His luck wasn't good enough for the hellfire simply to sputter and die.

Proving his point, the flames swirled and danced, as if a sudden breeze had swept through the cavern.

"*A knight in shining armor?*" There was a huffing sound, as if the fire was laughing. "*You are a disaster. Everyone knows it.*"

Levet flinched, his wings drooping. Was he a disaster? Certainly, there'd been occasions when his magic was not as dependable as he desired. And he had a habit of following his heart, not his head. But surely he had proven that his skills were worthy of respect? He had, after all, saved the world. More than once. And he was only in this awful place because Styx had sent him on yet another rescue mission.

"That's not true." Levet sniffed. "They all depend on me. Even the vampires."

"They laugh behind your back."

Levet turned in a circle, trying to locate his tormentor. "Who are you?"

"I see you, Levet. I see into your heart," the voice retorted, ignoring his question. *"You are not a hero. You are a small, worthless creature who should have been destroyed the second you were born."*

Levet blinked. He'd heard those words before. They'd been hammered into his skull for the first months of his life.

"Mother?"

"Leave, gargoyle." Without warning, the fire began to part, revealing a narrow pathway. Suddenly Levet could see the opening in the far wall of the cavern, a visible promise of escape from the netherworld. *"Leave and never return."*

Levet scowled. Did the voice truly believe he would forget about Troy and scamper down the pathway to freedom? Or was it a trap? Did the flames hope to lure him forward so they could suck him into some new chamber of horrors? Levet folded his arms over his chest.

"Non. Not without my friend."

"He's not your friend." There was an unexpected blast of heat, as if Levet was pissing off the flames. *"No one is your friend."*

The words were perfectly designed to strike at Levet's worst fears. After his family had driven him out of the Gargoyle Guild, he'd spent endless centuries roaming the world alone. To most demons, he was a freak. Or worse, a pest that needed to be destroyed.

"You lie," he forced himself to say, but even he could hear the uncertainty in his words.

The flames soared to the ceiling. They looked as if they were soaring in triumph.

"They endure your company," the voice mocked. *"Nothing more."*

Levet stomped his foot, his tail twitching. "Stop it."

"Not even Inga truly cares about you."

"Inga," Levet softly repeated the name of the female who'd become the light of his life. Inga. The oversized ogress with tufts of red hair and a fondness for outrageous muumuus. The female who could cuss like a drunken troll at the same time she was painting the most exquisite murals on the walls of her throne room. The female who could destroy entire cities with the power of her magical trident, but sob in betrayal when she overheard one of the mermaids whisper a cruel insult. The female who looked at him with a loyal devotion that he tried every day of his existence to deserve. Levet squared his shoulders, the fear and despair that had threatened to smother him abruptly shattered. Eagerly, he clung to the memories that gave him unimaginable strength. *"You are wrong."*

The flames seemed to dim. "I am never wrong."

Levet firmly shook his head. "You can claim that others find me annoying. And that my family has chosen to banish me because I am different." A smile curved his lips. "Never Inga. She cares for *moi*. It might not make sense, but she does. And she believes that I am a hero."

The pathway closed, and the flames began to creep in around him. *"Turn back,"* the voice commanded.

"Non." Levet didn't know where the voice was coming from, but he was realizing that this was another test. The underworld had peeked into his heart. It understood that he always feared that he wasn't good enough, or strong enough, to accomplish his goals. And that a part of him was always waiting for failure. What it hadn't seen, however, was that Levet was never going to quit. He would keep trying and trying until he somehow found a way to succeed. Squeezing his eyes shut, he pressed his wings against his back and forged his way through the flames. "Troy!"

Chapter 18

Bertha strolled out of the casino with a bounce in her step. She'd enjoyed the show. Who wouldn't? But it was the festering annoyance she could feel from Hades that was responsible for her smug enjoyment. Hey, he'd invaded her mind without invitation. Like a parasite. He'd even forced her into her current form. She had to get a small amount of revenge whenever the opportunity presented itself.

She weaved her way through the throng of human tourists who flowed along the sidewalk with the force of a tidal wave. She didn't bother to conceal her presence, and several men paused to glance at her as she passed. Thankfully, they all stepped aside to give her ample space to pass without touching her. She'd like to assume it was because they could sense her awesome power, but she was pretty sure it had something to do with her invisible passenger.

It wasn't every female who was carrying around a god in their head, after all.

Not that she wanted Hades taking up residence in her brain. In fact, she very much hoped she could find a way to get rid of him. The sooner, the better.

"Wasn't that a yummy show?" she asked in overly innocent tones.

"Yummy? Half-naked men gyrating on a stage?"

"*Gorgeous* half-naked men gyrating on a stage," she reminded him, just in case he'd forgotten how delicious the dancers had been. "With fabulous music and flashing lights and screaming women. Oh yes, it was very, very yummy." Bertha's amusement dimmed as she heaved a sigh. "And a reminder that I have been alone for a long time."

She felt something tingle through her that might have been surprise, as if Hades was caught off-guard by her words.

"You're not alone," he protested.

Bertha frowned in confusion. "Of course, I am. It has been years…" Her words trailed away as she grimaced. "It's been centuries," she corrected herself, "since I had a companion."

"I'm with you."

"An annoying voice in my brain? Bah." Bertha shook her head, refusing to acknowledge the flutters of excitement. She was trying to get rid of the unwelcome god, wasn't she? "You aren't a companion; you're a curse."

"Do you want me to be your companion?" Hades sounded more curious than wounded.

"I'm not sure I would survive," Bertha muttered.

"Neither am I."

A shiver raced through her. It wasn't fear. Not exactly. Anticipation? Bertha hissed in annoyance. Surely not.

"Perhaps it's best you are in the netherworld," she said, speaking more to herself than to her mental companion.

"You could join me."

The sudden image of the male's unearthly beauty and smoldering ebony eyes formed in her mind. At the same time she could feel the searing heat of the flames that danced over his slender fingers. Was Hades reminding her of what he had to offer?

It was working.

Too well.

This was no time to be distracted by the sizzles and crackles of pleasure that were zigzagging through her body.

"Um. No thanks."

Dodging past a large party of humans wearing matching T-shirts, Bertha veered off the main sidewalk onto a narrow pathway that was lined with palm trees.

"We could meet in the middle."

"Middle of what?"

His low chuckle sent more pleasure zinging through her. "Ah, now that is an interesting question."

"You…" Bertha heaved a deep sigh.

She didn't know what was worse. When the voice in her head was nothing more than a mysterious entity. Or now that she knew it was attached to a gorgeous god who seemed intent on stirring up unwelcome sensations.

"What?" Hades demanded.

"Nothing."

There was a momentary silence as she rounded a bend in the pathway to discover a large glass-and-steel hotel that soared toward the star-speckled sky. It didn't have the flashing neon lights or spewing fountains as some of the other resorts, but Bertha felt a strange compulsion to see inside.

"Where are we going now?" Hades groused.

Bertha tilted back her head to read the discreet sign hung above the entrance.

"Dreamscape."

"Another casino?"

Bertha frowned, struck by a vague memory. "There's something familiar about the name. I wonder why? I don't think I've ever been here. Have I?"

"Does it have male strippers?"

"Oh." Bertha hurried forward. "Let's find out."

They entered the building through a revolving glass door, stepping directly into the casino. There was the scent of fresh paint, as if the place had been recently redecorated.

A quick glance around the long, open room was enough to reveal that it was more sophisticated than the others in the area, with polished black floors that reflected the glittering chandeliers that hung from the ceiling. There was less glitz and more glamour, she silently decided.

Still, it was thickly crowded with humans who were gathered around slot machines that blasted music and blinked with blinding lights. Or pressed against the roulette tables screaming at the top of their lungs.

To Bertha, the chaos was exhilarating. Obviously, Hades didn't share her enthusiasm.

"Can we go someplace where there isn't so much noise?" he grumbled.

"No way." Bertha sucked in a deep breath, her barely-there wings fluttering in excitement. "I just hit the jackpot."

"Jackpot?" The voice sounded confused. "You aren't even gambling."

She sucked in another breath. "I just caught the scent of a buffet. Do you suppose it's an all-you-can-eat? I do hope so." She hurried forward, following the mouthwatering smell. "Can you imagine how much a gargoyle can consume?"

"Replenishing your strength is a wise decision," Hades reluctantly agreed. "But are you sure we can't find someplace else for you to enjoy your dinner? Perhaps in another dimension?"

"Fah. Party pooper."

"Excuse me?"

Bertha spread her arms to encompass the crowd. "This is a glorious location. So much excitement." She lowered her arms, the nagging familiarity distracting her enjoyment. "I just wish I could remember where I've heard the name Dreamscape before."

"Perhaps in your nightmares," Hades muttered.

Bertha blinked. Dreamscape. Nightmare. "Was that…a joke?"

"I'm not without humor."

"Hmm." Bertha was distracted as they rounded a line of slot machines to stand directly in front of the open buffet. A tiny quiver raced through her. "Oh, do you smell that?"

"I smell so many things. Most of them awful."

"Awful?" Bertha clicked her tongue. This male thought the casino was stinky? He lived in a place that genuinely smelled like hell. Bleck. "There is roast beef. And green beans with bacon. And apple pie. Mmm."

"Smoke. Sweat. Vampire," he dryly added.

"I…" Bertha's words dried on her lips. "Vampire?" Bertha furrowed her brow. Why would a vampire be at a human casino? There were several fabulous demon clubs in Vegas. And some less-fabulous ones that offered lots of naughty entertainment. Then, she stiffened as she finally recalled her fleeting visit to Hong Kong. "Uh-oh."

"What's wrong?"

"I remember why the name Dreamscape is so familiar."

"Tell me."

"When I traveled to help Levet in Hong Kong, we stayed at a hotel called Dreamscape Resorts. I think the vampire who owned that hotel also must own this one."

"Is that a problem?"

Bertha made a sound of impatience. "Have you forgotten that Styx sent a vampire to force me back to Chicago?"

A sharp flash of anger sent heat sizzling through her. An anger that came directly from Hades.

"No one is forcing you to do anything."

Was he being serious? He'd been treating her like a mindless puppet for months.

"Except you?"

"Only because it's necessary." He sounded genuinely offended by her accusation.

"Tyrants always say that."

Hades ignored the insult. Or maybe he didn't think being called a tyrant was an insult. He was a god, after all. They were notorious for possessing oversized egos.

"You need to get out of here," he commanded.

Bertha turned toward the nearest exit. Not because she was obeying Hades. But he was right. She had no idea whether Styx was still searching for her, but she wasn't in the mood to have another confrontation. Not when her tummy was rumbling. It was past her dinnertime. She would have to find another buffet to satisfy her cravings.

She hadn't managed to take more than a step, however, when a male abruptly appeared directly in front of her. He was attired in a tailored suit that molded to his slender muscles. His dark hair was neatly trimmed, and his black eyes smoldered with power. His features were finely sculpted and stunningly gorgeous. Of course. He was a vampire. They were always gorgeous.

"Too late," she muttered.

"It's never too late."

Bertha had no idea what Hades meant, until the heavy pressure of his power began to build.

"Don't you dare," she snapped.

Unaware of the danger he was in, the vampire offered a smooth dip of his head. "Aunt Bertha, this is a pleasure."

"Chiron," she murmured, relieved when the power slowly faded. She wasn't sure she could have stopped Hades if he'd chosen to injure the vampire. "We meet again."

"Welcome to my humble establishment."

Bertha glanced around. "Hardly humble. How many of these resorts do you have scattered around the world?"

"A dozen. So far."

"Nice."

Chiron shrugged. "I'm glad you decided to drop in. Our king has been searching for you."

"Not my king."

"Fair enough." Chiron grimly held on to his smile. "That doesn't change the fact that he wishes you to return to Chicago."

Bertha heaved a sigh. Why was Styx being such a pain? Was it truly because he was in debt to her nephew?

Levet had often told her stories about the numerous times he'd saved the leeches from almost certain disaster. But honestly, she'd only been half-listening. She adored her relative, but he did tend to yammer nonstop.

It could be a little overwhelming. Still, it appeared that Levet's claim, that the vampires were deeply in his debt, was genuine.

Or maybe he had been such a nag that the leech would do anything to get him off his back.

Whatever the cause, it was obvious the king wasn't going to be happy until he had her back in Chicago.

Which meant that she was going to have to tread lightly. There was no way she was meekly leaving Vegas. Levet might be worried about her, but she wasn't going to put him in danger. Then again, she wasn't willing to provoke a fight when she had a god lurking in her head.

Clearing her throat, she took a cautious step backward. "I was just about to hit the buffet."

"What did you do to Satin?" Chiron abruptly asked.

Bertha was easily distracted. "Who? Oh, the pregnant leech." She stared at Chiron in confusion. When she'd left the bar, the leech had been standing there looking as if her world had been turned upside down, but there hadn't been anything wrong with her. Well, beyond the fact that she was carrying a child that should never have been possible. "I didn't do anything to her. Why?"

"She's disappeared."

"Really?"

"And not only her," Chiron said, an unmistakable edge in his voice. "The King of Were's cousin, Marco, who was following her, has disappeared, along with Troy, the Prince of Imps, and Levet."

Bertha felt a stab of fear. She didn't care about the others, but she was worried for her nephew. Clenching her hands, she silently reached out with her mind. Gargoyles with royal blood had the ability to speak mind to mind. It took a second, as if Levet was far away, or perhaps in another dimension, but she could discern he was alive. And as far as she could tell, unharmed.

Disguising her relief behind a baffled expression, she tilted her head to the side. "You have misplaced all those people? You should have a better system of keeping track of them."

Chiron's jaw tightened. Good. She wanted him annoyed. Perhaps she could drive him away without any need for messy violence.

"They all had one thing in common," he ground out. "Do you want to guess what it was?"

"A game?" She clapped her hands together, bouncing on her tiptoes. "I adore games. Let's see. What did they have in common? Hmm." She pretended to consider her answer. "Were they all wearing sexy red vests?

Satin was, I know. It was lovely. I plan to buy one while I'm in Vegas. Do you have any shops here in Dreamscape?"

Anger flashed through Chiron's dark eyes. "No, they were—"

"Hey! I'm not done guessing," Bertha protested.

The vampire's fangs lengthened, a sure sign he was struggling to leash his temper.

"They were all looking for you."

Bertha stomped her foot. "This is a stupid game."

Chiron shuddered, his hands clenched at his side. "You truly are related to Levet."

Bertha wasn't shocked by the male's obvious distaste for her relative. He was like a fine wine. An acquired taste.

"Of course, I am. He's my favorite nephew."

"Then where is he?"

"I have no idea," she answered in complete honesty. She took a step backward. And then another. She wasn't as fast as a vampire in this form, but she had the ability to petrify Chiron for a short time. Hopefully long enough to make her escape. "Maybe I should go find him."

"Absolutely not." Chiron narrowed his eyes. "You're going back to Chicago."

Bertha slammed her hands on her hips, genuinely annoyed. "Why does everyone suddenly assume they're the boss of me?"

Chiron stepped forward, the cold swirl of his power wrapping around her. "I'm just following orders."

Bertha gave a sharp shake of her head. The idiot was going to provoke Hades into doing something stupid.

"I wouldn't if I were you," she warned.

"I won't," Chiron promised. "But she will."

The vampire glanced over her shoulder. Bertha hesitated. Was this a trick? Possibly. But she couldn't stop herself from turning to see what he was looking at.

At first, she was confused. All she could see was a group of humans who were laughing and calling out to the other guests as they headed toward the buffet. It wasn't until they'd stumbled past that she noticed the tiny female with lush curves and untamed golden curls standing a few feet away. Her eyes were a swirl of gold and green, and her round face held a sweet expression that made her appear harmless.

Always dangerous.

"Who are you?" Bertha demanded.

"Lilah. Chiron's mate." The female lifted her arm, revealing a small satin pouch.

Bertha studied her in confusion. At least until she caught the scent of lavender and foxglove and honey. The bag contained a spell.

"Witch," she breathed.

Lilah grimaced. "Sorry about this."

Bertha turned to flee, but the witch had already tossed the spell in her direction. It hit the back of her head, the bag busting as it connected with her skull. Bertha coughed as lavender sprayed through the air. She was allergic to the stupid stuff.

Not that it mattered.

She hadn't managed to take more than a step when the magic wrapped around her, clinging like a spiderweb. The harder she fought against the invisible strands, the tighter they clutched.

"Crap." Bertha stopped her struggle as darkness filled her mind.

There wasn't any point in fighting the inevitable. It wasn't a dangerous spell, and she would soon be awake again.

But she wasn't going to be happy.

Chapter 19

Marco jumped from one frost-coated rock to another, his massive body moving with more power than speed. He could see the jagged outlines of the fortress above him, but the last thing he wanted was to rush into an ambush.

Eventually reaching the top of the high peak, Marco cautiously circled the ruin that had once been a formidable citadel. Over the centuries, the stones had crumbled and were charred from at least one fire. The wooden floors had rotted away, and the roof was now a pile of shattered slate tiles littered across the ground. Cautiously moving through one of the gaping cracks in the wall, Marco followed the stench of sulfur toward what had once been the far corner of the inner courtyard.

He discovered Satin bent over a pile of rubble, digging through the broken stones and layers of dirt. Her dark hair tumbled down her back, tangled by the crisp breeze, while her red vest was torn and coated in a layer of dust.

Her untidy appearance troubled him. They'd spent hours running through the woods, not to mention rolling in the dirt, during their wild bouts of sex, and she'd always managed to stay immaculate. It had something to do with being a vampire. The fact that she looked a mess could only mean she was unable to use her powers.

With a burst of magic, Marco shifted into his human form and slowly approached her. He'd nearly reached her side when she abruptly whirled toward him, her fist swinging toward his face.

"Stay back."

Marco hastily ducked. The blow would have broken his jaw if it'd connected.

"Satin."

She stared at him, the flames burning in the cognac beauty of her eyes. But Marco thought he caught a glimpse of recognition.

"I'm no longer in control of my body," she said, her voice strained. Was she fighting against the ifrit's compulsion?

He cautiously straightened. "Can you hear me?"

"Yes."

Relief jolted through Marco. As much as it might piss him off to know that the evil demon had taken over Satin's body, he at least was assured that the bastard hadn't managed to wrest complete control. It gave him hope they could banish the creature back to hell.

The question was…how?

"What did you discover in the human's memories?" he asked, his jaw tightening as she jerkily turned back to shift through the pile of rubble.

"Mila, the human woman, was a willing slave to the ifrit," Satin answered. "She sacrificed her own parents to gain control of the fortress. She even had her cousin thrown in the dungeon when he arrived to take command of the duchy."

It was more or less what the frost fairy had told him, which reassured him that Satin had managed to gather vital information during her journey through the human's memories.

"What happened to her after the creature was banished?"

"It wasn't."

Marco studied her profile, confused by her answer. "Zephyr lied?"

"No, Elwha had already suspected it was a trap. He allowed them to capture him and retreated far enough from the world to convince the elementals that they'd succeeded in banishing him."

Marco considered her words. It made far more sense that the ifrit had never left than to believe it had managed to infect Satin from the netherworld.

"I assume it kept its connection to the human?"

"Yes." She tossed a large chunk of rock to the side, nearly hitting Marco. Was it on purpose? Was the ifrit listening to the conversation and trying to stop it? Or was it focused solely on whatever it was trying to reach beneath the rubble? "Mila was supposed to remain hidden in the cellars beneath this fortress until Elwha could regain his strength and eventually achieve his ultimate goal," Satin revealed.

"Do you know what that is?"

"To be fully in this dimension."

Marco narrowed his gaze. He could sympathize with the desire to be out of the netherworld. He'd never visited, but he was guessing it wasn't paradise. But would the need to escape be overwhelming enough to go to such an effort?

"That's it?"

Satin dug through a thick layer of dirt. "And to hold dominion."

Ah. Now, that sounded more like a creature from hell. "Over humans?"

"Over everyone."

"Typical." Marco rolled his eyes. Did every evil demon have fantasies of ruling the world? "So, what happened?"

There was a pause as a visible shudder raced through Satin. Was the ifrit trying to keep her from answering the question? The possibility intensified Marco's interest.

The nasty stench of sulfur swirled through the air, but Satin managed to force the words through her stiff lips.

"Mila hid as he commanded, but eventually the duchy was overrun by a rival family who burned the fortress," she told him, explaining the brutal fate of the once-proud structure. "She was forced to flee into the tunnels her father had created as an escape route in times of danger. She didn't know a vampire had built a lair in the darkness."

Marco arched a brow. He could easily imagine a young woman huddled in the tunnels, assuming she was safe from an invading army, when the true danger was lurking in the darkness.

"Your sire?"

"Yes."

Marco briefly wondered if the ifrit had any warning that his human was about to die. Surely not. Otherwise it would have done something to try to protect his property.

"So, you were transformed into a vampire with no memories of the past?"

"Exactly."

Marco had a thousand questions. How had the ifrit kept his hold on Satin after she was turned? Why had he remained under the radar until the past few weeks? How did he expect to gain dominion over the world? But he was distracted from his train of thought when Satin abruptly returned to the task of clearing away the pile of rocks and debris.

"How did the Elwha gain control of your body?" he asked, resisting the urge to reach out and pull her away from the pile. Her fingers were cut and bruised from the relentless digging, but it was obvious she didn't feel the pain.

"I'm not sure." Her features tightened, as if she was trying to grimace. "I have glimpses into his mind, but it's distorted."

Marco's breath caught in his throat. "You can read his thoughts?"

"It's not clear," she warned. "They flash in and out like a strobe light. Most of the time, they flicker so fast it's hard to grasp them before they're gone."

Marco tried to temper his hope. There was too much at risk to be anything but terrified. Still, he'd feel a hell of a lot better if they could discover the creature's plans.

"Do you know why you're at this fortress?"

"He's searching for something."

That seemed fairly obvious. Why else would she be digging in the dirt? But glancing around, Marco couldn't believe anything of value hadn't already been hauled away by raiders long ago.

"Do you know what?"

"No…" Her words trailed away, then he could see her jaw tighten. The ifrit was attempting to silence her.

"Satin?"

It took a second, but at last she pried her lips open. "I caught an image of a gold medallion," she managed to rasp.

"Gold medallion?" Marco repeated the words more out of confusion than fear that he'd misunderstood.

"Yes." She started to dig faster, as if the ifrit understood it was giving away too much information.

Marco took a covert step closer. "Why would it search for a medallion?"

"I'm not sure, but I could see it in his mind, and it's weirdly familiar."

Marco frowned. It was possible that it was a common necklace worn by certain demons. Like an amulet or charm. But if that was the case, why would the ifrit be going to so much trouble to find it? And why wouldn't Satin instantly recognize it?

He stiffened as he was struck by a sudden thought. "Is it the anchor?"

"No."

The answer came without hesitation, and Marco grimaced. It would have made everything so much easier if he'd been right. Not only would they know why they were standing on the frozen mountaintop, but he would have a chance to destroy the ifrit's connection to this world.

And to Satin.

"You're sure?" he couldn't stop himself from asking.

She didn't answer; instead she hissed through her tightly stretched lips. "Mila."

"The human?" Marco shook his head in confusion. "What about her?"

"She was the anchor."

Marco hesitated. Was it possible the ifrit was screwing with them? It obviously couldn't prevent Satin from peeking into his thoughts or sharing the information with him. So maybe he'd decided to divert them with lies.

"How is that possible?" he demanded. "She has no magic."

"No, but she's a creature of this world," Satin reminded him. "An empty vessel he could fill with his essence."

Ah. Now, that made sense. A human was not only created in this dimension, but it had no power to fight against a demonic possession. As Satin had said, Mila would have been an empty vessel.

"Until a vampire killed the human and claimed the body." He spoke his thoughts out loud.

Satin turned her head, revealing the eyes that flared with a furious fire. The ifrit clearly held a grudge against the vampire who'd stolen his anchor. Satin's voice, however, remained eerily devoid of emotion.

"Elwha had no choice but to abandon the body as Mila died."

"Where did it go?"

"Into the medallion."

Marco released a growl. Ah. So the ifrit could hide inside an inanimate object. No wonder the elementals assumed the bastard had been banished. Distracted by his thoughts, Marco was barely aware that Satin had pulled away the last of the rocks to reveal a circular hole in the ground. Not until she stepped forward and casually dropped through the opening.

Cursing his lack of vigilance, Marco sprang forward to dive headfirst through the hole. It probably wasn't his wisest decision. He had no idea where he was going, or what might be waiting for him. Then again, it hopefully wasn't his worst decision. Like the night he'd challenged a troll to a drinking contest. It'd been during the full moon, and he hadn't been thinking clearly. After the sixth round of grog, he'd passed out and hadn't woken up for over a week. It took another week to remember his name.

Flipping in midair, Marco managed to land on his feet, crouching low to avoid a hidden assailant. When nothing leaped out of the dark, he glanced around the open space. It appeared to be the old cellars of the fortress. Or maybe the dungeons. There was nothing left beyond the stone floor and walls that were coated in layers of filth.

Assured that he hadn't landed in a trap, Marco searched the darkness for Satin. He caught sight of her just as she was heading out a narrow doorway.

"Wait!"

"I can't stop."

Marco scurried forward, squeezing through the opening. He was forced to hunch forward to avoid smacking his head as he entered the passageway that was roughly carved into the mountain.

"I'm here," he assured Satin as he walked directly behind her. It was too narrow to be side by side.

"I recognize these tunnels," she said.

Marco wrinkled his nose as he fought back a sneeze. The dust was so thick in the air it was hard to breathe.

"From when you were a human?" he asked.

"Not just then," Satin said. "They open into the caves where I stayed when I was a vampire...oh."

Marco frowned, hating the fact that he couldn't touch her. He ached with the need to pull her into his arms and reassure her that everything was going to be alright. But he wasn't stupid. He knew the second he reached out, the ifrit would knock him away. Or worse. He couldn't risk being injured.

"Talk to me, Satin," he urged.

"I was staying in the caves when I acquired my strength."

Marco's stomach twisted in dread. The fact that she'd come into her powers in the same location that Elwha was hiding from the elementals couldn't be a coincidence.

"The ifrit," he breathed.

"It must have been." There was a sharp edge in the words. She was obviously disappointed at the realization it was the evil spirit who'd given her the strength she needed to face the world. "The power was never mine."

"Why did you come here?" Marco demanded, attempting to distract her.

"At the time I'd been searching for a place to hide, and I had a vague memory of being in these caves after I'd been turned. It'd been a long time, but I recalled enough to know they were remote and would provide a measure of isolation. Which is exactly what I desired."

"This is where he infected you." The words were a statement, not a question.

"Yes. I think Elwha called me to this place."

"Why not choose another human?"

There was a long silence as they continued to creep their way through the cramped tunnel. Was Satin attempting to peek into Elwha's twisted mind?

At last, she made a sound of frustration. "I think he tried to find another vessel, but while Mila had technically died, her body was still alive. That meant his connection to her was unbroken."

A hard smile curved Marco's lips at the thought of the infrit's fury when he discovered he was trapped with a vampire.

"So, he was forced to reestablish his connection to his anchor, even if it was otherwise occupied."

"Yes."

"What happened after you returned to the cave?"

"I was there a few days before I found the medallion. It was hidden beneath a pile of stones, and for some reason I reached down to pick it up. I was holding it when the power surged through me."

Marco didn't doubt the discovery of the medallion, along with her impulse to pick it up, had been the work of Elwha.

"You left it behind?"

"I never considered the possibility that the two were connected."

Marco silently sorted through his thoughts as the tunnel widened and they stepped into a large cave. The ceiling was still low enough to brush Marco's head, but the area was large enough to move around freely with an opening that revealed they were still high on the mountain with the forest far below. It was no wonder Satin had sought this place to hide from the world. It was as remote a location as she was going to find.

Walking with jerky motions, Satin moved toward the far side of the cave.

"Why didn't he gain control of you then?" Marco asked, following behind her.

"He tried, but the vampire rejected his attempts."

Marco smiled in satisfaction. "That must have been frustrating for him."

"Exceedingly." She bent down, grabbing rocks and tossing them aside.

"You said it's been gaining strength for the past few weeks." A rock flew near his head, and Marco was forced to duck. The stone smashed into the wall and blasted into a dozen pieces. Marco straightened, refusing to be intimidated. "Do you know how?"

She grabbed another rock and threw it aside. Her eyes flared with crimson flames.

"It's so jumbled," she at last ground out. "His fury. His fear that he was trapped in the netherworld for eternity. And then..." She hesitated as if shocked by what she'd just peeked at inside the ifrit's mind. "Joy."

"Joy?" Marco felt a stab of unease. "Why?"

There was another pause. This time Marco suspected it was Elwha attempting to halt her words.

"The baby." She managed to force out the words.

Marco jerked back, feeling as if she'd just hit him with one of the massive rocks. "What are you talking about?"

"He intends to use the baby as his new vessel."

"Did he create the child?" he rasped. Not that it mattered. In his heart, the child was his. Nothing would ever change that. Nothing. And he would destroy the world before he allowed the ifrit to infect it with his evil.

"No, but the magic he put inside of me allowed the possibility of a baby. It was his only hope of gaining a vessel he could control."

Marco muttered a curse. As relieved as he might be that the bastard had nothing to do with the actual creation of the baby, it appalled him to think of Satin being infested with the creature's toxic evil. Then, with a shake of his head, he leashed his burning anger. Later he would deal with his fury that Satin had been callously used by the ifrit. Once the creature was burning in hell.

"You gained your power centuries ago," he pointed out, his voice remarkably steady. "Why did it take so long for you to get pregnant?"

Satin picked up another rock. "He doesn't know."

Marco absently ducked as the rock sailed directly toward his head. He was distracted by a sudden, blindingly obvious realization.

"I do," he assured her, a warmth flowing through him.

"You do?"

A vivid memory seared through his mind of chasing Satin through the dark woods outside his lodge, followed by a savage coupling that left them both bruised, bloody, and deeply sated.

It hadn't just been sex. It had *never* just been sex.

It had been life-altering, soul-defining, never-be-the-same-again sex.

"The only explanation is that you're my mate," he said with a simple conviction that came from the very center of his being. "And I'm yours. The magic from the ifrit combined with the primitive enchantment of the mating bond to create a miracle."

He watched the shudder race through Satin, as if she was desperately attempting to regain command of her body.

"Marco, we can't let it have our baby," she hissed.

"Never gonna happen," he snarled. "I promise you."

He impulsively stretched out his hand, but before he could touch her, Satin was bending down to snatch something off the ground. He caught a glint of gold before Satin's hands closed around the item, warning him that the medallion had been discovered.

That couldn't be a good thing.

The thought had barely time to form before the cave was polluted with the gagging smell of sulfur. Worse, a cruel smile was twisting her lips as she turned to stare at him with her fiery gaze.

"At last," she breathed, holding the medallion over her head.

Accepting that Satin had again lost control over her body, Marco spread his legs, prepared to defend himself. He didn't doubt that Elwha was anxious to get rid of him. One way or another.

Instead of an attack, however, a glow began to surround the medallion. Marco's eyes widened as the glow moved down Satin's arm like a coating of fire. No, not fire. Magic. There was a spell in the medallion. Fey magic, he belatedly realized as he caught the faintest scent of citrus.

But why?

The question was answered as a portal opened directly in front of Satin and she stepped forward.

"Shit."

Satin was about to disappear. He had no idea where the ifrit was taking her or what was going to happen when he got her there. The only thing he knew was that Satin wasn't going there alone.

Shifting into his wolf form, Marco soared into the unknown.

Chapter 20

Satin cursed in silent frustration as the ifrit grabbed the medallion and created the portal. She could still see and feel what was happening around her, but the creature had taken complete control. As if she were nothing more than a bundle of awareness tucked in the back of the creature's mind.

On the bright side—or at least as bright as any side could be under the circumstances—she was sharing Elwha's thoughts. Which meant she knew he was standing in the middle of the Mojave Desert because there was a portal to the netherworld. It wasn't open, but it was the point where the ifrit had managed to thread his tether of power into this dimension. It was also the spot where he intended to rip a hole large enough for him to fully enter.

Also on the bright side, the sun had just set behind the nearby mountain range.

At least she wasn't going to be fried to a crisp.

Intent on peering into the ifrit's muddled thoughts, Satin was distracted by the sound of a familiar growl. Marco. As if on cue, a large werewolf padded out of the darkness. She felt a strange burst of relief, swiftly followed by a sharp-edged sense of regret as the ifrit lifted her hand and shot a blast of hellfire directly toward the Were. Marco dove to the side, but she couldn't miss the stench of singed fur.

"Stop!" she silently commanded.

Unsure if the creature was aware of her presence, Satin was caught off-guard when Elwha spoke to her directly.

"Give me the child."

"Never."

The ifrit sent out another blast of hellfire. *"Give me the child, or the dog dies."*

Marco crouched low, avoiding the flames as he inched his way forward.

"He's not so easy to kill," she informed Elwha, feeling a flare of hope as she sensed the ifrit's desire to avoid a battle with the wolf.

It wasn't fear of Marco, she realized as she caught a glimpse into his mind. It was a reluctance to waste his waning energy. The creature had expended a considerable amount of his power to use the medallion to travel to this location. And it was taking even more to try to open the portal to hell. Once he was fully drained...

Satin wasn't sure exactly what happened, but she sensed that the ifrit would do anything to avoid the potential fate.

"The Were won't hurt you," Elwha muttered, as if to reassure himself.

Satin silently acknowledged that was a possibility. When Marco looked at her, all he could see was the female he claimed was his mate and the mother of his baby. It would be difficult for him to accept that she was now consumed by an evil spirit.

"He will if it's the only way to stop you," Satin warned, hoping to keep the creature distracted.

She needed a way to drain his powers, but how? The last thing she wanted was for Marco to be hurt. But without the ability to control her body, she was stuck trying to bait him into losing his concentration long enough for Marco to...

What?

She didn't know. But she had to try something. It was that or giving up.

"Why would the wolf try to stop me?" Elwha demanded, as if genuinely confused. *"I'm not his enemy."*

"You invaded my body."

"It wasn't your body. It was mine."

Satin silently agreed that the ifrit had a point. The body had first belonged to Mila, but Elwha had staked a claim while she was still alive. And as difficult as it was to accept, the powers that had given her the confidence she needed to make a place for herself among the vampires belonged to him. Still, she wasn't going to concede anything to the evil creature.

"First come, first serve," she informed him.

"I don't know what that means."

"It means that this body belongs to me."

She sensed his stir of anger, but he managed to maintain his focus. Keeping a cautious gaze locked on Marco, he bent down to place the medallion in the center of the portal. Instantly it started glowing.

A small trickle of hope wriggled its way into her unbeating heart. She'd assumed the medallion was just to create the portal to travel to this spot. Obviously, it was more than that. It was also some sort of key to allow the creature to enter this world. She was going to assume that if something happened to it, the ifrit would remain trapped in the netherworld.

"Fine. Keep your body," the ifrit snapped, as if annoyed by her resistance. "I only want the child."

"Never."

"And how are you going to stop me?"

Satin struggled to break free of his control. The bastard wasn't going to steal her baby. But how the hell did she stop him?

"The Were is my mate," she desperately said, the words ringing true in the demon's mind. Probably because they were true. Even if she had tried to pretend that she hadn't accepted Marco was destined to be in her life for all of eternity. "We can communicate without speaking. I can convince him to destroy me." Now she was forced to try to hide the lies. "Along with the child."

Thankfully the creature didn't question her assertion as he hissed in outrage. *"What is wrong with you?"* The words echoed through her brain. *"You should be pleased."*

"Pleased?"

"Your child will allow me to regain my former glory. What better fate could it desire?"

A sudden vision of a slender male with black hair and smoldering cognac eyes seared through her mind, a cold, ruthless expression on his pale face. Was that her child?

"No," she muttered, horror twisting her heart.

"If you don't desire glory, what do you want?" Frustration pounded through her. *"Power? Treasure? To rule at my side?"*

Her answer came without hesitation. "I want you dead."

There was a startled pause, as if the creature couldn't believe she was being so stubborn. Then, without warning, the image in her mind slowly changed from a stranger into a familiar male. *"You prefer this form?"*

"Marco."

Strong arms wrapped around her, the warm scent of musk filling her with a sense of peace.

"Stand with me," a voice whispered. *"Together we can be invincible."*

Satin struggled against the urge to sink into the fantasy that was weaving through her mind.

"A trick," she muttered.

"See for yourself."

Suddenly she could see the glowing medallion that was lying on the desert floor. Beneath it a black hole formed, growing wider and wider. Was that the portal?

Without warning, flames spewed out of the hole, twirling toward the sky like a tornado.

"What are you doing?" Satin demanded.

"Creating an empire." The hellfire rose higher, as if hungry to spread outward in a storm of ruthless destruction. *"We will rise from the ashes."*

* * * *

Bertha wasn't surprised when she opened her eyes to discover herself lying on the hard floor of a cell. Endless centuries had taught her that nothing good could happen when a witch was tossing spells at your head.

"Are you okay?" Hades demanded, clearly still hanging out in her mind.

"No, I'm not okay. That witch hit me with a spell."

She thought she heard him heave a sigh. "I meant, are you harmed?"

With a low grunt, Bertha forced herself to sit up and glance around. A waste of time, really. There was nothing to see but four barren walls with a narrow door chiseled into the stone.

There wasn't even a bed. Clearly the hospitality of Dreamscape Resorts was highly overrated.

"My feelings are hurt," she muttered, pushing herself to her feet. "That wasn't very nice. What did I do to her?"

"I believe she intends to hold you captive until Styx can arrive to take you to Chicago."

Bertha clicked her tongue. The question had been rhetorical. Moving across the stone floor, she reached to grab the doorknob.

"Locked." She yanked on the knob, but it refused to budge. "Well, that is inconvenient. How am I supposed to get to the buffet?"

"There's no time to worry about dinner."

Bertha's stomach growled in protest at being denied mounds of yummy food. "That's easy for you to say," she groused. "I suppose you are seated on your throne devouring platters of roast beef and apple pie. And bacon." Her mouth watered. "Stacks of bacon."

"I don't consume human food."

Bertha sucked in a horrified breath. "What's wrong with you?"

"I'm a god."

"Oh, right." Bertha wrinkled her nose. It was easy to forget that the voice chattering in her brain was the lord of the underworld. "A pity."

"It's a pity?" She sensed he was blindsided by her response. "That I'm a god?"

"*Oui.*"

"You are so very strange."

"Hey." Bertha gave another yank on the knob. It was bad enough to be stuck in the cell with her belly grumbling. She didn't need to add in being insulted.

"That's a compliment," Hades protested, his tone oddly defensive.

"Seriously?" Bertha rolled her eyes. "You really suck at those."

"I'll get better."

Bertha stiffened at the unexpected reply. Had a god just promised her to get better at complimenting her?

"How?" she asked, genuinely curious.

"How what?"

"How will you get better?"

"Oh. Practice, I suppose."

"That's…"

"What?"

A shiver raced through Bertha as she considered the notion of Hades staying around long enough to perfect his complimenting skills.

"Terrifying."

"Yes," he readily agreed.

Bertha shook her head, dismissing the ridiculous conversation. She had more important matters on her mind.

"Let's talk about the buffet and how I'm going to get there," she said, considering how best to get rid of the door. A fireball would be the easiest means. She could blast it to smithereens. But the stench of smoke always clung to her clothing.

"Later."

"Later? I'm starving now."

"First we have to finish what we started."

"Bah." Bertha sniffed. "You have been saying that for months."

"It's time."

Bertha remained wary. "Now? Right now?"

"Yes."

"Oh." Bertha released a sigh of relief. She was ready to be done with the mysterious mission. "Thank the goddess."

There was a momentary pause. "Are you so anxious to be rid of me?"

Bertha didn't bother to answer the question. Of course, she was anxious. Who wanted a god rattling around in their head? Especially one that treated her like a puppet. On the other hand, she couldn't be absolutely certain that she wouldn't miss the aggravating creature. Ridiculous, but there it was.

"I can get us out of here," she said, squaring her shoulders as she faced the door. "Did the stupid leech think I could be held captive in such a flimsy cell? It's an insult to my powers."

"Don't worry," Hades drawled. "I've got this."

"What do you mean?" About to insist that she be allowed to knock the door down with one of her fabulous fireballs, Bertha caught her breath in amazement. The stone walls surrounding her started to melt. Not literally melting, but that was what it looked like as the cell disappeared and they were suddenly standing in the middle of the desert.

They hadn't moved through a portal. Or even a gateway.

They'd simply been in one place, and now they were in another.

"Oh." She turned in a slow circle. She could see the skyline of Vegas in the distance. She'd stepped out of the portal a few hours ago in this precise spot. "This is where we started. Why are we here?"

"There's an opening to the netherworld."

Bertha grimaced, recalling her brief visit to Hades's homeland. "*Non.*"

"No what?"

"I'm not going back to the netherworld," she informed him, her tone stern. "Been there, done that, have the T-shirt. Okay, I don't have the T-shirt, but—"

"You were never actually in my realm," Hades rudely interrupted.

"I still don't want to go," she stubbornly insisted.

He heaved a sigh. "For now, I just need you at the portal."

Bertha slowly relaxed. "Fine. Where is it?"

"Just over the ridgeline."

With a shrug, Bertha headed toward the jagged rocks that looked like the spine of a dragon. Actually, they looked like the spine of a dragon she'd once dated. Cadmus had been a great time, with a fabulous treasure horde and the ability to use his dragon-fire to stir her deepest passions, but they both had a tendency to roam away and fall asleep in random places. It could be decades, even centuries, in between their hookups. Eventually she simply forgot about him, and they'd lost touch.

Reaching the top of the ridge, Bertha gazed down at the strange sight of a Were in his wolf form circling the female vampire who'd been sent by Styx to force her back to Chicago. What was her name? Satin. Yes, that was it. And next to the vampire was a swirling tornado of vivid crimson flames reaching toward the sky.

Satin appeared indifferent to the massive inferno that burned next to her. An unusual sight, considering that leeches were highly flammable creatures.

"Yuck." Bertha wrinkled her nose as a hot breeze brushed past her, bringing with it an unpleasant stench. "What is that odor?"

"Ifrit," Hades whispered, as if afraid of being overheard.

"Really?" Bertha eagerly searched the desert for some sign of the rare demon. "I've never seen one before."

"He's not fully in this dimension."

"Oh." Realization hit Bertha as the wolf crouched low and started inching his way toward the female in front of him. He was preparing to attack. "The vampire?"

"For now," Hades said. "But he's trying to use the child she is carrying to flee his prison and consume the world in fire."

Bertha's curiosity about the ifrit swiftly became concern. She knew enough about the creatures to fear what would happen if one fully entered this dimension.

"That would be a bad thing."

"Very bad," Hades agreed. "That's why we're going to stop him."

"We?" Bertha questioned in dry tones. "Or me?"

"Both."

Bertha clicked her tongue. It wasn't that she was opposed to a battle. It'd been far too long since she'd enjoyed kicking some demon booty. But she had never fought before without being a massive gargoyle capable of crushing her enemy.

"If you brought me here for a battle, why did you put me in this human form?"

"I need you to appear vulnerable in order to approach the ifrit."

She held out her arms, wondering if he'd seen how thin and feeble they were. Nothing at all like her ten-foot leather wings that could create small tornadoes with a single flap.

"I *am* vulnerable."

"Not for much longer."

The words caught Bertha off-guard. "What does that mean?"

"You'll know when the time is right."

The familiar words sent a flare of frustration sizzling through her. "Argh."

Chapter 21

Marco snarled as he crouched low, his gaze locked on Satin. His wolf was fully prepared to attack. It could no longer detect his mate in the slender form standing in front of him. There was nothing but the irritating stench of sulfur and the glowing crimson eyes that revealed the ifrit was in full control. Thankfully, his human half refused to accept defeat. He was convinced that Satin was still inside, battling against the invading demon.

That hope, however, made it impossible for him to do anything beyond watch and wait. Two things he detested. He was a wolf of action. He leapt first and asked questions later. A habit Salvatore had tried unsuccessfully to curb when they were young.

Now he quivered with the need to do something. Anything.

Firmly caught between a rock and a hard place—or rather, an evil demon attempting to escape the netherworld and his mate—Marco nearly missed the warm scent of gingersnaps.

It wasn't until he heard the soft tread that he belatedly whirled to discover a delicate human female approaching. *No, not human,* he silently corrected as he caught sight of the nearly transparent wings. This had to be the gargoyle whom Satin had been tracking.

A low growl rumbled in his throat, the fur rising along his spine in blatant warning. It couldn't be a coincidence that the gargoyle was making an appearance at this precise spot at this precise time.

"Easy, wolf." Coming to a halt, she lifted a slender hand. "I'm Bertha. I'm here to help you."

Help?

Releasing a burst of magic, Marco shifted into his human form. He was still suspicious of the female, but he was desperate. If she really was there to offer assistance, he wasn't in any position to refuse.

"How?" he demanded.

She glanced toward Satin and then the spiraling flames, which had widened and changed from crimson to a vivid gold. As if they'd become so hot, they were draining of color.

"I'm not sure yet," she admitted.

"Great." He stepped toward his mate. Soon the flames would be broad enough to consume her. "Satin!"

"She can't hear you," Bertha told him.

His jaw clenched. Was she implying that Satin was gone? Or just that she was currently unaware of the world?

"How do you know?"

She tapped the side of her head with a finger. "I have a voice talking to me."

Of course, she did. Any other time he would have written Bertha off as an aggravating pest. Just like her nephew. But there was a reason she was here, right? And he could only pray it was to destroy the ifrit.

"What's it telling you?" he forced himself to ask.

"The ifrit is using the baby to open a portal to the netherworld."

Marco cursed, but he grimly blocked the black tide of fury. The ifrit wasn't going to get his foul hands on his child. Or Satin. It didn't matter what he had to do. Or whom he had to sacrifice.

Including himself.

"How do I stop him?" he asked the gargoyle, his gaze locked on Satin.

"We need to drain his power."

Marco frowned. Actually, the suggestion made sense. If the flames were anything to go by, the creature was expending a lot of energy to escape the netherworld. No matter how powerful the ifrit might be, there had to be a limit. And once he reached it, he would be vulnerable.

"Any ideas?" he asked.

"Destroy the vampire—" Bertha jumped back when Marco released a savage snarl. "Okay, okay. Maybe not."

Marco returned his attention to Satin, searching for something that might provoke the demon. There was no way in hell he was harming his mate or child, but maybe...

His brows snapped together as he caught sight of an object lying on the ground next to the fire. It was easy to overlook with the vicious flames that swirled and danced.

"The medallion," he breathed, his eyes narrowing as it pulsed with an inner glow.

At first, he'd assumed it was a mere reflection from the fire, but the closer he looked, the more confident he was that the light was coming from inside the medallion.

"The ifrit is using it as a conduit to open the portal," Bertha told him.

That was exactly what Marco wanted to hear. "That should be a good start," he muttered.

"What are you starting?"

"This."

Not giving himself the opportunity to consider the danger, Marco darted past Satin to snatch the medallion off the ground. It was hot enough to scorch the skin of his palm, but he ignored the painful blisters as he scurried backward.

Fiercely focused on Satin as he prepared for the ifrit to attack, Marco was forced to dive to the side when the flames reached out like arms to try to drag him toward the center of the fire. A roar of frustration echoed through the desert, vibrating against the distant mountains.

"I think you pissed him off," Bertha murmured, suddenly standing at his side.

"Now what?" he asked, sweat beading his brow as the flames once again reached out and he was forced to dance backward.

"How should I know?"

"You..."

His words died on his lips as a heat seared against his back and he turned to discover more flames erupting out of the hard ground. They didn't head toward the sky, however; instead they aimed directly at his heart. Marco jumped to the side, but like a heat-seeking missile, the flames followed. He jumped again. And again. Each time the flames followed, inching even closer.

He had zero doubt that if the fire touched him, he would die. They weren't regular flames. It was hellfire from the pits of the underworld.

Trying to outwit the deadly fire, Marco faked a leap to the right before quickly diving in the opposite direction. He had no idea if his desperate attempt would work as he stumbled on a rock and fell flat on his back. Shit. He tried to scramble to his feet, but he could already feel the sizzling heat as it arrowed straight toward him. Prepared for the blast that would no doubt be his end, Marco was stunned when he was abruptly knocked aside as a massive creature abruptly appeared from thin air.

No. Not thin air, he realized as he hit the ground and rolled onto his back to study the gray demon with leather wings that stretched out as wide as a dragon. This was Bertha in her natural form. He had no idea when she'd changed, but she was glorious.

Blinking away the dust that threatened to blind him, Marco watched as Bertha positioned herself to take a direct hit from the hellfire, absorbing the terrifying blast. Even at a distance, he could feel the pain that was radiating through her body from the fire, but her lumpy gray features remained stoic. As if she'd accepted that this was somehow her destiny.

Still clutching the medallion, Marco cautiously climbed to his feet. He didn't want to accidentally distract Bertha, but then again, he wasn't going to sit on his ass as the female risked her life to protect him. Then, without warning, the throbbing pain in his hand abruptly disappeared. With a frown, he glanced down at the medallion clutched in his fingers. He hissed in surprise as he watched the glow flicker and then start to dim.

That had to mean the connection to the ifrit had been severed.

Parting his lips to assure Bertha the demon's power was being drained, he watched as the hellfire sputtered and died. More proof that the ifrit had overextended his energy. At the same time, the massive wings drooped, and the creature swayed to the side. Marco leaped forward, but before he could reach her, the gargoyle was crashing to the ground with an earth-shattering thud.

"Bertha." He rushed forward, leaning over her.

The misty gray eyes slowly opened, the pain she had endured now etched on her face.

"Satin," she rasped.

"What?"

"The ifrit...has her."

"Has her?" Marco turned his head, glancing back to where his mate had been standing.

The fire was gone.

Along with Satin.

* * * *

Levet boldly marched through the flames, convinced he would soon discover Troy. If this was a test from the netherworld, then he'd surely passed? He had proven his heart was pure. Or maybe he'd proven he possessed the courage of a dragon.

Whatever.

And if this was just an annoying obstacle...

He shrugged. He had climbed over obstacles his entire life. He had always succeeded.

Well, most of the time, he conceded. There had been a few flops, but who could claim to be flopless?

He was busy justifying his occasional mishaps when the fire around him abruptly disappeared. Seconds later, he spotted Troy stretched on the hard floor. The imp's eyes were closed, and he was as motionless as a mannequin. Levet shuddered. He hated mannequins.

With a heroic effort, he forced himself to move forward. At the point of bending over the male, Levet heard a soft snore.

The idiot was sound asleep.

"Hey!" Levet pulled back his foot and kicked Troy in the side. "I have been battling through hellfire in search of you, and you're taking a nap?"

Troy sat up, stretching his arms over his head and parting his lips in a wide yawn. "I was tired," he said, utterly unrepentant. "And I knew you would stumble across me. Eventually." With an elegant ease, he rose to his feet. "What took you so long?"

"You are a..." Words failed Levet. Perhaps for the first time in his very long existence.

"Yes?"

"I hope you stay here and burn," Levet groused, stomping across the cavern to the opening he'd spotted before the wall of fire had blocked his path.

"No need to be pissy," Troy drawled, his absurdly long legs allowing him to catch up as Levet reached the doorway and climbed the stairs that were carved into the stone.

"I am not pussy—"

"Pissy."

"Pissy." Levet reached the top step, relief blasting through him at the dry, gritty scent of a nearby desert. They had to be near an exit. "I am hot and tired and in need of a shower."

"Yeah, me too."

Levet stomped through the short passageway that spilled into another cavern. This one wasn't as large, but there was a welcome breeze that lured him forward.

"There is a portal nearby," he murmured.

"I can sense it." Troy sniffed the air, his expression troubled. "It's hidden behind an illusion."

"I can find it." Before Troy could start his predictable complaints, Levet created a fireball and tossed it toward the center of the cavern.

With a hiss, it smacked against an invisible barrier. There was a shimmer of brilliant colors, and Troy hastily ducked. For once, however, there was no hideous explosion. The barrier simply shattered and collapsed as it was supposed to.

A blessing. And a curse. As soon as the dust cleared, they could see a large demon with leathery skin and spiral horns that were coated in hellfire.

"An ifrit," Levet breathed in shock.

"And Satin," Troy added, pointing toward the female vampire who was crumpled on the floor next to the demon's feet.

Levet spread his arms wide. "Ta-da."

Troy sent him a scowl. "Ta-da, what?"

"I was sent to retrieve Satin, and that is precisely what I have done." He flapped his wings. "You are welcome."

"You haven't retrieved her yet," Troy warned. "There's a very large, apparently very angry demon to get past."

As if on cue, the ifrit turned in their direction, his eyes glowing with power.

"I am certain you will be capable of rescuing her before he can fry you to a crispy crater."

"Critter."

"Critter?" Levet frowned. "That cannot be right."

Troy folded his arms over his chest. "You just claimed you were the hero. You go get her."

Levet clicked his tongue. "I cannot do everything. Someone must stop the portal from closing." He waved his hand toward the ceiling, where a swirling darkness was rapidly shrinking. Soon it would disappear entirely. "Unless you desire to be stuck in this dimension?"

Troy tilted back his head to study the portal. "Fine," he muttered. "You hold the opening, and I'll get the leech. But if my hair gets singed, you're paying for a new weave."

"You can put it on Styx's credit card," Levet blithely assured him, flapping his wings to wobble upward. "I have one hidden in my lair."

Once at the portal, he squeezed his way into the opening, holding his arms wide to keep the stupid thing from closing.

"Hurry," he grunted, glancing down to see Troy darting between blasts of hellfire that the ifrit was shooting at him.

"Shut up, you stupid creature," Troy snapped. "You're distracting me."

Levet groaned as the portal ruthlessly pressed against his hands. "I am about to be squashed."

Troy cursed as the stench of burnt flesh filled the cavern, but just as Levet feared the imp was truly injured, he was leaping upward with the unconscious vampire clutched in his arms. With a grim effort, Levet widened the opening, allowing room for Troy to escape.

Gasping at the effort, not to mention sheer panic, as the ifrit released a bolt of hellfire in his direction, Levet felt himself slipping. His derrière was too large, he ruefully acknowledged. Or his wings were too delicate.

"Come on, gargoyle," Troy shouted.

With a heave, Levet shoved himself up and through the portal, barely getting his tail clear before it snapped shut.

Lying on the sun-baked ground, he trembled in fatigue, patting his round belly.

"Tomorrow I start my diet," he rasped, closing his eyes and allowing the exhaustion to consume him.

Epilogue

Satin stood in the center of the clearing, her face tilted toward the full moon. The silver light pooled over her, causing the child that continued to grow inside her to kick in delight.

"Already a Were," she murmured, touching her belly, which was swollen beneath her loose satin tunic. "Craving the magic of the moon."

"Like father, like son," Marco murmured, stepping from the shadows of the tree.

Awareness sizzled through Satin. It had been two weeks since they'd returned to Marco's club, the Hunting Grounds, but for several days Satin had remained unconscious as she recovered from the invasion of the ifrit. And the purging of the evil spirit.

During that time, Marco had never left her side, and she sensed his presence even when she was surrounded by darkness.

Even after she'd wakened and regained her strength, he kept close to her side. He claimed he was worried for the baby, and that was no doubt partially true. But she'd known it was his wolf driving him to be so vigilant.

Until they were officially mated, he would suffer.

Satin had hesitated. Not because she doubted Marco was the male that destiny had chosen for her, but she wanted to make sure any taint from the ifrit was gone. The thought that the creature could once again take control of her and put the male she loved in danger was unbearable.

As she'd healed, they'd invited Zephyr to come and make certain that the evil was well and truly gone. The elemental had quickly confirmed there was no hint of the ifrit. And still Satin had hesitated. Without Elwha's spirit, she possessed a niggling fear that she might become weak and vulnerable again. What if she became a burden to Marco?

It had taken some time, but Satin was finally convinced that she had retained her powers. She could be an equal partner with the male who not only held her soul, but had stolen her heart as well.

With a smile, she stepped toward Marco, framing his gorgeous face in her hands.

"Tonight is the night," she said in husky tones.

His eyes glowed with anticipation. "You're ready to play?"

She stepped closer, allowing his heat to wrap around her. She absorbed it with a tiny shiver. She had become addicted to his warmth. And his musk. And the glow of his wolf in his beautiful eyes.

She'd grown addicted to *him*.

"I'm ready to claim you as mine."

He stilled, as if afraid he had misunderstood her.

"Your mate?"

She pressed her mouth against his in a slow, lingering kiss.

"My mate, my lover, the father of my child." She kissed him again. "My everything."

"Yours forever," he whispered against her lips, his words a solemn pledge.

She ran her hands over the hard muscles of his chest. "Are you ready?"

A growl rumbled in his throat. "I've been ready from the moment I first saw you."

"Good." She smiled, pressing her lips directly against his ear. "Run."

Printed in the United States
by Baker & Taylor Publisher Services